THE
WEATHER
MAN

ROYSTON REEVES

NO EXIT PRESS

First published in the UK in 2023 by No Exit Press,
an imprint of Bedford Square Publishers Ltd,
London, UK

noexit.co.uk
@noexitpress

ISBN
978-1-915798-57-2 (Paperback)
978-1-915798-54-1 (Hardback)
978-1-915798-55-8 (Trade paperback)
978-1-915798-56-5 (eBook)

2 4 6 8 10 9 7 5 3 1

Typeset in Janson Text LT Std by
Palimpsest Book Production Ltd, Falkirk, Stirlingshire

Printed in Great Britain by
CPI Group (UK) Ltd, Croydon CR0 4YY

For Carly-
Your energy and encouragement
makes me want to create things.

One

I'm going to tell you about the worst thing that ever happened to me.

But first I must give you some context that's important: I am not a bad guy. I do my best to be nice to everybody, I never cheated on my girlfriend and I have three or four of those charity direct debits coming out of my bank account every month. I like children and I'm not a racist or any rubbish like that. I'm a normal person.

I get the depression. That much is true, but you wouldn't know it. I keep that shit well smothered. Most of the time you wouldn't know it anyway. I get three or maybe four horrible days in a month and I can deal with that, no need to go on about it.

It was October last year and I'd had a real shit day at work. I work in advertising, which was supposed to be fun and creative, but it's mostly just sitting in awkward, boring meetings and coming up with reasons you can't meet unrealistic deadlines and arguing with pedantic people about minutia that doesn't matter.

The social side is ok. Most lunchtimes there'll be three or four of the old boys from work going to The Three Kings across Clerkenwell Green for a couple of jars of Camden Hells or Birra Moretti. I tend to go, when I can. And after work on a Wednesday or Thursday there are usually a few people going somewhere for post work drinks. I normally go to those. I'll say, 'I'll come for one' and end up having four or five. It feels quite liberating to drink and chat shit late on week nights. Puts all the work stuff in its place.

This was October. My least favourite month probably (October or January). It's like the month of announcement that the nice weather and long days are finishing; but it's not close enough to Christmas yet to feel in any way good or fun or festive or whatever so everyone shuffles around with a long face. I bet part of it is also our brains triggering with some chemical that it remembers from the days of all that 'Back to School' guff.

We used to go back after the big holiday in September, so October would've been the month when it's dawning on everyone: *'It's so miserable and now I've actually got to do this all winter.'* I remember as soon as those 'Back to School' posters went up I'd feel a bit gloomy. They'd come out way too early. Sometimes they'd start appearing in Lakeside shopping centre in like, June and I remember thinking, *'Come on guys, take it easy with this.'*

Typically for that time of year, I was feeling down. I take Fluoxetine 40mg to help with that, but it only does so much. Prozac is very good but it's not a magic formula. On Wednesday night I went to The Three Kings with four work colleagues. Some kids from the Social Media team and the Client Services Director who was always up for a pint. You could rely on him.

The Three Kings is an old-fashioned pub run by this passive aggressive Welsh guy called Pat. He's ok but he has an inflated self-opinion. He once told off one of my mates for moving the speakers to charge his phone out of one of the plug sockets.

He has this girl Rochelle there who works the taps. She's cheerful and nice, you can easily lose half an hour chatting to her.

We sat right next to the entrance around this small table because it was the only one free. We all drank pints and got merry, chatting about the dickhead clients and re-telling everything that had happened in the day to make ourselves feel righteous and immaculate. I had a bet on as well, so I kept checking my phone to see the scores.

At about half nine I decided to go home. The Three Kings tended not to have hand wash in the Gents. It would routinely run out and they wouldn't replace it, so I'd have to wash my hands with just water when I had a piss, which made me feel a little bit dirty and eventually a bit cranky. I also don't like going to sleep too much after eleven if I have work the next day, and it was an hour's journey home.

My friend Clem left at the same time as me but went home in the other direction, so I was alone. I wasn't in the mood to listen to music, so I put my headphones on and chose a podcast about this kid who'd disappeared in Vermont. I forget about some of the American states – some of them just never really get talked about enough.

I knew a short cut to the Tube station that took a few minutes off the walk. You had to walk down the side of a café and cut through a building site. It meant you didn't have to walk all the way round the side of the station to get to the entrance.

Anyway, I'm walking down there listening this podcast and talking to my work mate Jack on WhatsApp. He'd lost the same bet as me. It was quite usual for us to back the same bet independently.

I guess we followed a lot of the same tipster accounts on Twitter and had gotten used to looking out for the same teams to do the same things.

I went down the side of the café, which was called Limon, and cut through the building site. It was unseasonably cold, so I was in a jumper and thin rain jacket, with gloves. I'd seen some people walking around with proper coats and scarves and hats on, like it was deepest winter (ridiculous).

I did have gloves on, yes, but I'll sometimes wear gloves even with a T-shirt. My hands get loads colder than the rest of my body, at least 60 or 70 per cent colder. So I'll normally start wearing gloves before I start wearing jumpers. I think, if it wasn't for social convention, more people would do that actually.

There weren't any people in the cut-through; it was really quiet. Maybe I wasn't supposed to go through there – but loads of people did it on the way to the station at about five or six, after work. The owner of Limon doesn't seem to care. Sometimes I see him out there watching everyone walk round the side of his café, frowning with his arms folded – but I've also seen him watching football in that same posture so that might just be how he likes to stand and watch things.

There were pallets of bricks and bags of sand everywhere and coffee cups that the builders had left. I don't know what they were building in there but there were loads of these massive yellow pipes running across the ground. Probably sewage pipes for a building or something, I thought. My headphones died. Ran out of battery, for fuck's sake. That's the problem with wireless stuff. I took them off and put them in my bag. I hate doing train rides without my headphones. End up having to listen to my own thoughts when I'd much rather detach and forget about my day than analyse it.

When I finished cramming my big headphones into the tiny space I had left in my bag, I looked up and saw this figure moving slowly towards me through the darkness. It was a man. He was walking pretty normally but not in a straight line. I guessed he was drunk.

4

A lot of drunk bankers would make their way back through here to Old Street station. So they could get their trains back to Hertfordshire or Essex or wherever. They could be arrogant dicks when they appeared in our pub. They'd look down on me because I don't dress up smart for work. But I don't need to. That's surely a good thing: the way I see it, if you don't need to wear a suit you're winning. But the bankers take it as a sign of weakness, like you're less important.

As the guy got within about ten or fifteen metres, he suddenly noticed me. He stopped and stood still. Then he laughed out loud to himself and said something (for me to hear, I think). Except I couldn't hear it, whatever he said. He spat on the floor.

Why do people do that?

Then he did something I didn't understand. He crossed over the path, so he was walking directly towards me, front-on. I could tell by his silhouette he was looking at me. I couldn't be arsed with any shit or anything, so I moved out across the path a little bit so there was enough space for both of us to pass without anyone having to move. As he got closer, under one of the few streetlights, I could see him a bit better. He was definitely a city boy of some kind, but he looked like shit.

Two

I have to quickly tell you about me and fighting. I give myself a five-point-five out of ten. *Not useless*.

Between five out of ten (survival level) and six out of ten (will occasionally come out on top).

Between the ages of 0-17 I think I lost every fight I got into. My dad reckons he never threw a punch in his life and he thought of 'knowing how to defend yourself' as somehow thuggish and coarse. My mum always had my back; she couldn't fight herself, but she had a fighting spirit at least and probably secretly wished I'd been a bit tougher.

Anyway, I used to get started on a fair bit by local groups of kids and I'd always end up getting beaten up. It wasn't that I was weak, but the adrenaline would be overwhelming, and it'd sort of paralyse me a bit and make my arms and legs feel all limp and useless, like I was in a dream. I never ran away from anything. I'd just stand there and lose.

The main thing was, I'd never really get wound up enough. I was such a laid-back kid I didn't ever feel angry enough to want to hurt anybody. I wasn't bothered enough. But then when I was about sixteen or seventeen, I started getting angrier about getting started on. I don't know why it suddenly happened, I think I'd just had enough of the whole thing, the whole liberty of it.

My lifetime fight record is probably something like four wins and ten losses. Maybe some draws. So, I can look after myself. I'm ok. But I won't be winning any title belts.

Three

His suit was all crumpled up; it didn't hang off him properly in a nice shape. His shirt had the top two or three buttons undone so his tie was hanging awkwardly, like it didn't know what form to follow.

He had short, mousy hair that was receding a bit and although he wasn't fat you could see evidence of a little beer belly gently pressing against his shirt.

His shirt was off-white with these thin, light-blue stripes on it. It looked like the kind of shirt that had been sitting there for years and he'd long since stopped liking it, but he kept wearing it because it was always there. It was the kind of shirt that made you think, *That guy doesn't live with someone who loves him*.

Single men have a high tolerance for worn out things.

I looked down as he got closer. Not because I was scared or anything, but I just was not in the mood for any sort of inter-action or drunk banter with this mumbling lone wolf. What's the best that could come out of an interaction like that? Even his walk set off alarm bells. That awkward, leaning stagger.

When he was about to pass me, I could see his face. He had little shrunken eyes; maybe a bit Slavic-looking in his features.

And he had this pointy nose like a little beak. Overall, a resting-bitch expression that looked sneery and hurtful.

Then out of nowhere, he took this sideways step, so he was walking straight in my direction again. Directly towards me, so I wouldn't be able to get past without moving.

Just to be clear about this: I'd made the effort to move out of his way to make it more easy and pleasant for both of us, and he's then deliberately moved to make it awkward again. *Think how disrespectful that is.* Seriously, stop and think about it. Someone going out of their way to cause a problem for you. And this guy didn't know me at all, remember. *So, why's he targeting me?* What is it about me that makes me a good person to pick on?

We were about to bump into each other, but I didn't try to avert it. *Fuck you, I've done my bit.* I stiffened up my back and braced to bump into him. I was just looking ahead, trying to look calm and casual. I even checked my watch, as if I was oblivious to this little cold war that had broken out and was just going about my business.

Now I could see that the guy wasn't any bigger than me. He was about my height, five-eight, and probably a fair bit slimmer and lighter than me overall. Adrenaline had started racing, but I wasn't feeling anything except pissed off at this prick who thought he'd just hassle me for no reason. Why's he chosen me? Do I give off a 'weak and vulnerable' vibe to this man? The thought sent a wave of anger through me.

As we crossed paths, he allowed his shoulder to swing into mine. We thudded together stiffly, and both carried on walking, neither of us giving the other the satisfaction of altering course in the slightest. I carried on walking without looking back. I heard him stop; the soles of his feet scraped the pavement as he turned to look at me. I just kept on walking.

Until he just calmly said, 'Pussy.'

It wasn't so much the word 'pussy' that annoyed me, but the way he'd said it. So much spite in his voice, overemphasising the 'p' to make it spikier and more sincere. Still walking, I turned my head to look back at him and laughed. I couldn't think of anything else to do, except pretend I found him pathetic. Idiot.

My blood was tingling. I kept walking but then my mind just flooded with feeling pissed off. My heart had begun racing: *why does he think he can just treat me like that? I've worked fucking hard all day and I feel like shit and now I can't even walk back to the Tube without someone taking a liberty with me, calling me names and shoving me around.*

Eventually, I turned around. I was grinding my jaws together really hard. Pointy nose's smirk dropped. He wanted me to know he was pissed off that I'd turned around. How *dare* I turn around, he's thinking. He's thinking, *'You're nobody. Don't answer back, boy.'*

As I approached him, I could feel my head nodding, for some reason. I got a few feet away from him and stopped. His face had dropped into a frown and he'd squared up his shoulders. I wanted to tell him he looked fucking dumb. His jaw was jutting forward now and the dim street light bounced off all the stubble around his chin, making it look burnt orange.

'Did you say something to me?' I said, in a low whisper. Deep as I could and just loud enough for him to hear. My voice box had shrivelled up a bit and I was physically shaking, I don't mind admitting.

He grinned and shook his head. 'No.'

I stared back for a minute and smiled a bit. 'Didn't think so.'

So, that's it, I thought. I can live with that. *I'll just leave it at that. I've had the last word now.*

But then another wave of this anger came over me. His grinning *fucking* face.

'Pussy!' I shouted and swung my fist at the side of his stupid fucking head. I had no idea why I shouted that. Just sort of matching what he said to me. Sort of saying *this is for what you said*, and so making it clear what I was doing him in for, so it was clear that I'm still the good guy in this thing. I'm the righteous one.

I got him right on the side of his face, on the top of the jawbone. *Bang.*

I heard his rows of teeth crack together on impact. He hadn't been expecting it. I don't know if it was the drink, or just arrogance, but he did not see that punch coming. He swung round with his arms out like a spinning top, one of those old-fashioned children's toys.

As he completed a nearly 180-degree spin, he tilted forward and sort of lean-dived headfirst down at the pavement. Then he goes quiet and he lets out this noise. Like a little wail. Like a little girl. I'm still pumped up with adrenaline, so I strode over and stood over him. I'm violently shaking with adrenaline and rage. I feel strong.

'Go on then. Say it again.' The words bundled out of my mouth so quickly that a load of spit came out and the word 'say' came out with a bit of a lisp. I was so hyped I couldn't even speak properly. It was raining. I hadn't noticed until then, but it had been raining for the last few minutes. Big globs of rain like spatters of paint.

He didn't move. Just stared up at me with an indignant face. Still smirking a tiny little bit. Just to be a rat about things. I muttered something, can't remember what, before turning and leaving him, shaking my head at this ridiculous thing I'd been dragged into.

Four

I got to the end of the shortcut and looked back. I didn't mean to. If I looked back, that would look like I'm scared that he's coming after me. (Which I wasn't). I knew he wasn't behind me anyway. I'd have heard his weird scratchy footsteps coming, for a start.

He was still down there. I knew I didn't knock him out, he was still making noises when I was standing next to him. He was clearly pissed. Maybe he'd passed out drunk? But he wasn't *that* pissed. You could tell by the way he moved; he wasn't anywhere near paralytic. He'd focussed his eyes on me too well, *he wasn't that drunk. Fuck him. I'm going home.*

A few minutes later I'd decided to go back and check on him. I'd kept walking towards the train station and eventually started thinking I'd wake up and feel bad about this the next day. Once the adrenaline had worn off a bit, I felt like I should check he was actually ok.

I doubted my punch could have done that much damage. But his head did hit the pavement so maybe he'd been concussed. He had landed on a slightly raised bit of concrete that separated the pavement from a concrete verge. Not quite a kerb; a design thing I think, a pavement border or something. I hadn't thought anything of it at the time. All of a sudden, I couldn't stop thinking about it.

I didn't know why, but I started panicking a bit. My mouth felt all dry and I had these sort of pins and needles in my tongue. He'd hit that bit of raised pavement and made a really weird sound. A sickly noise, like a sudden, blunt *cruck*. Come to think of it, I'd never heard a sound like it. My pace quickened. My adrenaline was rising again, but this time in a different way. Before it made me all hot, this time it was making me all cold. As I neared the corner to get back into the shortcut, I noticed I'd started to run.

Five

He was still there. He hadn't moved at all. Still lying propped onto his side, arms out in front, hands almost palm-to-palm, legs in a sort of running man motion on the ground. I got close to him and slowed down to a tentative walk.

'D'you want an ambulance?' The words sort of spilled out of my mouth before my head had fully approved the question. No response. I walked up a bit closer. Not too close, in case he was going to swing at me or something. I kept about a metre away.

'Fucking call me a pussy for no reason.' I said it slowly and quietly. I said it to try and level things out before he reacted. I wanted him to know it was one-all, he didn't have a score to settle.

I walked around him (always maintaining my metre-berth) and looked at his face. He was staring in my direction, expressionless. Looking right through me.

'Mate,' I said. The authority draining out of me.

I felt like a kid, waiting for an adult to come and take charge of the situation. I couldn't think of anything else to say. I looked up and down the walkway. Absolute silence, absolute stillness.

Fuck the metre. I stepped up to his face, knelt down and put

14

my gloved fingers out towards his face. Using my left hand to prop myself up, I reached over with the forefinger and middle finger of my right. I gently pressed my fingers into his cheekbone. He didn't react.

I waved my hand in front of his eyes and whispered, 'Hello?'

I didn't know how to check for a pulse, so I pushed him over onto his back and as I did, I revealed a patch of blood that had been hidden under the side of his head, just below his temple. I reeled back and gasped. I couldn't see where the blood was coming from but there was quite a lot of it. All gathered up and smeared across the side of his face. The stubble down the side of his face now looked jet black where it'd been darkened by blood and shadow.

Heart racing, I pulled my phone out of my pocket. Still looking at this guy, I tried a few times to unlock the screen before realising I had my gloves on and it wasn't going to work. I reached for the wrist cuff of my glove to pull it off but stopped myself. *Did I need to keep my gloves on?* Holy shit.

I looked up and down the alley again. I could hear myself breathing really heavy and fast. Trying to gulp in more air, like I couldn't get enough all of a sudden. I heard myself say something but I'm still not sure what I said. I couldn't hear myself; it was like my ears had shrivelled up a bit.

I stood up and walked past him, glancing up and down the walkway the whole time, squinting in the dark to see if anyone was around. I looked out across the building site and up into the pale-yellow office block windows in the middle distance. No movement, anywhere.

I looked down at him again. He actually looked peaceful in the middle of all this. I turned and set off towards the station again. I kept my phone out, so if anyone saw me walking away from him, I could say I had found him there and was trying to get help. And then, when I'm back home and far away I'll ring up 999 and say, 'Oh, it's probably nothing but I saw this drunk guy lying on the ground sleeping when I walked past.'

But I'd already decided that I wasn't going to stay there. It's not like I could help by staying.

And the bottom line was, I'd punched this guy – I'd punched him and he'd fallen and bashed his head because he was drunk. But if I hadn't punched him, he probably wouldn't have fallen over. (But he might have).

My DNA and little threads of my clothes would be all over him. I watched enough crime documentaries to know that, once they found out I was there at the same time as him, it wouldn't take long for them to close the net on me. Bits of wool off my gloves or teeny bits of cotton off my jacket. A bit of my hair or an eyelash or some skin cells, or something like that.

I'd heard a few fables before about big-faced lads in Ben Sherman shirts in the 90s who accidentally killed people with 'lucky punches' in street fights. The most tragic cases were the ones where it'd just been a nice guy and one single punch, and the guy ended up in prison for ten years and his whole life ruined.

I staggered up to a bin and puked.

Six

The train ride home seemed like it took about three hours. In fact, it was probably more like half an hour, because I got a direct one. I kept a fast walking pace, without ever breaking into a run. I was like one of those Olympic racewalkers, swirling my hips for momentum.

I wanted to run but I didn't. I kept thinking about all the cameras on me that would probably later be used as records of *my behaviour after the incident*. It felt like the whole world had suddenly turned to look at me. If they started tightening the net on me, that kind of detail would become important. So I walked as casually as I could, with my hands in my jacket pockets. I kept shaking my head, like a dog trying to straighten out its fur.

I got home and closed the front door. Straight to the kitchen for a long glass of water. As I reached for the cupboard with my gloved hand, I stopped myself. I carefully took my gloves off, delicately placing them into a Morrisons bag. I decided I was going to take that down to the bins.

I washed my hands. I took the rest of my clothes off and put them in that carrier bag. Then I went for a long, hot shower. When I came out, I put the boots I'd been wearing into a bin liner. Then I crushed that into the Morrisons bag, too.

I necked the last quarter of a bottle of wine that was in the fridge and smoked a joint in my bedroom. It was a blunt and I smoked the whole thing in probably ten minutes, without coughing. I took two Night Nurse and lay on my bed staring at the ceiling. My heart was still racing, but I felt like I was starting to think a bit clearer. A bit more logically.

An hour later I was asleep.

Seven

I had forgotten to set an alarm and slept right through until nearly 11 a.m. I woke up, grabbed my phone to look at the time, and sat bolt upright. *Shit*. Night Nurse will do that, if you take it with alcohol and don't set an alarm. Two missed calls. A bunch of email notifications running all the way down the screen.

I quickly bashed up an email calling in sick and sent it to my boss. Then I immediately sent a follow-up email to her explaining that the first email had been stuck in my email Outbox since I tried to send it at 7 a.m. Having done that, I felt a bit calmer. *Breathing space*.

I went through the late-night messages and glanced over the emails that'd come through. Nothing. As I breathed in the relief, I absent-mindedly switched over to the BBC app to see what all the final scores were. No idea why I thought the football scores were important in that moment. It was almost a reflex action to fire up that app in the morning.

Then I saw something that made my stomach drop. And I realised nothing would ever be the same again.

Eight

Everything is as simple as you make it. If you concentrate, you can simplify most situations down to something manageable. That's why people talk about breathing exercises and all that. It does help. No task is too complicated if you really break it down into things you can manage. You just need to learn the techniques.

I'd just killed a person, though. I'm not sure how you even go about breaking that down.

It was the BBC's second most viewed story in London.

Breathe.

Even from the small picture attached to the story I could see it was something big. Two police vans and a car parked outside the alley. I got a weird flutter of excitement when I saw an ambulance. *Maybe he's not dead after all.* But the headline says a 'fatal incident'.

Breathe.

Maybe there was a *different* incident? This could all be a big coincidence? For fuck's sake.

A spontaneous hot flush had me power-walking to the bathroom. I splashed my face with cold water over the sink. I glanced up at myself in the mirror and couldn't believe how old I looked.

I thought for a minute about how trivial my usual problems were. This time on Monday I'd been stressed about a pitch presentation for a craft beer brand. Craft beer doesn't matter, in the grand scheme of things.

I could hear my phone buzzing on the bedside table in the next room. I ran to answer it. Maybe I wanted some feedback from the world to distract me from my thoughts. It was one of the girls in my team, Anna, giving me a heads up that my boss wasn't happy about my vanishing act. She must not've seen my frantically crafted email yet.

'I'll come in,' I said. 'I'm feeling a lot better now; had some stomach problems.' Good old stomach problems. I suddenly felt desperate to go into work, and normality. Nothing unusual or out of turn.

I threw my wardrobe open and chewed my nails as I scanned up and down the rail. I kept glancing back at my phone – God knows who I was expecting to call. I eventually put on a grey shirt, with a pair of black jeans that were hanging over the end of my bed. I spent ten minutes looking for my black boots before remembering I'd had to 'bag' them, which sent a horrible chill down me.

The fuck have I got myself into.

An hour later I arrived in Farringdon. London was grey and rank. Walking around London alone can get you down, if the weather's wrong. It's a different city in the summer. Although the rain had finished coming down, the roads were stained a deep black by the damp and puddles ran up and down the edges of the street.

Farringdon was prickling with people out for lunch. Being a Thursday lunchtime, the pubs were half-full. I walked faster than everyone else. Charging left and right on the pavement to carve a path for myself between the slow walkers.

As I turned the corner onto the main road next to the station, I couldn't bear to look up ahead. When I eventually glanced up, beyond Express Dry Clean, towards the shortcut exit from the night before, I couldn't see anything unusual. It looked pretty normal, which gave me a gentle, momentary endorphin rush. *Had it all been a misunderstanding? Had I got it wrong?*

As I passed the opening to the alley, I casually glanced down it. I couldn't see far in, but I didn't notice any activity except for a single traffic cone about three metres down. The cranes were moving though. The building work was going on. That was surely a good sign? I was scanning the faces around me, trying to get a feel for the vibe. The whole time I was acting cool but under the surface I was taking everything in, glancing around at the position of all the cameras, scanning facial expressions, straining to try and listen to what people might be saying to each other.

There were quite a few cameras around. I counted at least seven but, in my efforts to appear relaxed I guessed I'd probably missed a few. There was a big pole at the crossing with three cameras on it, all facing different directions. One of them directly faced Limon café which flanked the entrance to the alley. I winced. Couldn't help myself. I rounded the corner at the end of the road and finally located the circus.

A police cordon; the alley blocked off with yellow tape and a sign requesting information. I didn't read any of it. I could feel the nausea rising, and I needed to keep my cool. I pushed on to work.

Nine

Work was not what I'd expected. But then again, I'm not sure what I'd expected. Everyone was in a pretty upbeat mood. I don't know why but I expected some state of semi-mourning. Nobody mentioned the activity going on down in Farringdon. But then, why should they? It had nothing to do with us. Meanwhile, something weird was happening to me. I noticed I was going out of my way to be extra nice to people. Super accommodating. I guess it was a like a weird side effect, trying to re-establish what a nice guy I really was. Trying to prove to myself that I was different from that whole situation last night.

But as the afternoon wore on, I ran out of focus. I sat in meetings daydreaming, with my laptop open Googling things like 'Farringdon', keeping it vague. Just a man finding out about 'Farringdon'. Twitter was quiet but there was a fair amount of local coverage from news corps. His name was Richard King. He was an insurance broker and, by all accounts, a decent, hardworking person who was well liked. (Yeah, right. When do they ever say anything else about someone who's just died?)

Someone asked me a question and I felt my head physically jolt upwards. *I'm in a meeting. Someone's asking me something about an email to procurement.*

'Yeah, I'll chase them.' I pretended to note something in my book. A couple of people nodded, and the conversation moved on. Nobody looked at me strangely or anything.

Richard King was from Colchester in Essex. He was a sociable man with a long-term girlfriend. He loved his mum, loved his mates and followed Blackburn Rovers. His dad was from Blackburn.

For the first time I began wondering if I should turn myself in. *Is that the best thing to do right now?* The best thing, *for me?* I could explain in detail that it was a complete mistake with no intent and that I'd only realised today he'd actually been properly hurt. They wouldn't do you for that. Not prison.

My whole body went cold at that thought. That thought was the manifestation of all the terror that had started bubbling in my gut. Me, in prison. I don't even like being away from my home for a single evening. I couldn't stand the thought of my life changing like that.

I yanked my phone out under the table and started Googling similar cases. After ploughing through a few articles, I stopped. *I'm leaving a fucking trail of breadcrumbs.* They can access all this, the police. It's all circumstantial evidence. They can get all your internet activities if they want. I quickly erased the History off my phone and work laptop.

Ten

When I got home, I took that bag of clothes from the night before, drove to the park near my flat and dumpēd them all in the charity bin, in the car park by the entrance. Somehow that felt safer and less traceable than putting it in a local bin. You put something in a charity bin, it gets cleaned and recycled back into humanity. It stops being 'an item of mine that's been discarded' and becomes just 'an item belonging to someone else'.

Tempted as I was to keep Googling the status of the police inquiries, I managed to stay off the internet all night. I made a quiet resolution to myself that from that moment on, I would behave like a normal person who didn't know anything about that whole business, or about Richard King.

I kept convincing myself that it wasn't my fault any of this had happened. From the few cases I'd seen, it was possible to get eight or ten or even fifteen years in prison for what I'd done; a rush of blood in a heated moment. There has in fact, been lots of precedent. It's been in the news a lot over the last few years.

The *one-punch death*, the alarmist tabloids have branded it. A pandemic that needs stamping out, like religious extremism or inner-city stabbings. The latest moral panic for suburban people to get twisted up in knots about. A little dose of fear to make us feel alive. A folk devil for us all to hide from. *That man cannot be me.*

After pacing my kitchen, thinking, for what must have been hours, I resolved that I needed to swallow all this up and draw a firm line underneath it. I'd take a day or two to feel regretful and sorry, and then forget the name Richard King and continue with my life completely as normal. It was the only way not to let this take over my life, forever. Because I didn't ask for any of this. I hadn't seen Richard King before, and I didn't know anything about him, twenty-four hours before. I didn't ask for him to come crashing into my life.

So, you can leave me out of it.

Eleven

I went in to work early the next morning. I woke up automatically at 4.30 a.m. and couldn't get back to sleep again; my mind was whirring. I kept reiterating it to myself: the only way to let sanity take grip of things again was to draw a line under this and take a permanent zero tolerance to thinking about it.

I thought, *I'll push back on any worry or anxiety about this stuff, as soon as it begins to emerge,* and that eventually it would be a speck on the landscape. Just distant, in the rear-view mirror.

Today's job was to put it firmly in the past. Archive it away in a part of my brain that I don't access often, and keep busy with work. But I had one last thing I needed to do first. I needed to check something.

On my way in to work, I went through the shortcut, which was open to the public again. Three or four metres from where the thing had happened, there were five or six bunches of flowers propped against the wall, and a Blackburn football shirt which well-wishers had written on in marker pen. I didn't stop to look at them or register any interest in them.

Outside Limon there was a police road sign appealing for information. Asking the public what happened has got to be really hit and miss, if nothing's been reported already. Nobody

27

is walking around paying attention to what's going on, really. *We're all too busy*. That thought gave me a momentary rush of positivity.

Most importantly, there were no security cameras down there. None at all. That's what I'd really gone snooping down there to investigate. I'd been vigilant the whole way through. There was no way anything could have been caught on camera. A little bit of good news. There wasn't even a line of sight to anything except the windows at the tops of tall buildings nearby. The alley was pretty well shielded by surrounding buildings and the void of the construction site.

The office was pretty empty, I had expected to be one of the first in but when I placed my fob over the sensor the front door jolted open. The deadbolt wasn't on, meaning somebody had got in before me. Normally the first thing I'd do upon entering the office would be to fill my water bottle at the dispenser in reception. Not today. I bustled straight through and made my way to my desk. It was in a corner beneath a big hanging sign saying *Planning*.

I could hear murmuring coming from the boardroom. I craned my neck to peep over the strip of frosted glass as I walked past. Couldn't see anyone. But as I walked further away, beneath the frosted area I could see four pairs of feet around the boardroom table.

I collapsed into my chair and flipped my laptop screen open. I punched the power button with my forefinger and threw my phone and wallet onto the desk. As I reached to pull half a stale croissant out of the open packet in my top drawer, some shuffling footsteps from the kitchen caught my attention. I saw my colleague Em emerge with a tray of coffees and glasses of water. I nodded and called out through a mouth full of croissant.

'Morning.'

Em widened her eyes at me and nodded towards the boardroom. She placed the tray down on her desk and reached into her handbag for a packet of tissues. Grinning nervously, she mouthed something at me as she picked the tray back up and whisked it towards the boardroom door.

'*What?*' I mouthed back.

She didn't reply, instead backing into the boardroom door.

Must be a client meeting.

After a few minutes, curiosity got the better of me. I could see an agricultural looking pair of shoes in there, with thick plastic soles. They weren't the shoes of your regular, polished Marketing Wanker. I got up and strolled round the side of the boardroom to the printer area. Pretending to look for a printout, I stood on tiptoes and peered into the boardroom. There were two police officers in there.

Jesus.

Twelve

One of them glanced up and locked eyes with me. Instinctively, I ducked down. She'd seen me. *Now what?*

I went back to my desk, inexplicably clutching a wad of blank paper from the machine. My mouth had gone dry. As I tentatively sat down, the boardroom door swung open. My boss leaned around the corner and gestured me in with a wave.

I swallowed hard and got up; my heart beginning to pound in my chest. I needed to get ahead of the sweat beads that would inevitably start emerging from my forehead in there, so I went to the bathroom first. I let the tap run for a good thirty seconds to let it go really cold, before scooping a few handfuls straight onto my red-hot face. I scooped a final handful of water into my dry mouth and grabbed some hand towels.

Breathe.

Would the police find it weird if I wore sunglasses to this meeting? I had an overwhelming urge to hide behind some sunglasses. I pushed the boardroom door open and there they were. My boss Julia, the Finance Director Brian and two police officers, one male, one female.

'Hello,' I croaked, 'what's going on?'

For a few horrible moments they all just stared at me in silence.

'This is Will,' announced Julia, pulling out a chair next to her. The female police officer looked up at me, blankly. The male one, wearing an expensive looking pair of silver-framed glasses, gestured with his palm towards the chair Julia had pulled out.

'Hello, Will. My name is Detective Inspector Matt Probert, this is Police Sergeant Sara Kane.'

I nodded at Kane and forced a smile at Probert.

'So, what's going on?' I blurted with feigned intrigue. In my effort to pretend I was finding the drama exciting and a bit fun I half-shouted it. Probert opened a pocketbook in front of him and took out a photograph, sliding it towards me.

'You may have heard about an incident on Wednesday night, up near the train station? We're trying to get a picture of the events going on around there at that time.' I blinked at the inspector, emotionless as possible. My mouth and throat felt like they'd been densely packed with cotton wool.

'Sorry... *which* incident?'

The police officers looked at each other and Kane answered. She had a hard, fucking face, oh my goodness. Those oddly angled, sarcastic eyes that let you know someone's going to be hard work. She was attractive, no doubt about it. Probably early or mid-thirties I thought.

She had lovely fresh-looking skin and shoulder length dark blond hair that curled a little at the bottom. Her mouth was perfectly formed, with a straight top lip framing a beautiful row of straight, white teeth.

'There was a fatal incident in the alleyway leading up to the train station on Wednesday night between 21:15 and 21:50,' she said. Her studious, brown eyes went right through me. She had a tone like an old schoolmaster, impatient and superior.

'Oh yeah! I saw the sign up next to—'

'Next to Limon café,' she interrupted. She must have known

I was going to pretend to claw for the name of the café. Somehow I thought pretending I couldn't remember the name of the place might detach me further from the inquiry. She seemed to be ahead of that, however.

Probert nodded towards Brian. 'You guys were in the pub across the green that night? Your colleague here mentioned you were there. Do you mind if we have a chat?'

'*Oh*… yeah, ok! Not sure how much help I can be though.' I smiled awkwardly and glanced around the table for water or something. Both Probert and Kane had glasses of water sitting in front of them, untouched. I imagined just grabbing one and taking a long sip from it. I could pretend I thought it was a spare glass. I could hear my own mouth clacking open and closed and I assumed everybody else could, too.

'Anything you can remember about that evening could be helpful,' Probert continued. He pulled a biro from the chest pocket of his jacket. 'Do you know what time you left?'

I puffed my cheeks out and raised my eyes to the ceiling. 'Ahh, half ten-ish?' My mind was whirring. Why hadn't I worked up a narrative yet? What was my *narrative*?

Probert glanced at Brian. Brian squinted at me slightly before looking up at the ceiling thoughtfully. He wasn't going to correct me, but his expression seemed to ask, '*Are you sure about that?*'

I resolved to get in there first. 'No, wait, hang on, it must have been earlier than that. The football was still going, so it must've been earlier. It must've been closer to half nine, quarter to ten.'

Probert nodded; Kane wrote something down.

'Yeah, because I left before you didn't I,' I said, nodding towards Brian as if I'd just remembered.

'Yeah, I think *we* left the pub at half ten,' replied Brian.

'Which route did you take home?' asked Kane. 'Do *you* pass through Farringdon?'

Probert intervened. 'Sorry to interrupt whatever you were doing, by the way. Won't take long, we're just trying to piece things together and get a picture of everything that night. The landlord at The Three Kings said you lot were in around that time, so we just need to know if anyone saw anything out of the ordinary, and if you're able to point us in the direction of anyone else who was in the pub… any details you can think of might help us build a better picture.'

My whole mood suddenly lightened. *He was apologising to me for this inconvenience. He's inconveniencing a law-abiding citizen (me) so he's apologising.* I felt liberated. *I was just another law-abiding citizen, helping out with anything I know. Nothing to see here.*

'Out of the ordinary…'

I rubbed the sides of my head and pretended to rack my brain.

Kane stuck her oar back in. 'What would really help is if you could just retrace the walk for us. Did you go through Farringdon?'

I'm a law-abiding citizen.

'Yes, I did.' I replied. 'I go through there on my way home.'

I resolved to explain my entire journey back to the station, just as it had happened, but without the banker. I told them about the shortcut; I told them I'd cut through there and I'd been chatting to a mate on WhatsApp. To show how helpful I was, I went back to my desk and got my phone. I showed them the conversation Jack and I had been having, pointing out the exact times of the messages, all the while knowing that this conversation had taken place minutes from the death of the banker. *When they eventually triangulate his actual time of death, to their mind, this conversation I was having with Jack about football will have been going on at exactly the same time.* It's pretty much an alibi. Nobody ever killed anyone while they were having a light-hearted chat with a mate on WhatsApp.

Julia's mobile phone rang. She apologised as she got up to answer it, explaining that someone was coming to fix the printer later that morning. I continued my story; told them I hadn't seen anyone or anything, but that I hadn't been particularly vigilant because I was texting and listening to a podcast.

I was in proper storytelling mode now, embellishing my story with little details to build out this parallel version of the truth.

With every passing second, I was growing in confidence. We'd reached the end of my usefulness to them. I began show-boating a little, probing with questions like a curious, innocent person might:

'How about DNA and all that? Could you get anything? Sorry, I watch a lot of documentaries.'

Probert smiled awkwardly, but neither he or Kane answered. Kane just continued staring at me, unwavering. I smiled at her.

Julia re-entered.

'Is it this printer that's broken?' asked Kane, gesturing towards the huge printer-photocopier whose form you could vaguely make out through the frosted glass.

'Yes,' replied Julia. 'And it's becoming the bane of all our lives, I'm afraid. It's been broken for nearly a week and it's supposed to be fully serviced.'

We all started to rise and collect our bits and pieces from the table. *Meeting over. We're into the small talk.* But not for Kane. She remained seated, still looking bemused.

'Weren't you printing something over there this morning, Will?' She half-smiled and motioned at the printer through the frosted glass.

Everyone looked at me.

'No,' I said.

She continued staring.

'Oh! Well... yeah. I sent something to print and then *remembered* it was broken.'

'Oh, I see,' said Kane.

For a few moments, everyone looked at everyone else. Eventually Kane came back.

'But it's been broken for a week?'

This weird stillness had come back into the atmosphere.

'Yeah, something like that,' I said, glancing at Julia.

Kane was still seated, still staring at me. 'Would you like some water?' she asked, pushing her untouched glass of water towards me.

I shot a bemused look at Julia and Brian. 'I'm good thanks.'

My mouth must have gone dry and started clacking again.

Thirteen

Kane and Probert came in again twice over the course of the day. They interviewed everyone who'd been in the pub that night. Nobody had seen anything unusual. There was some talk about the angry bible thumper (a local celebrity) who'd been shouting at people outside the station earlier in the day through a traffic cone, but that was about it.

We all talked about it in the office after lunch. By all accounts, it was *mental* that a guy had been killed and I must have passed the exact spot where it happened a few minutes before. Em started going on about the banker. Talking about how he just seemed normal, 'like one of us'. It was pretty normal for Emily to over-emotionalise situations.

By the end of the day I'd had enough of feeling so uptight. My muscles had seized up and I'd felt like my back was full of old, rusty springs all morning. I bought a bottle of prosecco from the off licence by the train station, went home and had a long, hot shower, stepping out every now and then to swig from my bottle. I got straight into bed and took a couple of Night Nurse.

• • •

Hours passed and I was still wide awake. I started to feel agitated. My mind wandered as I began rolling a joint. I thought about handing myself in again. I kept replaying this fantasy to myself, where I hand myself in and the police are like, *'Mate don't worry about it! You'd be surprised how often this happens!'* And I end up at home that same night. And I can just get on with my life, how it was.

Fourteen

A few days passed. I didn't see another living soul all weekend and Monday passed without incident.

I was still keeping my eyes open through Farringdon and was beginning to wonder if the police would ever be able to associate me with that had happened. The more I broke it down and examined it, the more I realised what a difficult job this was for the police to actually do anything about.

There were no cameras covering that alleyway and there were no witnesses to what had happened except me and the banker. The situation of that alley, flanking the building site on one side and the back of a row of shops on the other, had made it a kind of blind spot to London's unblinking, eye. When I broke down what the police had, it wasn't very revealing at all:

- *Drunk banker passes through Farringdon at night, probably heading for Old Street station to get a train back to Essex. For whatever reason he doesn't get on the train at Farringdon, he goes straight past the station and down the street next to it. Maybe he just wants the walk to Old Street. Maybe he feels sick from the booze.*

- *He takes a shortcut down an alleyway where somehow, he has a bad fall and hits his head.*
- *Loads of other people use that alley every day and it isn't covered by CCTV, so the police can't know who was down there at that time, but they do know that nobody witnessed the crime. Someone found the guy, hours later.*
- *Mr Will Cox happened to be one of the people who passed through the alley at a similar time, but he must have just missed it. Everyone missed it. It happens. The banker had been drinking. Fatal drinking accidents happen all the time.*

No witness, no fingerprints or anything. A black hole of an incident, with a strong suggestion of drunken misadventure. For it to be anything more than that, they'd need a confession, or a slip-up.

All I needed to do was keep my mouth shut, forever. I must never tell a living soul. That would be my part of the deal.

On Tuesday afternoon I was working on a pitch document with Jack. We heard Brian say something at the back of the room that got people talking and flocking around his computer screen. I leant back in my chair in their direction and frowned at Brian inquisitively.

'They've found the bloke,' Brian shouted over to me.

Moments later I was power-walking to Brian's desk, trying to look calm.

'They arrested someone. Must have found him on the CCTV,' said Lauren, one of the Social Media lot. 'You just can't escape it now; you can't get away with anything.'

The story on Brian's screen was something of a surprise.

They'd made an arrest in *The Farringdon Shortcut Killing*.

Since when did this fucking thing get its own name like that?

The Shortcut Killing is a bit dramatic. How many *actual, deliberate* killings happen every day and don't get this much news coverage? Not to mention get a little nickname like that.

The reality occurred to me at that point that some poor bastard was currently being interviewed somewhere about this thing he had nothing to do with. But it didn't make me feel as guilty as you'd think. Even though I admit I did have this simmering sense of guilt-laden relief in my stomach, I'd also had this other thought. Basically, I wanted to know more about the bloke they've pulled in, before I did anything else.

See, I'd had this reality check over the previous few days while I'd been wringing my hands and pacing my kitchen each night. The world isn't fair. It isn't fair on anyone, including good people.

Bad people don't always get what they deserve, and good people don't always get what they deserve. The world is sometimes fair but really often, it's not. A lot of the worst people in our world don't ever actually see any consequences for having bad intentions. I don't believe in karma or fate or anything, we're all just bumbling about. Some of us have good intentions, some of us have bad intentions, but it doesn't necessarily mean you get what you deserve.

Sometimes it's random and sometimes it's far from random. There are darkly clever people who prey on good nature in the world and trick good people into difficulty or uncertainty for their own gain. There are powerful people whose every-day approach to life is about bullying and corralling those weaker than them into corners from where they have to pay their way out. There are clever, devious people who live by exploiting and profiteering off the graspings of others. There are greedy people who knowingly make themselves rich off the hard work of others (and are often lauded as icons for doing so). And there are those people who just get a kick out of causing upset and exerting all kinds of dominance on the world. For personal gain or just for fun. And there are thousands of others who go about their days with bad intentions for the world.

And here's the thing: I knew I wasn't any of those things. I'm a person who does his best to be good to everybody. I've never knowingly, deliberately exploited anybody or taken anything valuable from anybody. I'm one of life's triers, pushing away at the grindstone, trying to be happy and to make other people happy, where I can. That's all I've ever tried to do; *to be happy*. That's the important thing to remember.

Just supposing for a moment, the guy who'd been pulled in is someone who's been on the police radar for a while; he could be a bad guy of some description. They could've been waiting for a chance to bring him in, but he keeps escaping justice. Some people have it down to an art form. Some people have a hold over the authorities, or just have the means to keep evading them.

I'd started to think about how this could be a rare example of the universe accidentally straightening out one of its inadequacies. A good guy has made a mistake; a bad guy was in the right place at the right time, and it ends up with a bad person being put away. It was just something I kept making myself think about. I was trying to make the thought more real.

How many good guys get locked up every day? And even outside of that: how many bad guys are just out there, living better lives than good guys, despite their bad intentions and bad behaviour?

Nobody interferes with that; we (the people without the power) just push on and grumble and accept that things aren't always fair.

Well, this time things might have accidentally worked out fairly. I told myself I wouldn't be upsetting the flow of things, until I knew more. I had resolved to act calmly and methodically and with respect for the fact that *I have always meant well*. I decided I would not be helping the police and that I would not be handing myself in. Just like the hundreds of *bad people* out there who do not hand *themselves* in every day. I was turning a blind eye – letting nature take its course.

Fifteen

Weeks passed and things began returning to something like normal. It's amazing how much ruthless direction you can muster when you feel your freedom has been threatened. The hot, sick feeling in my stomach settled down to a casual simmer and I threw myself into work. The signs and cones and yellow police tape lingered for a while until it all became a low hum. I just stopped walking that way. I stopped looking that way.

People quickly got on with their lives. London is good at that. I made a big effort to make that business none of my business. And I really did manage to make it work. It started to become real: that principle that it was *nothing to do with me*.

I continued with my strategy of never Googling it, never mentioning it, never allowing it to cross my mind. If it ever popped into my mind, in any capacity, I got into a habit of instantly saying *no* to that line of thought and turning my back on it, mentally. I'd drawn a great, thick black line under the whole thing. I'd left it behind.

Christmas decorations began appearing in shops. Minds were turning towards the upcoming break. It had been a long year and we were all ready for relaxing, eating and drinking. Taking a week or two off to recharge.

I started going running in the evenings when I got home from work. I'd put some music in my earphones, as loud as my phone would let it go, and run a big lap of the area surrounding my flat, which took about 45 minutes. I didn't lose any weight through this enterprise. About an hour after running, I'd be starving and would cook myself an enormous portion of food or order a pizza. But the process of doing it felt a bit cleansing and helped me sleep.

While I didn't spend any time thinking about what had happened, I knew deep down that I was experiencing a sort of pent-up energy effect. That dark, miserable period had created this energy in me that I needed to keep disposing of. I was permanently moving, always occupied with something. That mindset was how I came to meet Ellie.

One night after work, a bunch of my colleagues went to Liverpool Street, to this pub called Dirty Dick's. When I was asked, I agreed to go along; I wouldn't turn down an evening distraction like that. I had to finish some stuff at the office, so they went without me and I joined them a bit later on.

I got there at about half eight and found my lot mingling with this other group. A cluster of about twenty. That made me a bit grumpy. I'd wanted to hang out and have a few relaxing drinks with my mates and wasn't sure I could be bothered meeting anyone new and telling them about my job or whatever.

I skulked to the bar and got a couple of pints of cider, scanning the group as the barman poured.

I wasn't sure who the other one was for but buying two drinks was something I'd learned to do over time. I didn't like showing up to a group with a single drink for myself in my hand, it felt selfish; but on the other hand I didn't want to push around the group asking who needed a drink because that process can last a hell of a long time when dealing with half-cut people. Turning up with two and announcing, '*I've got two actually, does anyone want the other one?*' would just cut through all that process. It's a good technique.

They were all perched around this table under a large stair-well. I attached myself to the edge of the group, hovering my spare drink around with raised eyebrows as I joined. Em saw me and bolted up, throwing her arms around my neck and splashing us both with cider. She'd had a few. She turned, still gripping me in a gentle headlock, and pointed at a girl standing next to my friend Jack, looking disinterested as he showed her something on his phone.

'It's Ellie!' Em squeaked, grabbing the girl's sleeve and yanking her towards us. Ellie and I smiled at each other, awaiting more information, which never came. Instead Em suddenly gasped, grinning ear-to-ear and thrust a pointed finger into the air. I didn't need to turn my head to know a bowl of chips had just arrived at the table. I'd seen that reaction from Em in pubs many, many times.

'Hey,' I nodded to Ellie as Em bounced away.

'Hey.' She smiled back. 'Thirsty?'

'Er, yeah,' I said.

Ellie nodded down at the two pints in my hands.

'Oh!' I said, forcing a laugh, 'Yeah! Do you want one of these?'

'What is it?' she asked.

'Cider. Blackthorn.'

She pursed her lips. 'How come you've got two?'

Jesus. Do I have to explain this? 'Well I just got here and felt guilty just getting myself one. I got another one for whoever…'

She looked confused for a moment and then smiled and extended her hand. 'Sure. Thanks.'

It seemed to relax her, hearing what a socially anxious male

I was. Her face softened, like she was suddenly interested in knowing more.

As the night wore on and the group gradually dispersed, Ellie and I talked and talked, barely moving from that spot where we met, except to occasionally visit the bar for fresh jars of cider. She was just my type of person: happy, bright and energetic, self-aware but not a show-off. She was cheeky and witty and a little bit dorkier than you'd think by looking at her. Hours went by in seconds.

When I'd first seen her, I hadn't pegged her for someone I'd get on with. When Em had pointed her out, she'd looked a bit full of herself. My first instinct had been that she looked like the kind of girl who'd had everything her way and that I'd struggle to find much common ground with her.

She was the same age as me, but I'd guessed her to be a few years younger. She was petite, around five-one or five-two, with lovely golden skin which was made all the more striking by a frame of bobbed, raven-black hair and impossibly dark brown eyes. As she spoke, a silver stud piercing in her tongue flickered in the candlelight around us. I found it hard not to keep staring at it. Her dark eyes were framed with thick, perfectly shaped, jet-black brows, the right brow would arch up a little when she was being ironic or self-effacing.

She had this amazing way with words. She worked for some company in Clerkenwell who sold golfing holidays to rich blokes. She didn't seem to think much of her job but at the same time didn't complain about it. She just had this clarity about her: this was what she was doing with her life at this moment, and it was supplementing her well enough and that she was satisfied with it. I found that so refreshing, that she was satisfied in life and just enjoyed living it, one day at a time. There's something so attractive about that.

At closing time there were still seven or eight of us about.

Em and Ellie were going to leave together. They left their bags with me while they headed off to the loo before the journey home. I stood by the entrance with these bags while staff wiped down tables and swept the floor.

A staff member asked me if I'd mind going outside. I didn't mind, even though it was starting to rain. I've never wanted to be one of those people who hang about when a place is trying to close. The staff have got homes to go to.

I stood watching drunk people staggering up and down Liverpool Street while I wondered how to ask for Ellie's phone number or to see her again or something. Despite talking to her for hours about a hundred different topics, I'd somehow managed not to find out whether she was single, or whether she was interested in me. I was worried about making a fool of myself. I didn't want to ask her out and be rejected because she'd tell Em. And Em would tell everybody at work.

After a couple of minutes, Ellie reappeared, minus Em. She smiled and came over to me, reaching out for her bag. I realised I probably had about thirty seconds before Em came bounding out and my chance would be gone again. I couldn't think of what to say.

I just stood there next to her in silence, as we watched some drunk blokes across the road who appeared to have dropped something down a drain and were gathered around a woman who was trying to retrieve it for them with a pen. Em reappeared and grabbed her bag from me, reaching out to hug my neck loosely with a single flailing arm as she turned to go.

'See you tomorrow, mate,' she said.

'Yeah, see you, guys,' I said, raising a pathetic arm up to motion at Ellie.

Ellie smiled. 'Lovely to meet you!' As she said it, I noticed her lips had changed colour. She'd topped up her lipstick in the bathroom.

'Yeah, you too,' I said, charging up a fake grin.

After the two of them had left, I turned to flag down a taxi from the busy street. As a black cab pulled up and I leaned towards the window I instinctively reached for my wallet in my back pocket.

It wasn't there. I slapped the side and back pockets of my jeans, wincing as I tried plunging my hands into my inside jacket pocket, knowing it wouldn't be there, because I never put it there. I apologised to the cabbie and sent him on his way.

First the lipstick debacle, now this. What should have been a great evening had turned into pure shit in the space of a few minutes.

The pub had now closed and bolted its front door, but I could see the staff still working inside. I pushed my face up to the glass and knocked gently. A girl who was wiping down a table turned and mouthed to me that they were closed. I shouted into the glass, 'I don't suppose you've found a wallet?'

She cupped a hand to her ear and I responded by mimicking taking a wallet out of my pocket and opening it. She came and unbolted the door to let me in.

'I think they did find a wallet, it's in the office. If you go upstairs and go right to the end of the corridor, my manager's in there.'

What a relief. There are few better feelings in the world than thinking your phone or wallet was lost or stolen, and then finding and seeing it there in the flesh again. The manager, who looked about thirteen years old, pulled it out of her desk drawer and checked my details against my driving licence before handing it back to me. I shoved it straight into my pocket, thanked her and left.

I felt exhilarated now, like I had this rush of good energy. Standing right there outside the manager's office, I pulled my phone out and messaged Em:

'Forgot to ask, is Ellie single? I was going to ask for her no but don't know if she has a bf or whatever?'

'Forgot to ask'. Yeah right. Because I was so busy watching drain club.

I hailed a cab for home. As we crept through the late-night traffic towards King's Cross, I must have checked my phone screen at least fifty times. Each time I pretended to myself I genuinely needed to know the time again. Just as the cab pulled up beside St Pancras, I saw the screen finally light up:

'Yeah single, she's asked me for your number.'

Before I got on the train back home, I sat for half an hour on a bench in the misty rain outside St Pancras, looking at Em's message again and again. Just marinating my mind in how good that felt.

Sixteen

The next few days were busy at work. I continued deliberately throwing my mind into as much action as possible. I was taking on more and more. I found it a really useful alternative to going home to sit alone in my bedroom with my thoughts, and people were commenting on what a good mood I seemed to be in. *If I'm leaving a trail of 'a good mood', that's fine by me.*

Ellie was this bubbling little distraction too. She had taken a couple of days to get in touch, eventually messaging me at about 9 o'clock one night, just saying 'Hi, it's Ellie'.

Come on, give me something to work with.

I tried hard to get some momentum going with her, but she tended to be slow in replying to my messages, or her messages were infuriatingly short. I guessed she just wasn't one of those people who liked to text.

I knew it was up to me to do something, but I didn't want to seem too keen. So, we had this weird, stilted conversation trickling along in the background. Sometimes you have to be patient with people when it comes to welcoming in new relationships. Not everybody finds it that easy, I think. It doesn't mean it won't eventually be good.

• • •

One Thursday evening I stopped at the fish and chip shop on my way home from work. I was feeling a bit drained and ready to collapse at home and eat a large portion of junk food. I ordered a large cod and chips and grabbed about nine tartare sauce sachets, shoving them into my coat pockets with both hands. I could see the lady looking at me funny out of the corner of my eye, but I didn't care. Those sachets are so small you need at least four, especially when you're having battered fish because it can be so dry. Maybe I did take too much sauce but so what? Nine sachets probably costs the takeaway literally about nine pence, cost price; what do they care? Especially when I ordered the large cod. As the lady passed me the bag over the countertop, I held out my bank card and smiled a little, to suggest that's how I'd like to pay. The lady didn't smile back; she just nodded at a little square of card sellotaped to the side of the till:

CASH ONLY SORRY

Great. So I have to go and find a cashpoint because you don't want to pay your taxes.

'Is there a cashpoint around here?' I asked the lady, wincing, as if I hadn't lived there for nearly four years. She leant across the counter and pointed a red-raw, greasy looking finger down the road. 'See where Iceland's is? If you walk down to that, about a hundred yards past Iceland's but on the other side of the road. Or there's one back at the train station.'

Perfect. I'd found the south of England's furthest point from any ATM. I sighed and nodded thanks.

As I stepped back onto the pavement, I resolved to have one last rummage through my wallet in case there was a rogue twenty in there. I don't keep a lot of stuff in my wallet but there's this one particular pocket in there that accumulates bits of rubbish. Receipts and old train tickets and whatnot. I shoved my fingers inside and pulled out the lump of stuff in there. A book of six First Class stamps and a folded receipt from somewhere or other. And then this other thing that I'd never seen before. It was a USB stick, one of those fancy super thin ones, where the bit you plug into the computer is sort of split in half to make it thinner. It was a slider, but I couldn't get it open, it was jammed. God knows when I must have acquired that. I looked around for a bin to chuck it into. There weren't any. St Albans was like that near the train station. The pavements are too narrow.

I carried on down the road towards this ATM, thinking about Ellie and what I should message her. All the while, I was fiddling with this thing in my hand. It was a fancy one, that's for sure; it had a soft touch finish. I just kept absent-mindedly sliding my thumb over it as I walked.

Further down the road, I felt the mechanism move in my hand. The thing had come loose. I frowned and looked down at it as I walked, sliding it fully open to expose the connection bit. I realised why it hadn't been opening: there had been a little slip of paper inside, blocking the mechanism. A thin, yellow slip; an edge torn from a Post-It note. One end of it was still sticky. I turned it over and saw that someone had written on it in very soft pencil. It was so faint you couldn't really read it in the darkness. I angled the note towards the light from a passing shop. The writing was clumsy and untidy, and it took a while to make it out but eventually I worked it out. It said:

I know what you did.

Seventeen

I abandoned my fish and chips. I didn't feel like eating; I needed to think. I walked straight home and paced up and down my living room, staring at this note. I suddenly needed to know what was going on. I had shut down that business because it was nothing to do with me, but now it felt like I needed to see what was happening.

Every minute or so I'd notice myself lifting the yellow note and staring at it, holding it really close to my face, as if I was about to make some forensic discovery. Suddenly it felt very important to me to get a feel for what was going on. This note was no doubt an unrelated thing; it looked old anyway.

But all of a sudden I just had to check in on it all, the Richard King thing.

I began carefully laying a trail of a person relaxing at home and reading the news. I went on the BBC website and clicked through a few stories. I'd 'read' each of them for a minute or two, before I eventually arrived at a story about an arrest in the killing of The Farringdon Banker. *The Killing of the Farringdon Banker.* That was how they perceived it.

I don't know why but somewhere deep inside I was still hoping the case might be perceived as *probably an accident.* I had been doing a decent job of consciously keeping it out of my mind's atmosphere from day to day. Reading about it all again sent this nasty, cold wave over me. It wasn't disappearing. This indignant feeling overwhelmed me for a brief moment. I felt angry that the investigators couldn't just leave it alone.

At the bottom of the story there were links to other stories about the case, including the one about an arrest being made. I wondered for a moment about whether I should Google the arrest. This happened in my proximity, literally on my way home from work. Of course I'm interested in what's happening. I see signposts about it every day. *Of course it's of interest to me.* To anyone looking at this situation from the outside, it would be stranger if I *didn't* Google it.

The guy the police had taken in was called Jacob Evatt. He was twenty-eight and had already been in prison before, for GBH and for being an accessory to a robbery. He'd fallen out with Richard King earlier that evening in a wine bar in Exmouth Market. The disagreement started over Evatt telling King's group to keep their noise down. It'd set off a chain of events that led to King insulting Evatt's partner as he left the bar.

The pair had a brief scuffle in the street (with Evatt, by all accounts, easily on top) before a group of men from outside another pub on the street separated the two. A coked-up Evatt had been more or less dragged away from the scene by his girlfriend. King by this point, probably wisely, had headed off towards Farringdon train station on his own. *Oh no wait, not wisely.* But he'd scuttled off that way and the theory was that Evatt followed him.

It was all over Twitter: a few different people had reported the incident to the police and Evatt was quite quickly identified. There was supposedly CCTV footage not long after he'd left the wine bar showing him walking alone, without his girlfriend.

He was a really intense character. The photos of him on the news made his eyes look so wild. And there was a lot to read about him on the internet.

Jacob Evatt was enormous, about six foot seven. He was white and had a closely shaved head. His hairline was just about visible and it reached down towards his forehead in this tight 'V'. His hair had receded a hell of a lot for a guy in his twenties. He had these thick, heavy brows that made it look like he was always frowning, and these two deep, thick brow wrinkles across his forehead, like a Shar-Pei. And beneath it all, these intense, burning-black eyes.

He didn't work. He was registered disabled because of problems with his back. By all accounts, he'd actually broken his back once. Someone had literally driven a car over his body – twice – forwards and backwards, during a fight. He'd also had metal pins put into his shoulder and back after coming off a motorbike.

For an unemployed guy he didn't half wear nice clothes though. He was always dressed sharply in designer jeans and tailored jackets. His girlfriend posted regularly about them eating out and drinking in the nicest places. He was clearly a man with a lot going on behind the scenes. He'd been in prison before for beating up a group of students after the screening of an England World Cup match in a pub in Barking. He'd smashed a chair over the head of one of those kids and left him with a fractured skull. He went to prison another time along with a guy called Jamie Keane, who had since been locked up for having half a kilo of cocaine in a broken fridge freezer in his garage.

Evatt was also banned from visiting Russia and the Ukraine after being arrested and briefly held there for his part in some football-related violence. The more I found out about this guy, the less I liked him. The girlfriend was nice looking and looked pretty normal. I wondered how women like that put up with it. If someone had to be taken off the streets over this, I was glad it was Jacob Evatt.

That's what I said to myself.

I picked up the yellow note and held it close to my face again.

I know what you did.

I sat for a moment and played out the scenario that someone did know what had happened and that this was their way of telling me. And then they'd found a moment to place this in my wallet.

So, why tell me? Why not tell the police? The note looked so old. Plus the fact it was crushed together with that USB stick I'd had in there. Surely something getting so crushed inside the casing of that stick would take months, not days.

I opened the stick and instinctively blew into the mechanism to clear it of dust. I actually read somewhere that you're not supposed to do that and that it makes matters worse – but I always find myself doing it. I wasn't sure I'd ever seen that thing before. I shoved it into my laptop.

The USB stick had just the one file on it, a video. It was a huge file and took a while to open. When it did, I saw a blank, grey background for a few seconds, and then a chillingly familiar image. It was a shot of a scene in Farringdon, taken from somewhere very high up.

It was night-time, but there it all was. You could see the building site; all the equipment and skips full of rubble. Down to the right there were fences and what looked like some office buildings – and the alleyway.

My shortcut.

I couldn't see the flowers and football shirt that well-wishers had since left in the alley, so the footage must have been from before. In the background, was just this series of high-rise buildings, whose lower levels were mostly obscured by obstacles on the building site. It took me a few moments to get my bearings, but I guessed that this was filmed from a top floor apartment in one of the buildings adjacent to the site.

The video was really clean and crisply shot. It definitely wasn't what you might be used to seeing off a CCTV camera or something. I didn't know much about cameras, but I knew this had been taken on quite a powerful one. It was shot from high up and most likely quite far away, but it wasn't grainy or pixelated. It was clear. The camerawork was really steady. Not moving or swaying, even slightly. I guessed it wasn't being held in someone's hands.

For a minute or so, nothing happened. I reached forward and turned the volume right up, in case I was missing anything. No sound. Eventually, a figure emerged. It was a person running, down the alley. It wasn't me or Richard King. A tall man, possibly a jogger, with long legs whirling beneath him like long helicopter blades eating up the ground. He disappeared and it was still again.

As I watched I became acutely conscious of occasional moving figures in high up apartment windows. I saw a person walk into their bedroom and sit on the edge of their bed while typing on their phone. I saw another person go into their kitchen and open the fridge. After a few minutes there was some more movement in the alley; another figure. This time it was unmistakeably the banker, Richard King.

My heart sank. There he was, clear as day. You couldn't see his facial features in any detail, but I could easily tell it was him. I didn't know him at all but even I knew that gait. That weird bird-man physique and awkward walk, flat-footed and leaning a little bit too far forward.

He walked up the alley in mostly a straight line. Even from that distance I could sense his nasty bird-eyes darting around in front of him. And then eventually, another figure. Me. I watched myself amble down the alley. You couldn't see my face, or make out my clothing very well. I wondered whether I'd know it was me, if I didn't know it was me.

You saw me amble down the alley and you saw me change course slightly to avoid King. As we approached each other you could see we were interacting, but there was no sound and you couldn't really make out facial features. You saw us bump together, then me turning around and taking a few steps back towards him. You saw him shake his head, slightly. Then a few seconds later I hit him, and you saw him go to the ground. You saw me leave and then come back and kneel next to the body. Then the screen went blank.

A few seconds later the footage came back, but this time much, much closer in on Richard King's prone body, plapped on the floor like a wet fish. And then it just stopped. That was it. The end of the video. I plucked the USB stick out of my computer and stared at it in horror.

Eighteen

I must've watched that video more than a hundred times. I became expert at skipping the lulls between the action. Knowing when it was time to slide the bar along and how far to slide it. I understood the message, obviously.

I spent hours lying face-down on my bed, half-hanging off the side, staring at the floor. I didn't even turn the TV on for background noise. I just lay there, thinking. I didn't stress, I didn't cry, I didn't move a muscle. I just lay there, thinking. Processing.

Night Nurse wasn't really helping me sleep as well as it used to. I'd got into a pattern of taking it, and I think the effects had started to wear off. Just this once, I decided to double-dose. I'd run out of weed and I needed something to slow my head down. I could get some sleep and hopefully have all my wits about me for the next day.

I took four tablets and opened a beer, changing position now to face the ceiling. Eventually, I turned the TV on and watched a subtitled Japanese documentary from the nineties. These villagers who were having some sort of memorial. A girl who was like seven had to smoke about fifty fish on a barbecue made of fashioned metal wires. She did brilliantly, as far as I'm concerned.

I'd stuffed the USB stick under the bottom layer of a box of biscuits in my kitchen cupboard. I needed to work out what I was going to do with it. What I was going to do *about* it was another thing.

On Friday afternoon I cancelled all my meetings and sat at my desk with my headphones on, pretending to be in deep meditation over something. Work felt like an out-of-body experience as I pushed through the motions of the everyday, my mind whirring noisily in the background like a broken ceiling fan. At lunchtime there was a small crowd heading down to The Three Kings for a drink, but I swerved it. Much as I wanted alcohol, I couldn't bear to make small talk. Or any kind of talk.

At about two thirty a weird feeling came over me. My body felt weak and tingly. It'd started from my fingertips and toes and edged up to my chest, making my lungs feel like they'd shrunk to the size of raisins. It wasn't really possible to take a deep, refreshing lump of air down. Everything felt tight, the rusty springs were back in my torso.

I decided to go for a walk, to try to clear my head. I'd made it part of my routine now to glance up at every street camera I passed, noting its angle and line of sight. I guessed most of these cameras either weren't on or contained film that gets recorded over every few days or weeks. I know that's how it works. If there was anything on those tapes that was useful to the police, I'd have heard about it by now.

I scrolled absent-mindedly through my phone as I walked to Itsu. It was a nice day; cold, but bright. I was going to get some duck dumplings bullshit with soy sauce, and a chocolate mousse. I couldn't face the shortcut and the homage to King, so I walked the long way around. I scanned news headlines on my phone. There hadn't been anything about Jacob Evatt in a while.

Then I felt something bump against the side of my left foot. It was like someone had bashed the side of my heel with a mallet. My heels knocked straight together and, even as I realised what was happening, my momentum carried me forward towards the ground. I didn't manage to get my hands up in time. My chin and left elbow smashed against the pavement, sending my phone spinning off in front of me. As I tried to get up, a hand grabbed my collar and pulled me back down towards the ground.

Nineteen

'Don't try to get up too quick. Stay there,' said a male voice.

'You all right? You're bleeding. Here.' A woman strode up from behind me, pointing a pack of tissues at my chin and lowering her arm towards me, as if I should use her as a frame to climb back up. I put my hand on my chin; it was bleeding, I could feel bits of rough skin peeling off it. My hand was scratched too.

'Are you okay?' the male voice asked.

I tried to answer and realised I'd bitten my tongue when I'd hit the ground. As the adrenaline wore off, I became aware I was in a lot of pain.

'I am *so* sorry,' the voice said.

I looked up and saw a middle-aged guy standing over me. He was wearing black corduroy trousers and brown lace-up brogues. He had a checked shirt on, done up to the very top, under a purple donkey jacket.

'I think we bumped feet,' he said. 'I was rushing.' He leant down and put his hands either side of my torso to help me up.

'Ooh!' He noticed the scratches on my chin and winced. His breath stank.

'I'm all right,' I said, brushing imaginary dust off my chest.

My teeth hurt where my jaws had knocked together. I started patting my pockets for my phone.

'Here!' muttered Donkey Jacket, scampering off ahead of me to pick it up. 'You dropped it.'

He brought it back to me with his head tilted to the side apologetically. He had an oily nose and silver-framed, oversized glasses. I didn't think he looked like a hipster, meaning he was wearing the hipster glasses unironically. Meaning they were just really horrible glasses.

'Cheers,' I said, reaching to take it from him.

He snapped his hand back and his warm demeanour dropped for the first time.

'I'm not a grass. Don't worry, I'm *not* a grass.'

I looked at him, then looked back down at his hand, where he'd withdrawn my phone. Slowly, he handed it back to me,

'Sorry, here!'

I snatched it and shoved it into my back pocket. I stepped back from him, warily. His whole demeanour was weird and excitable. He edged towards me again, glancing over his shoulder first to check for who might be listening. Then he grabbed my wrist and lowered his head, glowering at me beneath his brow:

'Listen, I'm not a grass but I know you saw my video. Just relax okay, Wilbur. It's fine. I didn't mean to trip you over just then.' He nodded back over his shoulder at the site of the accident.

Accident?

What was I supposed to do? This was *gone*. I'd finished with all this. I wanted him to know I had absolutely no idea what he was talking about. *Absolutely no idea*. I glanced around me to see if he was alone, then blinked back at him, feigning confusion. He let go of my wrist and slowly opened his palms at me in a motion of surrender.

'I just want to talk to you about what happened; I haven't told anyone. I promise I won't.'

Twenty

He called himself Solly. He walked with me the rest of the way to Itsu. He explained through excited whispers that he'd 'caught everything on camera from his balcony'. I just stared ahead and listened to him. I couldn't work out if he was insane, or trying to help, or threatening me or what.

He said he was a filmmaker and had caught the whole incident on film by accident. He said he 'recognised me from around Farringdon' when he saw me in the video. Apparently, he wanted to talk to me about it before he deleted the footage. He said he felt bad for witnessing it and he 'just wanted to get some things off his chest, without it going any further'.

I didn't really know what to say to this. I mean, I understood that the guy felt guilty or whatever, but I was blown away by the fact he'd come and found me to talk about it. How on earth had he found me?

He was a weird guy, no doubt about that. He looked like a creep. His thin, dark hair was swept back revealing a shrivelled forehead crowning those glasses. His eyes were big, green and pathetic, with deep crow's-feet stretching out across his temples. He seemed bent on letting me know that he 'didn't want this to go any further'.

'I need someone to talk to, so I can move on.' He kept going on about not being a grass. That part seemed important to him.

He pushed a hand into his coat pocket and thrust a folded Post-it note at me.

'Call me. Please. Call me when you finish work, yeah? Solly, yeah? Nice to meet you.'

I didn't know what to say. I was still a little bit in shock from falling over. I held my hand against the cut on my chin and snatched the piece of paper.

Of course, I did contact him. I couldn't not. Since the second I'd seen that video, I'd been obsessing about ramifications and what the risks were. Now I had an answer. *I'd been seen.* Not only that, but I'd also been caught on camera. *He only needs to turn that film over to the police and I'm fucking cooked.*

It didn't seem like he wanted to, though. That's one thing he'd been completely clear on. He'd have done it by now and from the few minutes I spent in his company I'd picked up on a sincere aversion to *grassing.* But he clearly wanted something out of me.

Just before 5 p.m. I text him.

'Hello Solly. Are you free for a drink after work?'

He replied seconds later with an address in Farringdon and the question:

'HALF 6?'

Twenty-One

At five o'clock I left work and headed to the address Solly had given me. When I found the place, I stood staring up at the top of the high rise for a while. I ambled into a pub on the corner, to wait until half past six. I sat by the window, watching people going in and out of the building across the road. By a quarter past six I'd finished two pints and decided to cross the road and ring the buzzer.

Solly's apartment was on the top floor of the high rise. He was waiting at the door when I came out of the lift, ready to receive me. I smiled at him as I approached him; some sort of lingering instinct to be nice, I suppose.

He showed me in. The place was disgusting, with stained walls and cheap, pocked carpets. I stood in the middle of his living room while he noisily shook a stack of plastic chairs stacked in a cupboard. Eventually, he emerged with one and held it out to me.

I took it from him and placed it in the corner, near the front door. I didn't feel comfortable sitting down yet, so I hovered in front of the chair as I scanned the room. It wasn't that untidy, but it was dirty and there was a pungent smell hanging in the air, like chip fat and dirty laundry.

He didn't offer me a drink – I didn't want one from that kitchen anyway. He excused himself and went to the bathroom while I looked around. The kitchen area was in the corner, partitioned from the living room by an untidy countertop. An awkward row of appliances sat covered in a dense, shiny film of grease. I made a silent promise to myself that I would never touch anything in that place. I kept my hands in my pockets.

You could see finger smears all over the hob, and the ceiling was a dark grey colour, perhaps caused by smoke from a fryer, or someone smoking cigarettes while cooking, over a long period of time. Across the room, opposite the kitchen four large, dirty windows glared out at Farringdon. Each of the corners of the floor had these little build-ups of dust and grime in them, like they hadn't been cleaned properly in years. The walls were mostly bare except for a wooden-framed painting of a landscape scene. (I guessed he'd painted that himself, it was absolute shit).

The weird thing was, you could tell the guy must have had money. There were clues everywhere. He had a huge Panasonic television mounted on a wall, and dotted around the place were lots of other little nods towards wealth. A Sonos sound system built into the ceiling and walls; a stylish design piece in the corner made of old metal beer kegs; and a big, brown leather wingback chair facing the TV. The chair looked nearly new from behind, but the seat was covered in what looked like key or knife scrapes and cigarette burns. Deep, black scars that looked like something hot had been dropped on there, badly burning the leather.

The smell in that place was making me feel a bit light-headed. Solly eventually re-emerged clutching a multipack bag of crisps. *Had he got them from the bathroom?* He awkwardly turned his wingback armchair to face me.

'Oh, my goodness,' he mumbled. 'What a thing! What a wild

thing, huh?!' He then jolted up and stepped forward, extending his hand to me. 'Solly.'

'I'm Will,' I said.

'I know!' he snorted. 'I know that.'

'*How* do you know?'

'I've just spent the best part of three weeks finding you,' he said, nodding, settling down into his chair. 'I've had this on my conscience! You know that guy is dead, right?'

I glared at him. 'Yes.'

'Yeah. Do you know about Jacob Everett?' he asked. He thrust his hips forwards as he fumbled in his trouser pocket. The insides of his corduroy trousers were shiny from wear.

'Evatt,' I corrected him quietly.

'He's got the rap for it,' he probed, scanning my face for a reaction.

I looked at the floor and shrugged.

'He's a fucking… He's a tough guy! No messing about,' Solly continued with a grin.

'I didn't *want*... anyone else to get the blame,' I muttered.

'Well, the guy's in the nick right now; if you don't want him to get the blame you can quite easily get him out!' he laughed. 'I'd say you can be pretty relieved someone else has got the blame – I know I would be!'

There was something in Solly's demeanour I really didn't like. He seemed excited by all this, not disturbed by it. It was like he was talking to a friend about a TV drama show. He wasn't being rude, but he clearly was asking things he already knew the answer to. He was *rubbernecking*. It all seemed a bit condescending, like he was dragging me back through it, because he could.

He pulled a bag of tobacco out of his pocket and straightened out a rolling paper on his thigh. I looked through the windows at his balcony. There were six or seven cameras out there, set up on individual tripods. A tarpaulin stood in front of them, hung from the balcony above, blocking them from the outside world, like what those nature botherers use when they're watching badgers at night. Again, it was a rich person's kit, no doubt.

'What's with the cameras?' I asked.

'Listen,' he said, now carefully placing pinches of tobacco on his rolling paper. 'I want to reassure you about something, Will.'

Here we go.

'I'm not interested in anything criminal or anything like that. My old Dad died at the hands of the police when I was a kid, so I won't deal with them.'

I took a proper, deep breath for the first time in about six hours.

'This is just about me and the way I feel, I just feel shocked about the tape. I need closure.'

It felt like cold, clean water being poured on my hot, dry head. He seemed sincere. I looked into his wrinkled eyes and he looked back at me and nodded, breathing out slowly. I believed him.

'It wasn't my fault,' I said eventually, staring at the dirty floor.

He didn't reply for ages, then he leant towards me and spoke gently, 'But it's okay isn't it. It ended well. You haven't got the blame.'

'I don't think anyone should get the blame. There's no blame except the—'

'Insurance,' he interjected.

'Sorry?'

He slowly reached into his inside pocket and pulled out a lighter. After lighting his cigarette, he gestured his hand at the window.

'He was an insurance broker, King.'

'Why did you send me the video?'

'If I hadn't, would you have come and met me?' Solly replied.

'I needed to get you round here, didn't I? Off the record, I mean; away from the' – he gestured around at the top corners of the room with his finger, as if to suggest some form of surveillance. He really was a bit nuts. I sensed he'd spent too long on his own.

'I need to ask you about it, so I can get my head around it,' Solly continued. He put his cigarette down momentarily and held the multipack bag of crisps out to me. I declined with a shake of the head. He took out a single pack of Ready Salted and placed the rest down on the floor.

He opened the bag and started taking crisps out, one by one. I noticed he'd hold them in his mouth and suck them for a while before chewing. Sometimes taking a pull from his cigarette while a soggy crisp mouldered in his mouth. The whole thing was revolting to watch. He breathed really heavily through his nose all the time, and it'd intensify when he ate.

Solly was about five foot ten and looked between fifty and sixty years old. His look was pretty much overshadowed by those dumb glasses. They ratted him out as a bit of an oddball. He had thinning hair and his face was covered in red blotches and little scratches and cuts from an inadequate razor. Although he was slim, his skin sat loosely around his jowls and he had these big, overgrown eyebrows and a slightly hooked nose, which pointed downwards to a thin, dry pair of lips. His skin looked pallid, oily and unkempt.

'Go on,' I prompted him.

'Tell me about it, from the start,' he said, raising his eyebrows and placing another piece of crisp in his mouth to suck. Again, it was this apparent excitement that got to me. But I knew I needed to indulge him and get it over with. So, I told him what had happened. He didn't react. His expression remained completely blank; he just listened. It was like he'd heard it all before.

When I finished, he heaved a deep sigh, nodded and placed his empty crisp packet down on the arm of his chair. 'I get it,' he said, reassuringly.

I held my hands out as if to gesture back that I didn't know what else to say.

'Do you feel bad?' he asked.

'Of course. But what can I do now, except feel bad?'

'Nothing,' he said. 'You can't do anything. But I'll tell you what: I feel a lot better now you've told me the story behind it. It sounds like he got what he had coming.'

I winced at that. No need to go that far.

Twenty-Two

I sat with Solly for another forty-five minutes or so. Despite the fact that this guy was patently odd, it felt good to talk it all through with someone. Felt like I was getting some of it out of me. But there were still some bits that didn't quite add up. I wasn't buying the whole *'I've seen you around Farringdon'* thing. How had he seen me in that video and then identified me? How had he found me?

I didn't see any point in holding anything back. I thought, I might as well finish all this off, today. So, I asked him: asked him how he'd really found me, how he got that USB stick into my wallet and whether he'd deliberately tripped me over in the high street. I asked him to tell me everything straight.

He stuck by his story, that he recognised me from having 'seen me around'. He said he had that alleyway under surveillance inadvertently, almost 24/7, so he'd see me going through there quite a lot. In fairness, he referred to a blue and white raincoat I wore on occasion. That surprised me and made it seem oddly credible. He obviously *had* seen me before. I hadn't worn that raincoat in months.

He explained that he was a regular in The Three Kings and said he would see me in there with colleagues, a couple of times a week. He said he'd go in there most afternoons and 'would regularly see people from my company'. He admitted once he recognised me in the footage, he'd followed me home from work one night with the intention of putting his note through the letterbox of my home later that evening. He said he was 'worried I might attack him' if he confronted me face to face.

But then he said that I'd detoured to that bar in Liverpool Street. He'd lifted my wallet while I was chatting to Ellie in the crowded bar and handed it in to the management with his note and USB stick, knowing I'd end up asking them for it. He said it 'made life easier for him' to do it that way. I told him it would've been easier just to come and talk to me.

And he completely denied tripping me over deliberately. He said he'd been waiting outside my office to speak to me but that'd he'd been distracted and ended up having to follow me into Farringdon. He kept saying he hadn't meant to trip me over, but he kept grinning while he was saying it. It was as if he was undermining his own sentiment. Reassuring me with his words, but nullifying them with his face. Without thinking, I touched the sore skin on the side of my chin.

'You followed me home? And wait – and... so, why are you recording the alleyway?' I exclaimed.

Solly slumped back in his chair and eyed me. 'I *don't*...' He looked thoughtful for a moment, before a corner of his lip curled into a grin.

'Look.' He launched himself out of his chair and scooped up two different remote-control devices. As he did so, he glanced back at me and grinned conspiratorially. 'I've got something on you, you can have something on me.'

I braced myself. *What fresh hell is this?*

Five minutes later I was watching in disbelief as Solly showed me his homemade pornography. Adjacent to the alleyway, a few hundred metres from Solly's balcony, was a new office block.

The top few floors were apartment space. Solly explained to me that 'eighty or ninety per cent' of the flats had 'a decent girl or woman' living in them, and that some of them 'had active sex' (whatever that meant) and that 'loads of them hadn't got curtains up' or didn't close their curtains.

I suppose, when you move into a new build, you have other priorities for the first few months. Especially when your windows are so high up from the street. He went on to explain that over the last thirty-five years, he'd accumulated a library of over 600 fully edited, high quality videos, with genres ranging from unsuspecting women having sex in their homes to other unsuspecting women having cameras angled at them on the Underground, in the supermarket or in various different changing rooms.

He'd invested in some serious equipment to fuel his hobby: he had all manner of tech (most of which looked brand new) including a Nikon telephoto lens with night vision that he reckoned had cost him over thirty grand. I didn't speak while he excitedly talked me through his setup. I kept realising I had my head in my hands and having to correct myself. What the hell, man.

I was quite pleased with how things had ended up and didn't want to sour things or rock the boat by appearing judgemental or broaching the idea that he was entirely mental. In a funny way, I felt quite lucky that it was a pervert who had seen this. In a funny way, I'd rather it was a deviant. It meant *he* had no incentive for anyone to know about what he has, either. I quietly resolved that I'd post an anonymous letter to all those ladies in that apartment, to let them know it was time to invest in some curtains.

'It's all just self-preservation,' he said as he walked me to his front door. 'Did you know, in China if you hit someone with your car and cause them an injury, you have to pay all their medical bills relating to the accident, for the rest of their life? If it's a serious accident and the person is seriously harmed but *lives*, then that could amount to hundreds of thousands of pounds – *who can afford that?* But if the person *dies*, you just have to pay for the funeral: as a one-off expense.'

I nodded slowly.

He continued, 'So, what's happened is this unexpected *hit-to-kill* instinct in a lot of people. A driver might accidentally hit a pedestrian because they're say, eating pretzels at the wheel, and their mind is instinctively like, "Oh wow. This poor human being, I hope they're ok", and then bang! Straight away their morality flips 180. Logic clicks in and they see the bald facts of survival. And just like that, instead of hoping the person is alive, they're hoping the person is *dead*. There are these videos of people hitting a pedestrian with their car and then reversing over the body to finish the job. I can show you, if you want.'

I shook my head.

'Do you understand me though? It's not that the person wants to kill anybody or has any negative intention at all. These are normal people we're talking about, like you and me. It's just self-preservation. We all do it. They've probably got kids to feed and put through school and parents whose medication needs paying for and they're just thinking, "Look, it's happened now, and I can't afford to lose all my money, so let's go", and they make a judgement in the moment that can keep their lives going. And not let it be overshadowed by that one mad moment they never asked for. But first they've just got to do something bad, really quickly.'

I didn't like this analogy. I wouldn't do that, I don't think. The reversing. That's not me. I nodded again, and sucked up my strength for one last push. 'Hey, thanks Solly. I mean, you've listened to what I had to say and I'm glad you understand. I've just got to let this thing rest, now. I've got to get on.'

He pursed his lips and nodded sagely. 'It's gone. Forget it. If you back someone into a corner where their livelihood is at risk, they're going to do what they can to escape. You got backed in and you've managed to escape it, so I'm happy for you. World keeps turning.'

I forced a smile at him.

As he reached to open the front door, I turned back to face him. 'Why go to all that trouble?' I nodded back towards the camera.

Solly smiled. 'Because I needed to get you to come here, didn't I. I needed to talk to you properly.'

I nodded but I still didn't understand the necessity for all this. He did not seem as wounded or confused as he was making out. In fact, he seemed very much in control of the whole situation. I looked him in the eyes for only about the third time since I'd met him. 'Look, I have to ask. The footage. The actual video. Can I take it? Then I can just dispose of it. I mean, I know it won't go anywhere, it'd just put my mind at rest if I know for sure it's *gone.*'

Solly looked perturbed. 'What d'you mean?'

'I… the video?' I detected a change in the atmosphere.

After a long, awkward pause he warmed up again. 'Oh! The video! Yes.'

'Yeah, I mean… if that's all right?' I didn't want to seem distrustful, but I needed to finally draw a line under everything.

'Cool,' he said. 'Yeah. I'll delete it.'

'Can… I see you delete it?' I asked.

'No,' he said firmly.

The atmosphere had definitely shifted. All that empathy had instantly drained from him. I strained a fake chuckle. 'Okay but… how will I know you've done it?' I asked.

'Because I'll tell you I've done it,' he replied.

I folded my arms and held his gaze. 'If I don't see you delete it, how will I know it's gone?' I asked.

'You'll know, because I'll tell you,' he repeated.

I forced an awkward smile. 'Look, please... it's important so—'

'Listen to me,' he growled. 'A bit of respect from you here, mate?'

I looked at him in disbelief. 'Solly I'm not... I don't mean to be disrespectful.'

'It doesn't seem like it!' he said. 'What, you want to stand over me while I delete it?' He was really shouting and the door to the corridor was open.

'No, I don't mean like that —' I protested. I was trying to bring the tone back to where it had been before.

His eyes darted wildly. He leant towards my face and whispered, 'Are you a murderer?'

'No!' I said.

'Good,' he said. 'Because I'm not a grass. Good night Will. Consider it done.'

He gently closed the door in my face.

Twenty-Three

Things became difficult. I hit an emotional wall. I think I'd
buried the initial trauma of what'd happened under this indignant feeling. A determination to escape that consumed anything
else. Over time, the defence mechanism lowers, and you start
to see things more for what they are. Or what they were. It
was starting to hit home that I'd caused a person's death.

Without going into whether it was deliberate or whether he
deserved it or whether I deserve it, when the anaesthesia of
shock wore off, I started to really feel the weight of it. The
police, Solly, Richard King... Something in my mind retreated,
like it didn't want to confront the world any more.

But not just this situation – any of the world. I took to
smoking more and would normally drink a pint or two at
lunchtime, starting the evening session before six, without fail.

Only now, I was doing my drinking sessions alone, in my
kitchen. I hadn't fallen out with anyone from work as such, but
I just didn't feel like I could face anybody. The folks at my
work have got quite good at knowing when to give me space.

This is what depression is like: it takes you in, rips your soul
out and takes control of your whole social outlook.

It makes a puppet of you: pulling you this way and that while you watch your relationships burn up as you alienate people more and more. You can see yourself moving from scene to scene and feel all over that it's wrong, and that you're not participating properly. But it's just not possible to change the thinking pattern and rescue yourself.

One of the things that I've noticed over the years is that when you have depression, you just want everything to *finish*. Every project you're working on, every night out, every conversation, every sexual experience: you're waiting to get to the end. And why? So you can go and do what? Nothing. So you can go and do nothing. Somehow doing nothing feels like the least-worst lifestyle choice. You don't feel like you should be finishing anything when you're doing nothing, because there isn't anything to finish.

One of the itchy features of being an introvert in the modern world is that people think talking is the answer to everything. So, my depression has always got this burning anger and resentment beneath it, because surely everybody can see the signs of a man struggling but nobody helps. Even though I know deep down nobody can help, I'm still angry at all of them. All those stupid people talking to me about stupid things and bothering me instead of helping me. In the full knowledge of course, that *I* don't even know how they can help me – so how can they?

And so, I retreat into a cocoon, where it's just me and some TV show. I sink into this vacuum in my mind where everyone around me is the enemy and the people who care about me most of all are all underestimating my problem and I cannot bear to see them or be near them.

Ellie became my only meaningful contact with the world. She kept me going. Little chats, text conversations that made me feel normal, even flashes of feeling good. In a funny way, I think my appearing to cool off when I went mute for periods intrigued Ellie. She started initiating conversations more. I just couldn't relax enough to want to spend time with her. I felt like I wouldn't be able to put on a good enough show, so I kept putting it off.

Solly had sent me into a spin. It was the vagueness of it all. And this creeping sense that he was revelling in it. He'd deliberately lured me there and made me sit through that whole weird meeting with him and then left me feeling like the matter wasn't closed. It was like he was *playing* with the situation.

A few days after I'd met him, I received a text message from him, saying, '**DONE**'.

There was something so arrogant and passive about the brevity of it. It was like knew he was in control. He knew I'd need more information than that, but I couldn't ask and risk implicating myself further. I replied, '**Ok**'.

I didn't believe that he'd actually disposed of the file. But I wasn't in the mindset of wanting to confront that problem. I sensed that he wasn't interested in telling the police, and that there was something else he wanted. But I didn't hear from him again after that. He just vanished, as quickly as he'd appeared.

Ellie came over one evening to watch a movie. I thought it'd give my brain some breathing space. She was great company, a calming presence. She told me stories about her days at uni and working in the City. She felt like this little pipeline of oxygen in the middle of everything.

She knew when I wanted to chat and when I just wanted to be silent. A great intuition for it. Sometimes we'd spend long periods in silence; it didn't seem to faze her. I wished I could tell her how fucking grateful I was to have her around. But it would have seemed a bit extreme, that early on.

One morning in early December, I got a text message from him. It just said, '**EVATT CHARGED.**' I Googled it but couldn't find anything, so I replied, **'Haven't heard anything about that.'** I was hoping he'd elaborate but didn't want to give him the satisfaction of knowing.

'HES BEING CHARGED WITH IT,' he repeated.

'Details?' I replied.

No reply.

Three hours later, the story was in the news. This guy Jacob Evatt was to be charged with the killing of Richard King, and was awaiting trial. This huge wave of simultaneous relief and guilt smashed into me. I was shaking uncontrollably.

As it turned out, not only did the police not have evidence to use against me, they had overwhelming evidence against this Evatt. I scrolled through stories and Tweets about it in utter disbelief. It was being talked about as an open and shut case. The police had CCTV evidence of Evatt and King fighting outside a bar in Clerkenwell, then of Evatt pursuing King towards Old Street station.

Then there was the CCTV blind spot down Turnmill Street and that alley. What they seemed to know was that King had gone down that alley, and Evatt had been following him in that direction. They knew Evatt was after him, and King's body and clothes were covered in Evatt's DNA from the scuffle they'd had previously. It became clear that everything the police had, pointed to this one guy. I started daring to think I might have been saved by this chaotic fluke of fate. I didn't know how to feel, or what to think. But I knew I needed to keep my head down.

Twenty-Four

At that time of year, it was difficult to bury my head in work. Ad agencies are like that – when clients start closing down, things go very quiet. And people were closing ranks for Christmas. I focused on Ellie. I needed more human interaction if I was to move forward and get back to normality.

She started coming over to visit me every few days. It was easier to meet at my place than hers; she lived in a house share in Mornington Crescent, where privacy was at a premium. We'd usually sit in my bedroom, drinking wine and watching films. Sometimes we'd venture out to the pub, but we'd hardly interact with anybody else. Neither of us really wanted to. We were in our own little bubble, away from the harshness of outside. We didn't need anybody else.

We'd sit and talk about the news or tell each other things about our lives. I'd tell her funny or cringeworthy stories from work. She had this elegant way of making me feel funnier than I am. She just seemed to *get* my sense of humour. Her humour was dry as hell. Just her mannerisms and reactions to things would crack me up. I told her I thought she could have been a comedy actor if she'd wanted to. She didn't like that. I told her, 'I didn't mean like *Mr Bean* comedy.' That didn't help.

The last Monday before Christmas, Ellie and I walked together through London to work in the morning. I kissed her goodbye and things felt good. I ignored any guilt that started creeping in. I never, ever allowed myself a thought about King, or that guy Evatt. It wasn't coming back into my world.

I hadn't heard anything from Solly; I was beginning think he'd genuinely lost interest in me. Nonetheless, I'd taken the step of leaving only £5,000 in a savings account and withdrawing the rest. This was just in case he decided to shake me down and I needed to prove that that was 'all I had'. Aside from that, I just tried to get my life moving again.

Everyone at work was in high spirits. I'd been helping a colleague run a brainstorm session with some clients. A brainstorm is one of those weird business rituals that Americans insist on us all going through, even though we all know nothing useful ever comes out of them. It's part of our job to do them, though; clients like them.

A biscuit company had briefed us to redesign their '*Iconic Christmas Tin*' (for the following year's Christmas) and we had to begin the process by pretending everyone in the team had contributed to the ideas, which we'd then continue to do until the Creative Director came up with an idea. Then we'd just present that and bin everything else. (Yes, that is how pointless most of my job is). I stuck some Christmas music on to create a bit of atmosphere and we got on with it.

We ended the day with a room that looked like a bomb had hit it and a big stack of A1 paper, all covered in illegible felt-pen scribbles and little diagrams. Everyone thanked me and fucked off. It was weird watching grown adults pretend those things had been really worthwhile and enriching. Deep down, we all knew they weren't.

An intern called Mascha eventually emerged and helped me tidy up. Mascha had a big mole above her left eye that nobody ever acknowledged. I always felt good after finishing one of those things and getting that process out of the way for a while. I packed up and by about half four, I felt I'd done my part for the day. I asked around if anyone fancied a quick pub trip (no takers) before heading off in the direction of home. I pulled my phone out to message Ellie; I wanted to ask her if she wanted to come to mine that night for dinner.

I made it a few metres from the office door, when a police car slowly edged around the corner, coming to a stop outside the front of the office. I could see Kane in the front passenger seat; Probert was driving. I waved to Kane and she nodded back. I wanted to continue walking but curiosity got the better of me, so I stopped and shouted over as they got out of the car, 'Back again?'

While Probert stopped to adjust the driver-side wing mirror, Kane started her way over to me.

'It's Will, isn't it?'

'Yes, hi.' I felt my blood pressure begin to creep up, but I was determined to stay cool.

'Will, I'm sorry to disturb you again; do you mind if we have a quick word?'

'Oh.' I looked at my watch and then back at her. 'Sure.' God knows why I checked my watch. I didn't have anywhere to be except home, drinking prosecco with Ellie. I led them into a vacant office, asking if they wanted refreshment and whether they wanted anyone else to join us. They declined both. As we sat down, I made a silent promise not to let Kane turn the mood sour. Whatever they had to say, I'd be helpful and positive and boring, just like a normal person.

I was going to be nice and forgettable, and get them to move on again, like before. *If they could link me to King, they'd have done it months ago. They've already got their man.*

'Will,' began Probert, 'as you've probably guessed, we're here about the death of Richard King.'

Twenty-Five

I sat motionless and listened while they went back over the basics. They told me King got hit on the head with something next to the building site near Farringdon station. An injury to his head had caused a hematoma, which caused his death. Apparently, the way he'd fallen probably resulted in an impact between the pavement, and 'the softer part of his skull'.

That turn of phrase made me so nauseous.

His body had been found between 9.50 p.m. and 10 p.m. by a resident of a nearby apartment, who was using the alley as a shortcut home from the train station. When I asked, Probert said the police were 'pursuing a number of leads' around the case.

What about Evatt? I was itching to ask. These things normally get solved early or not at all. And they'd already solved it. They had their man. The likelihood of finding meaningful new evidence at that stage must be really low. And yet, here they were, in front of the guy who did it.

The guy who did it.

On the plus side, there didn't seem to be any urgency or the sense of trepidation I'd imagine comes with apprehending a *suspect*. They were calm as cows. They both gave off this settled vibe of *going through the motions*, which relaxed me a bit. Neither even took their coat off before sitting down. I concentrated on keeping my breathing slow and steady.

Probert opened a notepad. 'Will, the conversation we're about to have with you is very important. I want you to forget everything that's gone before and treat this as your first involvement with us.'

Kane instantly glanced over at him as he said that. You could tell she was pissed off about something. Probert pulled a piece of paper from his pocket and began slowly unfolding it as he spoke. 'It's not easy to remember things from a specific time in the past,' he continued. 'I bet if I asked you what you did on your way home this time last week, you probably couldn't tell me.'

I smiled and shrugged.

'But we're going to need you to really *reach*. Our team's been looking at CCTV from this area and we've mapped out routes and timings for everyone who passed through there during that time.

You're one of only three people who – whether you remember it or not – almost definitely crossed paths with Richard King and almost definitely crossed paths with the person who assaulted him.'

He finished unfolding the piece of paper. It was a zoomed-in, cropped map of northeast London. He pulled a black biro from his pocket and drew a little circle halfway down St James's Walk next to Clerkenwell Green, where my office was.

It suddenly occurred to me that once again, I'd found myself in a dry-mouth situation without a glass of water. I instinctively glanced up at Kane as I tried to re-moisten my mouth from within.

'Now, that's *here*,' Probert continued, swirling his finger to clarify what the word 'here' meant. 'And that's The Three Kings pub,' he said quietly, as he drew another circle.

I could feel my temperature beginning to rise. My face was getting hot. One of the features of my office is that it's almost always oppressively hot, especially when it's cold outside.

'I'm sorry,' I interrupted, 'do you mind if I quickly go to the loo? I'm busting.'

'Yeah, of course,' said Probert, putting the biro down on the table.

Kane sighed, audibly.

'And maybe start thinking about last October for me,' Probert said as I got up. 'All we need you to do is talk us through your route and remember every detail you can. *Every* thing you saw or heard.'

Twenty-Six

When I got back, bottle of mineral water in hand, I felt calmer and more ready. At the very least, I felt confident that I wouldn't leave clammy sweat-marks on his map. I'd washed my hands with cold water, and it had temporarily cured my clamminess. I traced my route with the biro without looking up at Probert and Kane. My hand was shaking a bit, but not much. Neither wrote any notes nor said anything; they both just watched me, dead-eyed.

I told them I'd left the pub and headed down Clerkenwell Close. There were a few people out there smoking, I remembered, outside the pub, but I couldn't remember anything about them, not even if they were men or women. I thought they were probably men.

I then crossed the square. I was walking directly across the roads as opposed to using crossings, as it was so quiet. I couldn't remember seeing many cars, or much activity. It was a quiet evening. I eventually got out onto the main road, where I thought I *had* used the pedestrian crossing, before turning into the alley down the side of Limon café.

'Ok, ok; great but slow down please,' interrupted Probert. 'The more detail, the better. Slow down the journey a bit. Even if you saw the back of somebody's head in a passing window, it's worth mentioning. Assume *everything* is worth mentioning.'

I puffed my cheeks out and widened my eyes at him, as if to signify what a big ask that was. The reality was, by now I'd rehearsed my eventless version of that evening so many times in my head, I wasn't up for embellishing it or going off-piste with my description. The way I saw it, the more rigid and minimalistic my version of events, the less chance they had of catching me out.

It had occurred to me of course, that I *needed* to have someone else there in the alley, or at least, on the route nearby. So, I kept that part of the story loose.

'It wasn't very well lit down there, but I was the only person in the alley, I *think*,' I continued. 'I didn't look behind me, though. I suppose there could've been someone behind me... I wouldn't have noticed. I wasn't paying attention.'

Kane glanced at Probert before breaking her silence: 'Can I ask how many drinks you'd had?'

I winced towards the ceiling. 'Four? Maybe five?'

'Ok. So, you were not completely drunk, but not completely sober?' she enquired.

I wasn't sure how to answer that, so I just said, 'Yeah.'

Once again, there was something about Kane that didn't sit right with me. She always conducted herself like she was doubting everything being said and she had this tone with me, like she knew something I didn't.

I told them I passed through the alley without interruption before emerging at the other side, then turned left down Turnmill Street and followed it all the way down to the station.

'Do you remember which side of the road you walked on?' Probert asked.

I rolled my eyes upwards and pretended to consider the question. 'No. Sorry, I can't remember that. I normally walk straight over the road though as I reach it, so I probably did that, probably walked on the station side most of the way.'

There was an awkwardness about the two of them, all of a sudden. It was like something suddenly didn't add up to them. I ran my mind back over my story and couldn't see anything that could be deemed too controversial. I could tell Kane was cooking up some theory in her head. She was leaning forward so she partially blocked Probert's eyeline to me, like she was taking control of the conversation.

'Why do you cross over Turnmill Street when you get to it?' she asked quietly.

'It's just... quicker I suppose. Cut across the road... It seems quicker.' I shook my head at her, to show I was grasping for something interesting to say about it.

'Can you say with certainty that you didn't stop, at any point?' Kane eventually asked.

I glared at her and swigged some water. I could feel my temperature motoring up by the second. I was shaking a little and I was no longer sure if it was because I was frightened or pissed off or what.

'No.' I said. '*Of course*, I can't be sure about that. It was months ago. I'm just telling you how I vaguely remember it. It wouldn't be normal for me to stop, it would take something *abnormal* for me to stop, and I don't remember anything *abnormal* happening, so no, I'm pretty certain I didn't stop.' I felt short of breath and I could hear deathly silence in the office outside. They were all trying to listen in, I could tell. Nosy bastards.

'And you didn't see a single person, the whole way?' poked Kane.

'No, I didn't say that. I didn't necessarily see anybody, but I might've. I mean, in all probability I *did* see people, but I *don't* remember them. It was so long ago; it could be any night.'

Flustered and hot, I took another swig. I was massaging my thumbs and forefingers together, under the table. It felt like it was helping somehow.

The fucking heat in that room was unbearable. I could feel drops of sweat coming up on my forehead and down the back of my neck. Kane had this ability to get under my skin. Some people just don't fit together. It occurred to me that I would *never* have got on with Kane if we'd been at school together or in a job together or whatever.

'Might you have stopped to buy cigarettes or something?' asked Probert.

I shook my head.

'Food?'

I shook my head and shrugged at the same time. I didn't want to commit to anything, and wanted to sustain this quietly belligerent, but very reasonable level of ignorance. Besides, I couldn't be sure there were any food outlets on that route that would've been open at that time. *They were testing me out, somehow.*

Without thinking, I held up both of my palms and rubbed my face. I hadn't realised how damp my face was. I must've been really shiny. I took a deep breath. 'And I think… yeah, that's about all I've got for you guys.'

I took a nice big gulp of air and leant back in my chair, as if to suggest we should leave it there. After a few awkward seconds, Probert nodded at Kane and put his map back into his breast pocket. I got up and made towards the meeting room door.

'Will,' Kane said suddenly. 'Will—' She stopped herself and looked up towards Probert.

My blood began to boil. *What now? What is it now?* I suddenly felt this huge, rush of adrenaline and hot nausea. 'Feel a bit sick,' I muttered.

I saw Probert nod back at Kane and say something, but my hearing had gone weird. It felt like my ears had closed up a bit. I kind of heard what he said but didn't register what it meant. It was like I could hear inside my own head, and the outside world was like background noise. My feet went tingly and heavy as lead, followed by my arms. And then finally, my head. It was like feeling really freezing cold, but without the coldness of it. My lungs shrunk really tight.

I heard Kane say something to me, then Probert say something loud. I could see these tiny little flashing lights. I turned to pull the door open, get some fucking air in. My vision was narrowing in like a tunnel. A Tube train going into a tunnel. Too fast, into the dark.

I don't know how long I was out for, but about a minute later I was conscious of the mayhem going on around me. My first thought was that I'd had a heart attack. They told me I'd tried to grab the door handle on my way down and missed, falling and crashing back-first into the plate glass door. My back and head hit the glass and sent a deep, resounding *pherdhungg* echoing around the silent office.

In seconds, Em was wailing like an alley cat and three or four people were around me from either side of the doorway. Brian had tried to help me up, then they all decided I should just remain sitting on the floor. They leant me against the wall and people rushed around getting water. A couple of minutes later I told myself, and everybody else, that I felt absolutely fine. Not that different to normal really, except for the embarrassment.

I eventually persuaded everyone to leave me alone. I explained that I hadn't slept properly that week and had been feeling nauseous all day and thought it was probably some rice I'd reheated the night before. For a brief moment, I went into a panic wondering if they'd check whether I'd actually eaten rice the previous night. Would I need to prove that? My mind was running at top, fight-or-flight speed. The police offered me a lift to the train station, but I declined, saying I needed some fresh air.

As I was leaving, Probert approached me, while retrieving something from his pocket. A business card. He handed it to me and asked me to call him in the morning.

'There's still something we need to discuss with you, it won't take long,' he nodded.

I snatched it off him, without looking at him. I'd had enough, at that point, and I was worried I was going to puke. Eventually, I left the office, waving back at my concerned-looking boss Julia framing the doorway next to that jobsworth, Kane.

As soon as I'd rounded the corner I burst into tears. Full blown, toddler-like tears, punctuated with short, desperate gasps. I hadn't cried for something like three years before that. I'd probably cried less than seven or eight times in the last decade. But now it was properly coming out.

I was trembling; my hands were shaking badly. I felt physically weak, like I'd been beaten up. I hurried to the station, so I wasn't seen again by anyone. As I pressed forward, I yanked my sunglasses out of my pocket, flicked them open and pulled them onto my wet, numb face.

I didn't ask for any of this shit.

Twenty-Seven

Ellie called me at about seven. Said she was bored and could she come over. Needless to say, I was not in the mood for going out, but I wanted someone around and Ellie was a calming influence. She was pretty quiet, like me, happy to sit in silence watching TV.

She arrived just after eight, wearing leggings, a thick jumper dress and pumps. She was clutching a bottle of rosé wine, the Portuguese stuff in the stumpy bottle. Even the sight of her was calming to me. This little conduit of oxygen among the fury. She came in and we headed straight to my bedroom. It was becoming our custom to sit on my bed in the dark, watching films or documentaries.

She noticed immediately that I wasn't myself. She'd done a big double-take on me as she came through the front door and asked me what was up. I told her I was tired from work. But it became more and more of a thing. I just wasn't relaxed, and she could tell.

She sat, trying to make conversation with me while I pretended to search for something to watch. My mind was somewhere else, of course. I couldn't stop wringing my hands, it was pathetic. Why were the fucking police back? They'd

94

taken that guy in and charged him. You solve these cases early, or not at all. They charged the guy, doesn't that mean it's over? I mean, in a legal sense, it's a closed case now, right? Who was I kidding, trying to second guess where things were, *in a legal sense*.

If the police were still interested in me, they must have found something new. But they hadn't said that. They were acting like it was still a fishing expedition. Like, they were still trying to get the lie of the land. *Evidence to charge him with?* But they'd already charged him.

I knew it wouldn't be Solly. What Solly had was stone-wall, rock-solid evidence that I did it. The police wouldn't be questioning me with maps and stupid peripheral shit like that. Not if they had me on camera. *They must have found something else.* I thought about that charity clothing bin, and how often it was emptied.

I became aware of Ellie poking my arm. 'So, what do you think?' she asked.

I tried to scan back over what she'd been saying. I am a trained master when it comes to appearing to listen to someone, responding to them at the right times, without actually listening at all. It's a sort of state of split consciousness I can get into. I learned it when I was a kid, because of how much my dad used to go on about horse racing.

My powers failed me. I couldn't piece together what Ellie had been saying. Something about someone's wedding.

'Sorry, about what?' I asked, innocently. 'The wedding?' *A smokescreen. Enough to get me through.*

'Yeah,' she said glumly.

'Sorry... what was the question again?'

Ellie got up and stood at the foot of my bed. 'Will, can I ask you something?' she said.

I felt myself wince involuntarily. I knew that sort of question wouldn't lead anywhere fun. Not when it started with my name like that.

'Sure,' I said.

'Well...' she started. 'My ex called me.'

Just like that, she had my full attention. For a brief, pathetic moment I felt horrified that she had an ex.

'Okay...?' I said, impatiently.

'I don't want to... I don't want to talk about him because it's all history,' she continued quietly, 'but he called me, and he's messaged me... a few times.'

I did my best impression of a person who didn't care about something.

'And...?' I shot back.

'Well he's... basically he's apologising, for how he was,' she said.

'Okay, that's nice of him,' I said, pretending to be interested in something on the seam of my jeans.

'I would never get back with him or anything.' She continued, grimacing, 'but... that whole thing was really shit.'

I nodded, still absolutely terrified about where this was heading.

'Our breakup lasted two years,' she said, 'he knew it was finished. The whole thing just drained my time and energy for two years.'

I nodded. I did not want this conversation. *Abort.*

'And now he's on his knees asking me to give him another chance. He proposed and everything.'

I snorted and rolled my eyes.

'Can I just... I know this is all history, and it doesn't reflect on you, but... I just can't put myself through any more... *I'm not a kid.*' It felt like she was gearing up to accuse me of something, which seemed premature. We weren't even properly a couple yet.

'I know you're not,' I said defensively. 'Do I treat you like one?'

'No,' she said immediately. 'No you don't. I'm not saying that.'

'So, what then?' I asked. Ordinarily I'd have reacted very differently to this conversation, of course. But I was mentally exhausted, strung out.

'Me and you, it's just a thing, like a fun thing, right?' she said. She was nervously playing with a scarf that was slung over the end of my bed. I didn't know how to respond to that. I had thought we were a bit further along than *a fun thing*.

'Yeah, of course,' I said. 'Of *course*.'

She rubbed her eye and looked out of the window. 'Can I just ask you... or *tell* you... sometimes I feel like you're a different person with me.'

'What do you mean, a different person?' I said.

'I mean, like there's an affectionate and kind side to you. But there's this other, really cold side that I sometimes feel. And it really feels different.'

I managed to keep my sigh of relief internal. She was just worried about my *mood*.

'Okay,' I said. 'I'm sorry.'

'No, wait,' she said, 'don't apologise, that makes me feel pathetic. I just... I dunno. I'm not an insecure person, but with you it's like, you can be really happy and chatty and upbeat and then, suddenly, you're all... until I go. And at first I thought I was imagining it, but...'

God knows how I let it become an argument, from there. She was so generous and polite about it. Not to mention she was absolutely right. I'd been this emotional windsock, billowing in the breeze, my mood going this way and that. One minute I'd feel guilty, then I'd feel angry, sometimes just scared. And I couldn't control when a change was coming on. It must have looked weird to her, from the outside.

I wasn't being horrible, just a bit vacant. I must have seemed to suddenly go disinterested. I can see that now. But that night, I was just this hot ball of trepidation and fear. I couldn't stop thinking about the police and what they wanted. I told her I was having a hard time at work and that I 'didn't want to talk about my personality flaws.'

'It's not about your personality!' she said. 'That's just it. I don't think it's you. It's like you... want to be somewhere else.'

'*What?*' I said. 'Surely you can't expect me to be chatty and upbeat all the time.'

She threw her head back and groaned with exasperation. 'I'm not talking about you being upbeat all the time... I just... can I ask you to promise me you'll be truthful with me? Just honest and straight-up,' she said.

'*Truthful!*' I gasped. I did not like the way this was going. My mind was racing at 200mph.

'That's all I'm asking of you, Will,' she said eventually. 'I don't want to argue with you, and I'm not saying I want you to be this happy, chatty person all the time; I just... don't want to feel like you're not really in the room. And if you do want to be somewhere else, then you should just tell me. Because it can feel like shit.'

This wave of sadness hit me. I realised how little I'd been thinking about Ellie's feelings. I knew what she meant about being *in the room* one minute, and not the next. I hadn't even taken her on a *proper date*.

'I'm so sorry,' I said. 'I'm sorry I've made you feel like that. I've been... distracted.'

'I know you have been, Will! I know you have been!' she said frustratedly 'And you don't have to tell me anything, but I would just like to know if your head's somewhere else.'

I understood the hint. 'I'm not seeing anybody else,' I said quietly.

'I'm not saying that, I'm just…' Ellie rubbed her face and let out an exasperated groan. 'I feel like you don't tell me anything. Like, what *is* on your mind. You can *talk* to me, you know.'

I looked up at her. She looked so vulnerable and sad.

'Yes,' I said, 'you're right. I'll talk to you more, I'm sorry.'

She walked around the side of the bed and climbed up to stand over me, like Peter Pan. 'You don't need to shut me out,' she said. 'I just don't want you to lie to me. I want to know where I am with everything and that's all I'll ask, is that okay?'

'Fine,' I said.

She looked at me expectantly.

'*Fine*,' I said again. I just couldn't think quick enough. 'So… the police came to my work today.'

Twenty-Eight

'There was this guy who was killed, in Farringdon. It turns out he was killed not far from my work. In fact, he was killed on my route home. And basically... I must have missed it by like, seconds.'

Ellie looked at me, wide eyed.

'Yeah, it was only a few months ago,' I continued.

'So... you saw it?' she asked.

'No,' I said, 'well not exactly... I guess I... must have done.'

Ellie stared at me in silence. She was absolutely motionless. Her eyes were like saucers.

'You... *must* have done?' she asked eventually.

'What I mean is, I walked past it, apparently. The police are saying I might have walked right past it.'

She eyed me cautiously. I saw a smile creep into the corner of her mouth. She was trying to work out if I was joking.

'I'm not joking,' I said. 'It really happened.'

She looked at me in shock. 'Oh my God, Will...' she said, 'that's just so... are you *okay*? When was this?'

'This was a couple of months ago. The end of October.'

'So, before you met me?' she asked.

'Yeah, sort of not long before that,' I said nervously. 'But I just can't remember anything that they're asking about and it's… it's stressing me out now.'

She pulled me closer to her and embraced me. It had been a matter of minutes since she'd asked me not to keep things from her, and there I was, telling her this heavily edited version of the truth. I felt shit about it, of course. I justified it to myself that I was somehow protecting what we had, by not telling her the truth. I told myself I hadn't lied to her, as such. Bullshit. I definitely had.

I couldn't handle her sympathy though, that was a step too far. I told her it was all fine, but the investigations seemed to be ongoing, and the police were stressing me out, asking me things I couldn't remember.

I felt a lump gathering in my throat, so I stopped talking. Ellie was so sympathetic; it was making me sick. She told me she couldn't imagine what it'd be like, but that she'd try her best to help me. She told me I could confide in her.

The worst part was, I believed it too. I was desperate to tell her the whole truth. I just wanted to completely unload on her, right there. But I stayed strong. I held tight. I'd made a resolution to draw a line under this, and to take it to my grave. However much I trusted Ellie, I could not let this become her problem.

We stayed up late; she asked me loads of questions about everything. The conversation about the police got her onto my parents, which led to my family, and where I grew up. To cut a long story short, my mum's long gone and I don't know where she went. She wasn't really cut out for mothering and she'd always had a sort of illicit agreement with Dad that that was *his* side of things, even when she'd been around.

She was a bit of a hippie and a part-time political activist. She spent the first twenty-two years of her life working between an independent coffee shop and this subversive bookstore in King's Cross.

She met my dad, who was also an active leftie at the time – albeit not as active as her – in the eighties and they lived together for a few years in Dad's little flat in Canning Town, surrounded by cracked paint, humming pipes and asbestos.

I told Ellie about my dad; how he was a nice guy and was pretty smart but had his head in the clouds. He trained as an accountant after school but didn't finish. He got bored and ended up quitting and going to work in his parents' café which is where he eventually met my mum. He liked it; we weren't well off and it was hard work, but he didn't mind, the lifestyle suited him. He appreciated not having a boss.

Despite not having much money, our house was always full of stuff, interesting stuff; some of it old, some of it new, some of it worth a fair bit. As a kid I used to think Dad was a collector of old accessories like umbrellas, scarves and briefcases. I found out later that in fact, he was a minesweeper on the London Underground. It was sort of a hobby of his. Ellie thought it was hilarious.

At about 8 p.m. most week nights, while everyone else was heading in the other direction, Dad would get on the District Line and ride into London. Then he'd follow one of a number of different routes through the central section of the Tube system, picking up things people had left behind in the carriages, on seats or window ledges, or propped up against carriage corners. Over the years he found loads of valuable and useful stuff. If he found anything with a name or address on it, or anything containing bank cards or money, he'd always take it and hand it in at Lost Property. He was principled in his sweeping, more of a womble than a vulture.

I told her how Dad had named me after an Antiguan guy called Wilbur Jerry. The story goes, my dad got invited to Antigua for his uncle's wedding. On his last day there, Dad had been drinking in a bar, chatting to this local guy, Wilbur. Dad

says he was half drunk but good company and a proper character: ancient looking flip-flops, a wispy, wayward beard and
huge buck teeth.

He carried this big brush around with him so Dad guessed
he must be a street sweeper. Then out of nowhere, halfway
through his drink he excused himself and disappeared. Then
he'd reappeared fifteen minutes later and bought a round of
drinks for everyone.

Dad later found out that his mate Wilbur Jerry was in fact
a professional athlete. He'd excused himself from the bar to go
and take part in a 100 metre World Championship qualifying
race down on the track. Half drunk, Jerry won the race and
qualified for the tournament (although there was no record of
him attending it).

The brush was what he used to clear debris from his starting
position on the track, before the race. He had to do it because
he didn't like to use starting blocks, like the other athletes. He
just didn't like them. Dad just thought this guy Wilbur Jerry
was the epitome of cool and self-sufficiency. So, that's how I
became Wilbur Cox.

I told her how Mum left us when I was twelve. We woke up
one morning and she'd gone. She'd put me to bed previous
night and had kissed Dad on the forehead before falling asleep.
There hadn't been an argument or anything (although the two
of them did argue).

She sent Dad a letter a month later from Liverpool, saying
she'd felt suffocated by her existence and wanted to find her
place in the world. We did see her after that. She turned up
for Christmas a few times and came to meet me outside the
school gates once; but her heart was never in it and that was
obvious. I think she met a new partner eventually and built a
new life up there, with no kids and minimal responsibilities.

Dad raised me not to feel bitterness about that whole thing. He made a concerted effort not to, I think. I think he understood that the situation was horrible for a little kid, so he tried to play it down. 'Your mum's gone away to try a different life and we must respect that.'

He talked about it honestly but flippantly, like it was just *one of those things*. Looking back, it must have really got to him inside, but he never let on. I was mostly raised in the homes of uncles and aunties, while Dad worked and paid the bills. He did his best.

I told Ellie about how, about a year previous, Dad had met a lady. He went to a residents' meeting at the building he lives in and got talking to a woman called Lisa who worked for the local council. They're sweet together; she's ten or fifteen years younger than he but they've got a real connection.

I said how one night I went round to have a takeaway with them and they both got drunk on red wine and started discussing really earnestly whether one day someone would invent a machine that could change piss back into drinking water. Lisa was a lot smarter than Dad, but she humoured him, and they made each other laugh incessantly. I told Ellie how great it was that Dad had found someone nice who was on his wavelength. He was so much more relaxed.

Ellie told me I didn't need to feel alone, and that I could always talk to her about anything. I wished to God that were true.

'Remember that I care if you're feeling alone, or sad, Will,' she said. 'I want you to talk to me. And even if you don't feel up to talking, we can just... hang out.'

We lay staring at the ceiling, talking until we both fell asleep at about two in the morning. I could feel Ellie breathing life back into my frazzled, worn-out brain.

Twenty-Nine

I woke up the following morning with a new resolve in me. The previous day's trauma had wiped me out emotionally, and it felt like that whole experience had drained some of the guilt I was feeling. My late-night talk with Ellie felt like it'd brought us closer. Things felt different.

I had this new fight in me. I found myself rushing to get showered and dressed in the morning. I wanted to go to the police station and get it done. I suddenly felt kind of driven by the injustice of it all, and how all this had been foisted on me. I resolved that I wasn't going to take it lying down any more.

I wasn't going to stand here while people fired things at me, and I have to duck and hide and scamper about in the shadows. I wasn't going to accept having my life changed forever by a nasty, aggressive man who fancied throwing shit at me for his own entertainment. *No. This is my life, and you only get one.* It was time to get rid of this thing.

I emailed Julia saying the police had asked me to go in and see them, and I headed straight over to the Islington address on Probert's card. I wore an ironed shirt and a sharp blazer. I didn't exactly feel strong, but I felt determined and ready to fight my corner.

As I walked, I straightened everything out in my head. I went back over my story I'd given them the previous day, visualising it all over and over. Visualising how it'd happened. Visualising what a smooth, eventless walk it'd been from beginning to end, and practising my frustration and disbelief that the police should still want to talk to *me*.

I got there about ten past nine and asked for Probert. They left me waiting for fifteen minutes before Kane's constipated face eventually appeared through the porthole of the door and she prized it open with unnecessary force.

'Hello Will,' she said. 'Are you feeling better today?'

I gave a pained smile and put a hand to my stomach. 'Yeah, a bit.'

I had already decided I was going to run with the food poisoning story. I told her I'd been up all night, vomiting and up and down from the toilet. A really human admission, I thought. Something that might make someone feel closer to someone. But nope, when I looked across at her, she was hard-faced as ever. She didn't say a thing more about it.

She led me up to a small office with a round table and four blue, felt chairs. Comfy chairs, for a police station, I thought. It's probably once you become a suspect that they make you sit on the hard chairs. I slid around the side of the table and sat on the far side. I felt like I didn't want my back to the door, for some reason. Kane followed me in and asked if I'd like a cup of tea. I said, 'No thank you,' but asked for a glass of water. While she power-walked off to get the drinks (as ever, with unnecessary intensity) I flicked through BBC News on my phone; I just couldn't think of anything else to do. I checked Twitter, then scrolled aimlessly up and down WhatsApp.

After a while I started to get bored and confused about where they were. I paced around the room until eventually, they both appeared. They'd had me waiting a really long time and neither of them apologised or even acknowledged it. I scowled at them both as they settled into their chairs. I momentarily wondered why Kane hadn't shaken my hand when I'd first arrived. *A bit of human courtesy.*

Probert opened a paper file and pulled out the wrinkled map from the day before. I could see the circles he'd drawn and the wavy line I'd added from The Three Kings to the train station. He put his finger on the line.

'Will, something about this isn't making sense to us.'

I raised my eyebrows as if to request that he elaborate. These two were creating a horribly tense atmosphere again.

I wondered if that was something they got special training in.

Thirty

'Did you know, the average man walks significantly faster than the average woman?' Probert asked. 'Almost a tenth of a metre per second faster, which is quite a lot.'

'No,' I replied.

'You don't think that's a lot?' Probert asked provocatively.

'No, I mean I *didn't* know that. Yes, I do think it's a lot. That's another metre every ten seconds, so another six metres every minute of walking, it's quite a lot really.'

'Yes, exactly,' said Probert.

I started wondering what he was driving at, but my hands were steady. He hadn't been like this yesterday, but I felt a lot tougher and more prepared. My eyes darted between him and Kane. *Are we not bothering with having a good cop, any more?*

Probert leant back and smiled passively. 'Thanks for coming in, by the way. We weren't expecting you to do that so quickly.'

I shrugged.

He nodded back down towards his map. 'How long would you say that journey normally takes you? From the King's Arms to the train station?'

I frowned and glanced between him and Kane as if I was confused. 'The… Three Kings?' I asked quietly.

'Sorry, yeah,' he said. 'The Three Kings, sorry.'

Have that. That tiny, pedantic victory had made me feel less like a schoolkid being interviewed by two adults. I leant back in my comfortable chair and tried to guess the answer to his question.

'Honestly, I'm not good at estimating things like this. But I reckon… probably ten minutes. Or maybe a bit less; I don't know.' I was a schoolkid again.

'Well,' replied Probert, 'according to Google it's six minutes' walk. But we walked it ourselves and it took us *seven* minutes, with no interruptions.'

'Okay,' I said.

'Do you know how long your journey took that night?' asked Kane.

I looked at them blankly.

'We've analysed a lot of CCTV footage from the area, and we've been able to piece together a pretty accurate journey of everybody's routes, that night,' said Kane.

My stomach started straining and undulating inside me.

Apparently, it'd taken me just over fourteen minutes to do the seven-minute walk between The Three Kings and Farringdon station. I didn't find that particularly shocking to begin with, but these two were suddenly prowling around that fact like hyenas. I could tell they were thrilled to have worked this out and that it was the reason they door-stepped me at work the day before.

Stay calm.

Probert added that that didn't mean I had been *visible* for the fourteen minutes, there were a number of blackspots without coverage. But from the time I left the pub and came into view of the private traffic enforcement camera pointed at the end of Clerkenwell Close, to the time I was seen on the camera facing outwards at the front of Farringdon train station, my journey had taken fourteen minutes.

I shrugged. 'Weren't there any cameras tracking me in between?' I hid the panic in my voice pretty well as I asked that question.

'Yes, sixteen on that journey, five of which covered your route,' Probert shot back instantly. 'Two working cameras, both of which caught you crossing the square, a third which caught you approaching the alley and two others down Turnmill Street that weren't recording.'

I glanced between their faces; this seemed like a critical moment.

'One of them was facing the alley,' muttered Kane.

'*What?*' I spat the word out a bit too quickly.

'One of the cameras on Turnmill Street was facing Richard King's entrance to the alley – the side you exited from – and probably would've caught the first thirty yards or so of the alley where he died, but it wasn't operational.' She was staring into my face as she said it, trying to read my reaction.

I didn't give her one. I couldn't. My face was frozen with fear and trepidation.

'So, Will,' continued Probert, 'there's this big gap.'

I looked back at him, straining to sustain a bemused expression, even though I knew what was coming.

'We can track the first part of your journey pretty well. Until you reach the alleyway. And that all seems logical: it took you two-minutes-fifty to get to the front of the alley, which seems about right.

But then there's a gap of eleven minutes until we see you again, arriving at the train station.'

'When the second half of that walk should've taken about three and a half minutes,' Kane said quietly.

There was a long, uncomfortable silence.

'We timed it out, and timed it out again walking extra slow, and then extremely slow,' Kane continued. She was on a roll now.

I waited for her to add to that sentence, but she didn't. She left the conclusion to my imagination.

'We can't know where those seven minutes went, but we know it was between you entering the alley and arriving at the train station. It means you probably stopped between those points, for a period, even if you don't remember it now.' Probert said, reclining in his chair.

I stared at the table with a frown. 'I don't… think…' I whispered rhetorically.

'Something made you slow down or stop, and we need you to remember what it was,' Probert said, poking at his map again. 'Because we've mapped your route against the victim's and basically… you were almost certainly twenty-five or thirty metres of him when he was beaten to death. Probably less.'

Kind of him to use the expression, 'beaten to death'.

'So, how… *how* can you have seen *nothing* and *nobody*, Will?' asked Kane.

There was no going back on my story of the events now. I just shrugged. 'Well, I walk slowly, I'm quite famous for it,' I mumbled. 'I probably walk even slower when I'm drunk so… that seven minutes gap is probably more like two or three minutes, if you account for my slow walking speed. And I don't know what I stopped for, but I definitely can't remember it.'

Neither of them looked satisfied by this.

'That was actually something we considered,' replied Probert.

'Obviously, we have your walking speed captured on this video, too,' interrupted Kane. 'We know what your walking speed is and more to the point, what it was that night – from the footage. You actually have a relatively *fast* walking pace, just so you know.'

I looked up at Kane sharply, and then back to Probert. *Oh Jesus.*

'Would you do the walk with us?' asked Probert, suddenly. 'See if it triggers anything?'

'I'd rather not,' I snapped back instinctively. I felt cornered. 'I walk that route pretty much every day, so if something was going to be triggered, it'd have been triggered by now.'

They both seemed a bit surprised at my flat refusal, but I pursed my lips. 'I might have stopped to text. I was texting my friend when I left the pub. I told you that, didn't I? You saw the messages. I also remember looking at the cranes on the building site, maybe I stopped to look – I don't know.'

'Do the walk with us, Will,' said Probert, gravely. 'It's important.'

Kane had been writing notes on an A5 pad. 'We're talking about seven minutes, Will. Not a quick stop, not even a five-minute stop-off. Seven whole minutes. And judging by the footage we do have, if you stopped for seven minutes, it was either *in* the alley – or just after you left the alley on Turnmill Street,' she said.

I stared at her for a moment, not knowing what to say. I cleared my throat and looked back down at the map.

'Do you understand what we're saying to you, Will?' said Probert. 'There's a good chance that whatever stopped you for that seven minutes might well be linked to the reason Richard King is dead.'

'It certainly happened at the same time and in the same place,' said Kane.

I shrugged again and rubbed my face. Didn't know what else to do.

'So, what happens now?' I said, after a brief silence. 'I mean, I understand what you're saying you need, but I can't really help you, it's—'

'Would you be willing to let us request your mobile phone record from your supplier?' Kane suddenly interjected.

'My... mobile...'

'We know roughly where you were, we just want to know

more about what you were doing, to get a full picture of what was going on at that time,' Probert added calmly.

'But what does that *mean?* Am I a suspect now?' I said it with a deliberate smirk, but those words pained me as they left my lips. I felt like I'd acknowledged that narrative for the first time, given it some credibility.

Kane and Probert looked at each other for a moment.

'No, you're not,' Probert said eventually. 'You were there, so you're a witness. You're the guy who is going to furnish us with the information we need to *find* the person who did this.'

I nodded and pulled my phone out of my pocket, placing it gently on the table in front of me.

'So, what do you want me to do?'

Thirty-One

They made me walk the route with them, in Farringdon. Kane drove us there. It was mid-morning so luckily it was pretty deserted. I set off from outside my office. Probert and Kane walked together behind me, slightly to the right.

I walked it as slowly as I possibly could. I stopped to look at advertisements, stopped to tie my shoelace. When we got to the alley, I looked back at them.

'I think I stopped here,' I said. 'At the top of the alley.' I knew it was the start of the CCTV blind patch.

'Why?' said Probert.

'I… can't remember.' I said. 'I just have this vague recollection of stopping here and… Yes! My headphones. My headphones stopped working.'

'They stopped working?' asked Kane, writing in her notebook.

'Yeah, they stopped working, and I stood here trying to get them working again. For a while. Probably a couple of minutes. Because I wanted the distraction, for my journey home.'

'Then what happened?' said Probert.

'Well, I couldn't get them to work. I didn't think it could be the battery, because I'd charged them that morning. So, I kept trying. But then eventually I guess I realised it must have been the battery. I guess I must have worn them down, through the day.'

Probert held out his palm as if to suggest I proceed.

'I put them back in my bag,' I said, 'then I carried on.'

'So, you think you were doing all that for more than a minute?' asked Kane sceptically.

'I don't know, I don't remember exactly,' I said.

We continued down the alley. I explained to them that I'd been texting my friend Jack at this point, about our lost bet. They had my phone records to verify that. I told them I hadn't noticed anything weird or unusual, but that I'd been 'immersed in my phone'. Neither of them found that very credible. When we arrived at the bottom of the alley, they probed me to re-member what I could see at this point. They wanted me to look up and down the street and consider all memory hunches. I told them it was really quiet, but there might have been a few people around. They asked if there'd been any cars around. I said I 'thought there might have been'. I don't know why.

I said I had a vague memory of there being a car, and that I could see its red brake lights on. I did remember that image, but I couldn't say it was definitely from that night. But the fact they'd asked me about a car just made me say I'd probably seen a car. I can't say that was a hundred per cent true. I can't say they didn't push me into confirming that. They really wanted me to put that on record.

Thirty-Two

I must've got about twelve hours sleep over the entire Christmas and New Year period. I had begun adding over-the-counter sleep aids like Nytol and valerian root to my now-normal dose of Night Nurse and weed, to slow my mind down and get some sort of rest. Needless to say, I felt like pure shit. I needed to make a new start in January. I wasn't heading in a good direction.

I resolved to go back to basics with Probert and Kane, stop letting them push me and poke me into speculating on their behalf. They had obviously come around to the idea that I was the key to the case, and they intended on continually trying to shake me down for information. I gave them access to my mobile phone records. I also allowed them to go through and record my activity on WhatsApp that evening. I doubted there could be much of interest for them to find. I'd already been through all my activity on there that night and there wasn't really anything to be revealed from there that could be of much use.

I'd left things open. The rogue seven minutes were left hanging, unaccounted for. The police left with my stubborn position of, 'Don't know, can't help, knock yourself out with my mobile phone records.'

Something had occurred to me. If they had any evidence at all on me, they wouldn't be going through this digging process. They'd said they thought there were three people in the vicinity of King that night: me, Evatt and one other person. They had isolated me as having this proximity to the crime, but they had an evidence gap. I guessed they couldn't progress that knowledge any further; they were stuck.

They wanted to cross my story of events with Evatt's until they had a detailed enough picture of the evening. Thing is, I had this fair assumption that this Evatt hadn't seen me, because I hadn't seen him. They had a blackspot in their event map, and they were worried about it. But nobody could incriminate me, because aside from Solly, nobody had seen me – and I'd left no evidence. And I couldn't incriminate Evatt, because I hadn't seen him. (And also, because he hadn't done it). That thought relaxed me. It felt like the police were grasping at straws. The only person who could reveal me, was me. All I needed to do was continue saying absolutely nothing. The more they could get me to say, the more chance of me slipping up.

Things slowly began to improve again, and I got back into thinking more clearly. I heard a couple more times from Kane and Probert, asking me to fill out witness statements for them and showing me pictures of different people to try and jog my memory about this and that. I remembered nothing. My story didn't deviate.

I was beginning to feel like I was in a position of certainty again. Fuck the seven minutes. The seven minutes were whatever I said they were, and I said they were nothing. A seven-minute void in the world's existence. And nobody could prove otherwise.

Thirty-Three

On the first Saturday morning of the new year, I woke up to a message from Ellie asking me if I wanted to go with her to her friend's birthday party in Barnsbury. I couldn't agree quickly enough – it was perfect timing. I had decided to push myself to get out and get in stride with everyone else, and what better way than going somewhere I didn't know anyone. It was all part of drawing a line under all this stuff from last year: step one.

I got home and pretended to watch the football results coming in, while I thought about the evening ahead with Ellie. I planned a few things to talk about, in case the conversation dried up. I went through my normal pre-date routine of clippering my stubble to grade five and cleaning my plimsolls. I chose a black jumper with blue jeans; plus my gloves and a leather jacket over the top to keep the new year cold out.

I met Ellie at Tottenham Hale Underground station at seven o'clock. I was waiting by the entrance to the station when she appeared up one of the flights of stairs wearing a blue denim jacket over a black dress and beige boots. She leant back and waved like an old friend as she walked towards me, which put me at ease. We hugged; she smelt amazing, like fresh fruit, ice cream and flowers.

I offered to order us a cab to her friend's house, to save her thin jacket and bare legs the freezing cold January evening. She said she'd rather walk and talk, which was fine with me. We stopped at a pub to get a drink together on the way.

We sat there and chatted for a good couple of hours, polishing off six large glasses of prosecco between us. We talked about her new flat, she'd just moved into a place in Battersea, a house share with three of her friends. She started reminiscing on some of the things we'd spoken about during that night at Dirty Dick's.

I was amazed at how sharp her memory was; I couldn't remember half the stuff we'd talked about, but that's pretty normal for me when I'm drinking. We had talked about our families and where we worked. She teased me a bit about how I hadn't asked her out and she'd had to initiate. I apologised. 'I had a lot going on...'

At about nine we headed off to the party, half-cut. During the time we'd spent in the pub, the temperature had dropped another few degrees. Ellie grabbed my arm and clung to my body for warmth, the whole way there.

As we approached the front door, I felt a bit nervous from wanting to make a good impression on her friends. I felt my phone vibrate in my pocket. I pulled it out and saw two messages from Solly. The air caught in my lungs for a second as I read his name.

He was back. The message said, '**COME TO MINE TOMORROW 5PM.**'

The presumptive tone of it got my back up. I was feeling semi-drunk and belligerent, and he was an immensely irritating man. I wasn't going to let him torment me again. I replied, '**Busy tomorrow**' before pushing my phone back into my back pocket.

Not tonight, perv.

Thirty-Four

The party was no more than twenty or so people. All crammed into the basement and garden of this three-storey town house. Ellie and I had stopped at an off licence on the way and had brought a bottle of prosecco each, as well as a bottle of tequila for the house. We stood at the edge of the garden avoiding the wet grass, chatting to these guys, one of whom lived there. It turned out Ellie didn't know anyone that well either. She'd been invited by her friend who went to college with the guy whose party it was.

They'd just finished college and were producing their own hip hop music. I thought they were cool; they struck me as rich kids, but they weren't pretentious or annoying. It was fun to chat and just lark around, forget about everything else. Ellie kept going back to the kitchen and topping up our drinks and by 10 p.m. the two of us were almightily pissed.

I started thinking about having something to eat, to save me from going over the edge. That's when Ellie came back from the bathroom clutching the bottle of tequila. I burst out laughing; I couldn't really say no. Everyone in the vicinity ended up doing a couple of shots each and things started to ramp up. Someone emerged from the house with a bong and the cheer that went up could probably be heard south of the river.

Ellie and I lost each other for a good half hour, during which time I got chatting to these two blokes standing by the toilet. One of them was talking about his brother who'd knocked someone out in a street fight the previous weekend. The guy was telling this story so vividly and with so much expression, you could tell how proud he was of his brother and what a great moment he thought it was.

I smiled and nodded as he spoke, but I noticed how much it struck me right in the gut. I didn't want to listen to it but somehow, I felt like I still needed to keep this pretence up. Like I still had to blend in and act like people being punched in the street didn't have special meaning for me. Eventually I managed to pull myself away from that pair and headed out into the back garden for some air. I sat down on a garden wall, facing away from the house and took big, deep breaths of the cold air, which made me feel less sick. I took my phone out of my pocket to text Ellie. As I did, she appeared behind me and put her hands over my eyes. I grinned and grabbed her cold little fingers in my hands, closing my fingers around them as if to warm them up. She sat next to me on the wall.

'Well… you can definitely hold your drink,' I grinned.

'Yeap,' she replied, staring into my eyes. After a few moments of silence, she took a swig from a can of Red Stripe.

'You passed the first test. Definitely Not a lightweight,' she grinned.

'The first test!' I said in mock surprise 'We've been seeing each other for how many weeks now? I'm only at the first test?' We smiled at each other for a moment.

'What's the second test?' I asked.

She ignored my lame question and leant towards me. She grabbed the front of my jacket and gently pulled my face towards hers. Her lips were cold and minty from her chewing gum; she kissed me really gently but deliberately, reaching up to hold the side of my face with her fingertips.

'No more secrets,' she said.

'No more secrets,' I replied.

We sat there chatting, with her hand gently resting on top of mine. It felt like she'd had some extra motivation today. It was like she'd decided to push things up a notch. We were both pretty obliterated by this point. We talked and intermittently kissed; god knows how long for.

Just after two in the morning, people were crashing or leaving.

'How are you getting home?' I asked Ellie. 'Are you coming to mine?'

'Let's go get something to eat first,' she said, pulling her phone into view.

We wandered to Caledonian Road and stood looking up and down the street. It was almost completely still; nowhere was open.

She held my hand as we walked and talked. Towards the bottom of Cally Road we crossed a bridge that ran over a canal. We stopped for a moment to stand and look over the edge at the murky water of the canal in the moonlight. It was so quiet and peaceful.

Ellie suddenly turned and grinned at me, biting her bottom lip and tugging my hand to request that I follow her. She led me by my arm down some steps into a walkway that ran down by the canal, into a natural alcove between beams of the canal wall. Her eyes looked charged as she locked vision with me at the bottom of the steps. She moved her lips as if she wanted to say something and I noticed how swollen they were. She grabbed the collar of my jacket and then swung around so her back was against the wall. As she yanked me close, I pressed her into the brickwork and she let out a little gasp. She pushed her hand up through the back of my hair and pulled my head into hers, wrapping her lips around mine – all the delicate intimacy had gone from earlier. We kissed a lot more intensely now, away from the view of the public, pushed tightly together in the dark.

She reached her hand around and unhooked the clasp of her dress, so the top part fell loose. I pulled the fabric off her shoulder and pushed my lips into her neck. She pulled my left hand down, onto her hip, hitching her skirt up so I was holding her warm thigh.

Suddenly, Ellie froze. I looked up at her and her eyes were wide open, staring straight past me. Her body went stiff, and her hands grasped tightly at my skin.

'Wait, wait, wait,' she whispered quietly, as she held the top of her dress anxiously and peered over my shoulder.

'What?' I asked, turning to see what had caught her eye.

Ellie stared at the bushes on the other side of the canal as she carefully clipped the top of her dress back into place. I walked to the edge of the canal, straining my eyes in the darkness.

'What is it?' I asked. I was weirded out, but I wanted to show Ellie how capable I was.

'Someone's there,' she whispered.

Ellie finished re-dressing herself without taking her eyes off a single spot on the other side of the canal. It was extremely dark down there; streetlights from the main road cast a little bit of light across the water, but the land that ran alongside them was dense with bushes and bracken. It was difficult to clearly define shapes. I pulled my phone out of my pocket and tried to shine a light across. It didn't achieve anything much; the light of my phone was no match for the dense North London dark.

'Did you hear that?' she asked, eventually.

'No… Hear what?' I hissed.

Then I heard it. Clear as a bell, there was the sound of a branch snapping. Not a small branch, that could be broken by some wildlife like a bird or a mole or whatever shit is scurrying about at that time; it sounded like a big old, thick branch snapping, like it had taken the weight of a human foot. Both Ellie and I fell silent and stared across the canal.

Eventually I turned and raised my eyebrows at her as if to signal that we should leave.

Thirty-Five

It was nearly 4 a.m. by the time we got home. We fell asleep in our clothes. I woke up at about 9 a.m. and chain-drank two pints of orange squash, then lay dozing for an hour or so with the TV on in the background. Ellie didn't stir.

The doorbell rang. I cursed myself for ordering stuff to arrive on a Sunday morning. I pulled on a sweatshirt and some track-suit bottoms and headed downstairs.

As I approached the door, I saw that it wasn't a delivery at all. I could see Police Sergeant Kane out there. I opened the door and there they both were, Probert and Kane. Both of them looked furious.

'Good morning, Will,' said Kane, emotionless. 'May we come in and talk to you for a moment?'

I led them into the living room and sat in an armchair, staring at the ground. I was too tired for this and I wanted them to know it. I didn't offer them a seat, but Probert helped himself to the end of the sofa, while Kane sat closer to me, placing a cardboard folder on the coffee table between us.

'Good morning, Will,' he said as Kane sat down.

I was still half drunk.

Kane looked at me blankly before gesturing towards the folder.

She edged herself forward in her seat and opened it to reveal a page emblazoned with a large image of two symmetrical polar bears, both pushing inwards against a large block of ice. It was the pattern from the jumper I'd been wearing that night – the night with the banker.

Kane examined my face for a reaction, before speaking.

'Do you know this design, Will?'

'Yeah... It's from my jumper.'

Kane looked across at Probert and then back to me. She leaned forward and peeled the top page aside to reveal a grainy CCTV image of me walking down a footpath in Farringdon. You could just about make out the same design across the front of my chest, framed by my brown jacket. I looked up at her and nodded. *I already said it was from my jumper, dipshit.*

Kane studied my face for a reaction, but I wouldn't give her the satisfaction. She then straightened the two photographs in parallel in front of me on the table. I stared at them.

'Yeah, it's from my jumper,' I repeated. My hungover voice was a deep, low growl.

Kane was moving slowly and deliberately. She didn't seem to be reacting to what I was saying. It was like she had this visit all mapped out in her head and she wasn't about to let me deviate her from the script. Maintaining eye contact, she held out her hand and Probert passed her a folded plastic packet, containing an A4 padded envelope, which had been torn open at the top. She placed it down on the table in front of me.

'What does it mean, Will?'

'What's what mean?'

She leant forward and pushed the envelope closer to me. For the first time I noticed the address on it: *P.C. Sara Kane, 19a, Something-Terrace, Islington, London.*

Someone had covered up the street name with masking tape,

but I could still make out the word 'Terrace' where it'd been written in such thick, dark marker.

'Your house?' I asked eventually.

Kane took the envelope and handed it back to Probert, who folded it and placed it on his lap. Kane looked different today, angrier; there was this acute sense of impatience about her. She picked up the folder and held the polar bears image up in front of me. 'Delivered this morning. To my private address.'

'Okay... That's weird I agree,' I frowned.

For what seemed like a full thirty seconds, we all just sat there in complete silence.

'Your colleagues know this is your case though, right?' I said eventually.

'My colleagues and I don't send each other things anonymously via post,' she smiled sarcastically. 'Did you send me this, Will?'

The mystery had punched a hole in my drunk bravado. 'Why would I send you a picture of a jumper logo?' I said quietly.

'I don't know,' she replied. 'I don't know, Will.'

It began to occur to me that this was actually a very serious thing. They weren't messing around. This coldness started to creep in. *This police officer is sitting in my living room with a picture of the jumper I was wearing.*

We sat staring into each other's eyes for a few moments, before she seemed to snap out of whatever she was thinking about and began putting the printouts back into her file.

'Someone wants us to think it was you,' said Probert. 'Surely you can see that.'

I forced an indignant scoff, which got caught in my throat and made me feel like coughing.

'*Me?*'

'Someone must have seen you, that night. And they don't

know we're already talking to you, so they're sending us clues to find you,' affirmed Kane.

I raised an eyebrow at her. 'The person who did it?'

She looked back at me sharply but ignored the question. 'Someone saw you clearly enough and for long enough, from front-on, that they could recollect this design. Do you understand the significance of that?'

Something tightened in my gut. *That bastard.* 'It means I crossed paths with someone,' I said, finally.

'Front-on, close-up,' repeated Kane.

'Front-on,' I shrugged, 'close up.'

'And you still maintain that you saw *nobody?*' she asked quietly.

'I said I don't *remember*; there's a difference,' I shot back.

'Well, someone remembers *you*,' she reached forward and tapped one of the polar bears.

I shook my head and shrugged again.

Eventually, she stood up, brushing down the arm of her jacket with a pale hand. 'Do you know what else the sender included, along with this picture?'

She produced another small polythene bag containing a tiny piece of cardboard. 'Iceberg Jeans, it says on it,' she said quickly, her eyes burning into me as she scanned for a reaction. 'Is this jumper with the polar bears from Iceberg Jeans? Do you have it handy?' she asked.

'I think it's probably...' my mind whirred as I spun through the possibilities. 'I'll go have a look.'

I shut myself in my bedroom and stood in front of the wardrobe. Ellie stirred and squinted up at me, confused. You could clearly hear their radios crackling in the living room. I pulled a wardrobe door open and eyes darted left and right. *What am I looking for?*

I just stood there in terror, staring at my own clothes. *Is this it? Have they got me?* I absent-mindedly combed the arm of a suede jacket with my fingers as I tried to rattle through my options. I didn't really have any. *The Iceberg jumper isn't in here because I got rid of it.*

'Is everything okay?' croaked Ellie.

My palms and fingers were suddenly damp with sweat. 'Yeah,' I replied quickly.

She must have been able to hear me taking those deep, panicked breaths. For some reason I kept on rustling through items of clothing, as if I was expecting it to materialise. After a few minutes I heard Kane shout up the stairs to me:

'Will, did you manage to find the jumper?'

'I'm just looking for it, sorry,' I called back. 'It's here some-where, I saw it yesterday.' I avoided eye-contact with Ellie.

I heard Probert say something to Kane.

'Can you not find it?' she called back.

I stared at the door of my bedroom.

'Would you be able to drop it in for us please? At the station,' she called up.

Relief. 'Yes. Sorry I just can't find it!' I replied, calmly as possible. 'I'll drop it in.'

As I came down the stairs, they were both standing by the front door.

'Could you drop it in for us?' she repeated, with a conde-scending smirk. 'Also, the other clothes you were wearing that evening, please.'

'Of course,' I said, knowing full well that they had been scattered to the winds via a charity shop somewhere by now. But it had bought me some time.

'Can I ask why? What's so interesting about this jumper?' I asked.

'That's what we need to see it for,' said Probert. 'We don't know yet.'

Thirty-Six

After the police left, I sat on the floor in the hallway and tried to take everything in. Solly had fucked me, that much was obvious. I knew I had to acknowledge the fact that this could well be the beginning of *game over*. A picture of my clothes from that night, sent directly to the police. Directly to Sergeant Kane at her home.

Something provocative: not enough to finish me off, but enough to turn the spotlight on me. He's *got their brains ticking* again. Kane had reacted instantly and instinctively, like he'd wanted her to. He's reminding me what power he has over me. *He's reminding me what he could do.*

I'd told him I didn't want to come and meet him at his appointed time, and he'd made this gesture in response. *Why send it to her home? Why not to the police station?* I racked my brain to try to remember if the envelope had had stamps on it. I didn't think it had. I think he'd hand delivered it. *How did he know where she lived?*

He must've followed her, like he had followed me. This nasty feeling had begun to brew in my gut about Solly. This was not in keeping with his tone and the way he'd spoken to me at his apartment. He didn't seem so much like this hapless, shocked bystander now.

I wondered about him. Who he was, what his story was. I'd been naïve about him, of course. This was a proper, full on uppercut into my world, and he knew it. This person was more dangerous than I'd given him credit for. This was an aggressive, instantaneous reaction. It showed a real bloody mindedness. He was speaking to me through the police. He was waving that prison cell in front of my face.

I picked up my phone and texted him: **'I'll come. 5pm.'**

'MAKE IT 7' he replied, seconds later. **'I WILL COOK.'**

Ellie appeared at the door of the living room. 'Was that the police?'

'Yeah,' I said. 'They just wanted… my clothes.'

'Your clothes?' she asked with surprise.

'Yeah, like… as in, the clothes I was wearing… that night,' I said.

'Why?'

'Because… I don't know. Because they're trying to work out where everyone was, from the CCTV and I guess they need to confirm which one is me. I don't know.'

Ellie stared at me for a long time, in silence. First, she looked confused, then pained, then she just looked back at me blankly. 'Confirm which one is you…' she repeated back to me, absent-mindedly. 'Do they come to your house a lot?' she asked.

'No, that's the first time,' I said, pretending to tidy up. 'They've found the person who did it,' I said, locking eyes with her.

'Yeah,' she said quietly.

'They're trying to, I dunno, build the case,' I said dismissively.

'Against… that person,' she said.

'Yeah. His name's Evatt, he's this nutter.'

'Why do they want *your* clothes though?' she asked.

'I don't know!' I snapped.

For the next twenty minutes I kept trying to make small talk.

Kept trying to gently guide the conversation away. But Ellie was deep in thought. She kept staring at the ground, like she was calculating something. My mind was straining in second gear.

She left, just before lunchtime. Said she had to help her friend who was revising for something.

I don't think that was true. She was preoccupied; I could see her mind was whirring. I didn't have it in me to lie to her any more, so I let her go.

Thirty-Seven

As soon as I was sure Ellie wasn't coming back, I ripped my phone from my pocket and called Solly. No answer. That bastard. I tried again three or four times, without him answering. He was trying to draw me to his apartment again.

Tempted as I was to bomb straight over there, I knew he wouldn't answer the door. I'd go at seven. I'd play his game, until I could get my foot in that door. When I got in there, I'd just fully go off at him. Tell him what a piece of shit he is. *If you can't keep to your word, what kind of man are you?*

I showered and dressed, drank a bottle of Lucozade and sat on my sofa, waiting for 7 p.m. I ordered a pizza but even though I was starving I couldn't eat it. I sat there grazing on bits of pepperoni and sweetcorn. I took two Nurofen for my hangover and eventually fell asleep on my sofa.

I woke at about half past five. I leapt up, grabbed my jacket and gloves and tore off towards London. I didn't sit down in the train; I was in battle mode. I was ready to tear strips off Solly for breaking the deal. I was going to try and make him feel like I wasn't to be messed with.

I toyed with the idea of just robbing him. Just taking his hard drive and then burn it or dump it in a canal or something. But that would be hard work. I'd need to subdue him somehow, for a start. That wouldn't be impossible, but it might be difficult.

I looked up what a hard drive looked like. I thought maybe I could take it when he went to the toilet or something; but they're not easy to get out. And of course, there'd be no guarantee he didn't have another copy somewhere else. I knew he'd transferred it, at least to that USB stick he sent me.

He'll have made another copy.

I thought about just plain threatening him. Telling him I was going to kill him or something. But that's a pretty heavy act to back up. I didn't feel capable of that, however angry I was feeling. Not of terrifying him into silence.

I was simply going to go there and play his fucking way, for a while. I was going to listen to him, play along and let him tell me what his game is. I'd nod along, laugh along if necessary, and let him talk. Then when he's finished, and he tells me how much he wants, I'll tell him what the rules are going to be. I knew what it was he was inviting me to: a shakedown. He was going to finally demand that I give him money for his silence.

As far as I could tell from my research, a 'one punch death' in the throes of a fight was likely to land you in prison for between five and ten years. That sort of a sentence doesn't sound like much, until you seriously consider serving it. Ten years is longer than I spent at school and college, put together. And those things went on for a goddamn lifetime. Ten years in prison. Ten Christmas Eves in prison, ten summers. Year after year of never getting to spend time with a girl or have couple of pints after a long day. Ten years, the difference between a young man enjoying the freedoms of his late twenties, and a father-figure in his late thirties.

And then there's the impact after that. The impact on everything. My career and the life I've started putting together. Having to start again, approaching forty, and all because of something I didn't want any part of. Something that got foisted on me one night, by some dickhead.

I'd pay Solly. I had savings, about £7,000, which was my house deposit fund. I made a few rules in my head for the whole thing:

1. The maximum I'd pay was £5,000. I wouldn't tell Solly that figure, I'd just keep it in my head as the upper limit. If he asked me for £100, he'd get £100.
2. This would be a one-off transaction, and I'd make that very clear. I'll pay the amount he asks for and then we're done. If I'm contacted again after that, I'll tell him, I'd rather he just shops me to the police, because there would be nothing to stop that dynamic going on forever; I'll play the game, but only *once*.
3. The same rule applies to Solly's silence. If he ever tells another living soul, I'll tell him the deal is off and I'll shop him, and myself, to the police. Because again, that dynamic could go on indefinitely and I'm not spending my life at Solly's mercy. I'll take my chances with the justice system.
4. After this, I would have no further contact or association with Solly.

Thirty-Eight

The lift up to Solly's apartment absolutely reeked of piss. The buttons looked filthy; I didn't want to touch them with my finger. I used a knuckle. As I approached Solly's door, I got this heavy waft of cooking. He'd said something about cooking. There was zero chance of me eating anything prepared by him, in that kitchen.

He opened the door in an apron and held his arms out welcomingly. It was like he was greeting a long-lost friend. I made a face at him as I bustled in and closed the front door.

'The fuck are you doing?' I scowled at him as I pushed past into his living room. I was trying my best to seem confident and assured. I wasn't going to let him know he'd succeeded in making me feel vulnerable. And he had been cooking, no doubt about that. His apartment was a hot, stinking hive of activity.

'Now Will, before we start anything else, what will I pour you to drink?' he asked innocently.

'I don't want anything to drink, I don't want anything to eat,' I said.

Solly smiled. 'That is the most delicious mackerel you'll ever taste,' he said. 'And I'm going to have to insist you have a glass of Sauvignon Semillon with it.'

He clumsily poured a glass and brought it over to me. 'Here!' he said.

I looked at the glass, then back at him. 'I haven't got time for all this,' I said, grabbing it from him.

He scooped up his glass and took an almighty gulp from it. He was half drunk, I could tell.

'Sit down,' he said, pointing to a small table he'd set up. It had those pathetic plastic chairs either side of it.

'I'm good, thanks,' I said.

He disappeared into the kitchen where he stumbled around for a few seconds before reappearing with a bright red oven dish, which he set down on the table. In the dish were two cooked mackerel.

To be fair, it looked like he knew what he was doing. They were scored all the way down the sides and looked well cooked. They had slices of lemon dotted over them. He went back into the kitchen and reappeared with a little pot of chopped onions. He poured them all over the fish and sat down at the table.

He took a sip of his wine and shifted in his chair. He looked across at me and exhaled heavily through his nose. 'You can at least sit at the table with me, Will.'

'I told you, I'm not hungry,' I said.

'Why don't you sit with me at least? So we can talk?'

I sighed, dragged the other chair a few feet back from the table and dropped myself into it, placing my wine glass on the table between us.

He ground salt over the fish, leaned over it and took a long, deep sniff, smacking his lips in anticipation. 'Are you *sure* I can't tempt you?' he said.

'Is that it?' I said. 'Just a fish, nothing else?'

He laughed to himself. 'The obsession with carbohydrates is a very working-class thing, Will.'

'Yeah and this is just pure nobility,' I said, as he peeled a piece of skin off the fish with his fingers and shoved it into the side of his mouth.

'Did the police contact you?' he asked, little fragments of wet fish skin shooting from his lips.

'Yeah,' I said.

He sniffed, picked a chunk of fish and crammed it into his mouth. 'What'd they say?' he asked.

Is this ape deliberately waiting until his mouth is full of food to talk?

'They said you sent a picture of my jumper design to the house of one of the officers,' I sighed. It was at this point I realised he hadn't even bothered to get a knife and fork out. *Had he intended for me to eat it like that, too?*

'They said I did it, did they?' he asked, without looking at me.

'Look, I can't be bothered to mess around like this Solly,' I said. 'You know what you did. What do you *want*?' I angled my head down a little, to interrupt his eyes which were darting around the fish in the red dish.

He stopped eating and looked up at me. He readjusted his glasses on his face. I noticed he hadn't cleaned any of the fish or oil off his hands first. He just carried on gesticulating and propping up his glasses and running his fingers through his gross hair. I guessed that must be why his skin was so oily. It's important to wash your hands after eating, everyone knows that.

He took a deep breath and pushed his plate to one side. 'Last night I asked you to come here, because I needed to talk to you.'

'You didn't politely ask me anything,' I said, 'you told me to come here.'

He shrugged, as if it were a pedantic difference.

'We don't have that kind of relationship,' I continued.

He stared at me and took another long draught from his glass of wine. 'What kind of relationship *do* we have?' he croaked.

'Well, it's like this. You filmed me without my consent and then you lied to me and told me you'd deleted the video, and now you've called me here to your apartment, so you can blackmail me. Oh, and you've cooked me a fish. That's our relationship,' I said.

He looked offended. 'I told you, I wasn't filming *you*; and I didn't lie to you, I deleted that footage, I did. You're a pretty ungrateful person.'

'So why call me here?' I asked. 'Why call me here now?'

'Because I'm worried,' he replied, 'and now *I* need *your* help.'

'Solly,' I said, 'what the fuck do you *want* from me?'

Thirty-Nine

Solly explained to me that he'd 'been conned out of some money'. In reality, someone had failed to pay him after he'd won some illegal poker tournament. He told me he was so skint he couldn't even pay his electric bill. I laughed out loud at him. 'Nice try. You must think I'm completely stupid.' I told him it wasn't necessary to make up any stories or convince me of anything. I told him I knew what I was there for, told him my terms and asked him how much he wanted.

'Go on,' I said. 'What do you want? Get on with it.'

'You're getting this wrong,' he said. 'I don't want any of *your money*.'

'No, Solly, let's not do that,' I shot back. 'That whole bit where we prowl around each other and you slowly reveal to me what you want. Let's finish this, right now.' I folded my arms and sat up straight.

'Will, look around you,' he said. 'I have lots of stuff, I am richer than you are. I don't need your money. I have my own money.'

'I'll give you two thousand,' I said, looking him directly in the eye. 'Two thousand pounds, cash.' I saw him stifle a laugh.

'I helped you,' he said, finally.

'You *helped* me?' I mocked.

'How many times do I have to tell you: I didn't film you on purpose. *You* came into my shot. And then... I deleted it for you. And you've never shown me any gratitude *what-so-ever...*' He reached into the red dish and pulled another chunk of fish out with his fingers.

'I'm grateful,' I said, 'if you really deleted it, I am grateful, Solly. I mean that.'

'I don't have any family,' he continued, 'I don't have many people I can call friends.'

I rolled my eyes.

'So, who do I turn to, when things get difficult?' he asked.

'Stop. Stop a second,' I said. 'You literally hand-delivered some evidence that incriminated me, to the police. Just to be clear, we aren't friends. I'm not here to listen to your problems.'

'And how the hell else was I supposed to get you to talk to me?' he asked, suddenly furious.

'You asked me *once*, while I was *out*, you gave me *one day* of notice. That isn't friendly,' I shouted.

He held his finger up to his lips. He winced and pointed at the wall to his left and whispered, 'You can't make too much noise in the evening, because he works earlies.'

'Yeah, you see, this is it,' I said, rubbing my face defeatedly.

'What is it?' said Solly.

'I know what you're doing,' I said, sitting back in my chair.

'Go on, what am I doing?' he said. 'I'd love to know.'

'You're going to try and make me feel sort of... *indebted*, so you can keep coming back and asking me for money in the future. You're going to try and become a *slow puncture* on me, aren't you?'

Solly took another gulp of wine and refilled his glass. 'You know how much I made last year, just out of poker?' he said.

'What do you *want*, Solly?' I snapped.

'A hundred and eighty thousand' he said, 'and the year before that I made two hundred and twenty.'

'That's great,' I said, taking my phone out of my pocket and glancing at it, 'well done.'

'That's a lot of money for a single man,' he said. 'And I also get my government money.'

'You mean you're claiming benefits?' I said. 'You're making all that money and claiming benefits?'

'I got my injury in a work accident!' he spat.

'Okay so, why are you bothered about someone conning you out of money?' I said. 'Can't you just pay your electric bills from your vast reserves of wealth?'

'I don't have reserves. I spend my money in case tomorrow I get hit by a bus,' he said.

'So you've spent all that money, and now you've run out?'

'No I haven't *run out*, it doesn't work like that. In poker it costs money to make money, you have to invest in the tournaments and stuff like that. I have investments.'

'If you're so good at poker,' I said, 'can't you just go on one of those online tournaments and win a load of money?'

He rolled his eyes. 'It doesn't work like that. Are you really that naïve?' He pushed my wine glass towards me. 'I don't have anyone who can help me,' he said. 'I don't know *anyone*... This has never happened before. I've had a difficult... run. This individual has £43,000 of my money and he won't give it to me. I won it from him fair and square. And he had sixty days to pay me, and now it's passed. It passed in August actually.'

'So, his deadline was four months ago?' I said. 'Yeah, he's not going to be paying you.'

'I know!' Solly said forlornly. 'Don't you think I *know* that?'

Solly came over to me and knelt on the floor next to my chair. 'Will, I don't have anybody to turn to, I don't have anybody who can help me.'

'Call the police,' I said, getting up to leave.

'Will, please!' he said, standing up. 'Please, be reasonable. This is not *licensed* stuff! I can't go to the police!'

'So what exactly do you want me to do?' I said 'Go round with my heavies and beat this person up?'

'No not…violence, nothing like that,' he assured me. 'Look, I just need somebody to go and talk to him,' he said. 'Let him know I'm waiting for him to pay, and he hasn't just got away with it. He's not a criminal or anything.'

'Are you asking me to go and reclaim a debt for you, Solly?' I said, with a smirk.

'*No!* I keep telling you, I just want you to let him know I'm waiting for him to pay, that's all.'

'Solly, why on *earth* would you want *me* to do this task?' I said.

'Because for once in my life I helped someone, and so for once in my life, I have someone to help me,' he said quietly. 'I don't expect you to understand what it's like, being on your own in the world.'

He began clearing away the food. He looked deflated, but I wasn't buying it.

'Goodnight Solly,' I said, heading for the door.

He followed me out into the hallway with a placemat in his hands.

'I'm not talking about a criminal,' he said. 'This guy is a schoolteacher, and he's older than me. He's a chubby little family man. He's weak. I'd go round there myself if my body wasn't knackered as shit.'

'You'll have to find someone else,' I said, opening his front door to leave.

As I went down the corridor towards the lift I called back to him: '*Don't* contact me Solly.' When I reached the bottom of the corridor I turned back. He was still standing there.

'I thought you'd be able to do it for me, because I know you are a tough guy,' he said. 'I've seen your punch, haven't I? It's impressive.'

He smiled at me and closed the door.

I could feel adrenaline and bile rising from my gut. *What the hell does that mean?*

Forty

Although nothing happened in the few days after that, the tension kept rising in me. I more or less stopped eating, I'd have to remind myself to eat. I had no energy or motivation to cook so I was constantly ordering junk food deliveries. My shit diet would not have been helping with my spiralling thoughts, which were pretty consuming.

I made a special effort to be as open as I could with Ellie. I was desperate to try to somehow hold on to her, however stormy it got. I didn't want her to lose any more faith in me. I wanted things to be normal.

We went to the cinema one night and saw a re-run of *Planet of the Apes*. She seemed more relaxed and didn't ask any more questions about the police. I hoped to god that stuff would just melt into the background. Of course, it didn't.

The next morning she messaged me, asking 'if I'd heard anything else from the police'. I told her they'd charged this guy Evatt, and I hadn't heard anything more. She asked when his trial was and if I'd have to be a witness. I said I didn't know. The thought chilled my fucking blood.

Sergeant Kane got in touch with me again. She called me and I just stared at my phone. I couldn't make myself answer it. She left a voicemail, asking if I'd had any luck finding those items of clothing. She asked if I could drop off the items she'd requested in to the station at Islington by the end of the week.

I don't fucking have them, you bitch. Leave me alone.

I was now beginning to feel fully trapped. I knew I had to do something. There was no more time to hide from the situation. She wanted my stuff taken in, and any more delay would only increase suspicion around me. I paced around, clawing for an answer.

I was a zombie most of the time, paralysed in my own thoughts. My advertising work, which had never been stuff of any real significance, was not something that was commanding my attention any more. I had a huge decision to make about my next step. I sensed the police knew something was up. They were on my trail, no doubt about that.

Solly was a problem. I knew deep down, if he could just disappear, they'd never have anything on me. I'd fluked this *immaculate killing* and they were relying on me to fuck up to give the game away. Solly was the outlier, the sharp little stone in my shoe. I just wanted him gone.

I thought about my other options. Just options, for if I really needed them. Nuclear options. Should I get out of there? Just disappear somewhere until this all blows over? *Where?*

I couldn't run from it. Nothing would make me look more guilty.

Forty-One

I woke up on the Saturday morning, thinking about Solly as usual. He knew I could punch, because he'd seen me. I'd taken that as a thinly veiled threat. He was referencing his video. Which, I had no doubt, still very much existed.

There was no chance of me doing his dirty work for him. There was no way I was going to go and threaten anybody. I cringed at the thought. Especially this tubby, old guy he'd described. If he needed money, I had it. I'd give him two grand as soon as he asked for it, I'd told him that. I was not going to get suckered into his game.

I went to the bathroom and stood shirtless in front of the mirror. I looked slim, in better shape than I'd been in for years, but my face gave away something different. My face let you know that this wasn't a healthy kind of weight loss. I looked old and tired. My eyes looked puffy and seemed to turn down-wards at the edges as if what I'd seen had etched a permanent extra degree of sadness. My skin was dry and pale. No wonder, it hadn't seen proper sunlight in far too long and I certainly hadn't been feeding it any vitamins. I scratched at my stubble with my fingernails.

Minutes later I was shaving. I wanted it all off. After I'd

finished, I slapped my face with cologne and let the wave of tingling pain tear through my face. It felt fantastic. Staring into the mirror I poured another handful of Gucci for Men and clapped it onto my neck. I gritted my teeth as the alcohol fizzed on contact with the freshly shaved skin. That pain felt fucking liberating.

I lay on the sofa and drank a bottle of Chardonnay that had been in the vegetable drawer of my fridge for months. That gave me a taste for it; I opened the only other thing I had in the house: a cheap bottle of champagne work had given me for Christmas. Drinking a couple of bottles of wine when your stomach's that empty of anything is a really different experience. It's like wine cut with acid or something. But it gave me this intense clarity.

I lay on my sofa playing Kane's voicemail back to myself, again and again. I needed to find an out. I thought of that torture thing that the Yakuza do, when they put a rat in a metal bowl on somebody's stomach, then slowly heat up the bowl with a blowtorch. The rat has nowhere to go but into the cooler wall: the flesh. So it starts burrowing into the person's body, to escape the heat.

I needed to find my way out of this. I knew I needed to do *something*. I decided to address this fucking jumper situation, head on. I came up with a plan. I'd tell the police I'd lost it. I'd tell them I'd lost a whole dryer full of laundry, at the launderette near the station in St Albans. The clever part was, it'd really happened before.

Something I've learned is that it's easier to make a lie more believable if you ground it firmly in real memories. The previous year my washing machine had broken. I'd had to take a load to that launderette and when I went back to pick it up, it'd been nicked. When I asked if they had CCTV, they'd looked at me like I had two heads. I'd had some decent stuff in there, nice jeans and t-shirts. I was fuming.

I decided to go down to the launderette and take a look. Just check what the CCTV situation was around there. I pretended I was going to the station to check the schedule on the board. But my eyes were darting this way and that, taking everything in, looking for cameras around the launderette.

There was nothing facing it. There were cameras in the vicinity but nothing facing the launderette. If someone were to drive right up to it, drop off their laundry and leave again in their car, you wouldn't see them on CCTV. The launderette was old as hell, it looked straight out of the 1930s.

So, that's where my jumper went. Of course, someone nicked it from there. In my drunken state I made this hasty change of plan. I went bumbling into the launderette and asked to speak to the manager. The old lady I spoke to was maybe Greek or Italian. Her English wasn't great, but she explained to me that she was the owner.

I told her I was looking for a load of washing I'd left in one of the dryers. She said she didn't know what I was talking about. I told her it contained an Iceberg Jeans jumper that was very valuable. She told me she was sorry but that items were left at the owner's risk. She said that sentence in perfect, accentless English, like she'd said it a million times.

I tutted and stomped about a bit. Made sure she knew I was devastated that it was lost. I asked her if there was a lost property and she pointed up to a giant orange basket of tatty old clothes, on a high shelf in the back room. I told her I wasn't going to inspect the basket. That felt like an unnecessary nightmare.

The lady could tell I was drunk. She kept suddenly jerking her arm out to catch me because she thought I was going to fall over. I must have been unsteady on my feet. She said her name was Dolores. I thanked her for her time and staggered back home. In my mind, I'd sorted my alibi for not having that jumper.

So, I phoned Probert to tell him the jumper was lost. I told him my washing machine hadn't been working one morning and I'd taken my stuff to the launderette – and someone had stolen the load.

He was silent on the line for a moment, and then said, 'The launderette?' He couldn't have sounded more sceptical.

I told him the name of the launderette, and that I'd been in to speak with the manager about it. I told him she'd said she'd keep an eye out. He asked me if *all* the clothes I was wearing that night were lost. I said no they weren't. See, I'd had this other idea: I was going to substitute everything else I was wearing that night with other, similar looking items.

I had a pair of dark brown boots that, from more than five yards away, would look identical to the ones I was wearing that night. The brown, lightweight rain jacket I'd been wearing over the top was easily substituted. I had the same jacket in a smaller size. Those jackets were two for £40 in Uniqlo so I got a Medium and a Large, so I could wear the Large with a jumper underneath. And as for the skinny black jeans I'd been wearing, I had three or four pairs, all identical.

I told Probert I'd drop them in, minus the missing jumper. He told me it was 'a bit of a problem', and he asked for the telephone number of the launderette. Which made this jumper suddenly seem terrifyingly significant. He wanted the phone number of the fucking launderette.

I kept telling myself though, there was nothing he could do. I'd neutralised the threat. I packed one pair of black, skinny jeans, one pair of very dark brown boots and one medium sized Uniqlo rain jacket into a bag and dropped them in at the police station.

Forty-Two

January passed slowly and payday took forever to come around, as ever. One afternoon Ellie and I were walking around Victoria Playing Fields. We'd taken to going for walks around those fields quite regularly. We'd talk about work and the things that were stressing us out. Ellie was having problems with her boss. He sounded like a real arsehole, the way he spoke to her.

It got to around four o'clock and we headed home. In January it gets dark so early, an afternoon walk quickly becomes a night-time one. We took the quickest route back to my flat. When we got there, I stopped at the communal post box by the building's main entrance. Ellie continued up to the flat; her feet were freezing, she said, and she didn't want to hang about. I couldn't blame her.

The lifts in my building were quite regularly out of service. You have to take the stairs up. It wasn't too much of a problem, my apartment is only on the second floor. It's good to walk up steps when you can, it's a great form of simple exercise.

As I approached the top of the stairwell with a stack of letters, Ellie was coming back from the other direction. She looked wide eyed, a bit panicked. She whispered to me, 'Will, your uncle's come over. He's really not well.'

I stopped dead. 'Sorry, what? *Who?*'

'Your uncle. He's really sick, Will. He said he's been trying to call you. Come on, quick!' She yanked me by my arm.

I plunged my hand into my pocket and pulled my phone out. Solly had called me, twice. Rage came over me instantly, right there in the corridor. That fucking fool had come to my flat. He'd spoken to my girlfriend. He'd stepped right over that line.

I shot past Ellie and ran down the corridor. When I got to the door my flat, I saw she'd already let him in. The door was still open, with the key in it. There was no sign of him, but I could smell him in the entrance. Musky old alcohol, B.O. and tobacco. And sort of pickled onion.

'Solly?' I barked, quietly as I could manage.

'In here,' he called from the living room.

'He's on the sofa!' I heard Ellie call down the hall to me.

When I got in, there he was. Reclined across my sofa holding the side of his stomach. 'Please, Will, please. Get me a glass of water, this is serious. This is serious.'

I could hear Ellie's footsteps following down the corridor outside.

His face looked gaunt and pale. For once, he looked deadly serious, no hint of a smirk.

'What the hell is wrong with you?' I whispered viciously. 'What are you *doing* here?'

'Calm down,' he said, jerking a finger towards the open front door and then to his lips. 'She'll hear you!'

'What are you doing in my fucking flat? Get out!' I whispered, through clenched teeth. 'I'm not joking, Will, I'm seriously in trouble, here,' he said, wincing and holding his side. 'Just give me a moment, please.'

'What the fuck are you doing here?' I repeated. 'What happened to you?'

His wrinkled, greasy face sagged into an even more pathetic expression as Ellie appeared in the doorway.

'Thank you so much, Ellie!' he called out, holding the back of his hand to his forehead. 'I think you just saved my goddamn life.'

'What's happened?' Ellie asked with genuine concern. 'I'll call you an ambulance, right now.'

'No!' he cried. 'I know exactly what this is, I just didn't expect it to happen today.'

Ellie stared at me, in complete shock.

Forty-Three

Solly told us he had a serious gastric condition that could flare up at any time. He said this happened around once a month, a sharp pain like being poked in the intestine with a knitting needle. He said it usually lasted about an hour, so he expected it to subside, shortly. Ellie rushed around him, brought him a glass of water and a warm flannel for his brow. He gradually calmed down.

As she placed the water down next to him, he gently took hold of to her wrist. 'Oh, what's that?' he asked.

'What's what?' she replied.

'Your tattoo. It's lovely.'

'Oh, thanks,' she said, pulling up the sleeve of her jumper dress a little to reveal a tiny tattoo of a swallow on her wrist. She then pulled down the collar of her dress to the side to reveal her shoulder, where she had another tattoo of another little bird. 'This is my new one. The one on my wrist is like ten years old.'

Solly lowered his glasses to the end of his nose and reached his hand out gently towards her shoulder, as if to ask her to turn a little, to give him a better view. She leant towards him to help him see.

'It's a little bird, a little bird of paradise,' he said. 'Would you look at that. Absolutely stunning.'

He propped himself up to look more closely, reaching to gently nudge the fabric of her dress a little lower with his fingers to reveal the entire design. 'So intricate,' he whispered.

'Yeah, it took about four hours,' Ellie said, holding her dark hair to the side so as not to obscure his view. He stayed there looking at her shoulder for far too long.

He was still gently clasping her wrist. 'Thank you so much for helping me in,' he said. 'You really are a darling. How have I not heard anything about you?'

He looked at me. 'Hello, Will,' he croaked. He was still trying to affect some debilitating illness. I could see right through it, of course. He was an absolutely shocking actor.

'It's so good to see you, my boy!' he said weakly. 'I'm so sorry about all this drama. I was in a terrible state when your girl-friend found me.'

I cringed as he eventually let go of Ellie's wrist; I knew what kind of shit was festering on those hands of his. I thought about calling him out, right then and there, spoiling his game for Ellie's benefit. But of course, I couldn't. Satisfying as that would have been, it would have been completely illogical. I just needed to focus on getting rid of him as quickly as I could.

'I wanted to surprise you, Will, I came to surprise you.' He called over to me, with his eyes pinched shut as though he were in terrible pain.

'Can I get you anything else?' asked Ellie. She looked at me helplessly. I had no idea Ellie could be this gullible. Or was it because I already knew him that this whole routine looked absolutely laughable to me?

'I'm okay my darling!' he said softly. 'Give me ten minutes' lie down and I'll be absolutely fine. I've had peptic ulcers all my life, I'm a martyr to pain in the guts.'

Ellie looked at me once again, as if she didn't know what to do. 'Take deep breaths,' she said to him. She shrugged at me.

'I was coming over to see how you are, Will,' he said quietly. His physical behaviour was really bizarre. He was trying to come across like he was about ninety. 'We're all worried about you, your mum's worried,' he croaked, wincing and holding his side. He turned to look at Ellie with a pained expression. 'I wish I could be meeting you in more… dignified circumstances,' he groaned, pulling himself into a seating position and rubbing his back.

'It's okay,' said Ellie. She was the exact opposite of him: a straightforward person with straightforward motives.

'How long have the two of you been together?' he asked, looking between us.

Ellie looked at me, then back at him. 'A couple of months,' she said.

'God bless you,' he said to her. 'You seem lovely. He's done very well.'

'Thanks.' she said. 'You seem nice too. Would you like another drink?'

'Yes,' he said, 'I would like a beer. But I would like the proprietor of the establishment to go and fetch it for me, to save your pretty legs,' he smiled at her.

Ellie grinned at me. 'You heard him,' she said cheekily.

I barged into the kitchen and grabbed a bottle of Rolling Rock from the fridge. He wasn't having the expensive beer. As I popped the cap off the bottle, I heard Ellie laugh out loud at something from the next room. His manner around her was gross. I sensed she was probably aware of it and was humouring him to avoid the awkwardness. As I returned to the living room, they were deep in conversation.

'We don't really talk about it much,' said Ellie. 'I think it's been on Will's mind a lot but he finds it hard to talk about.'

'Oh, but you *must* talk about it,' he said. 'You *must*. The essence of any relationship is communication. Don't you think so, Will?'

I put Solly's beer on the table in front of him and took a seat. I could feel my teeth grinding together. This was my *home*.

'We talk,' I said sharply.

He smiled at her. 'He's not a sharer, is he? Likes to take on all the problems himself, right?'

'You know him well!' she grinned.

'I've told him: just tell the police the truth about what you saw; tell the truth and nobody can ask any more of you.'

Ellie glanced at me, confused.

I looked back at him in disbelief. 'Wait, what? What are you talking about?'

'The stress!' said Solly. 'The problem! This case the police keep bothering you about. You sent me that email about it, didn't you.'

I glared at him. He winked at me and sipped his beer.

'I've been this young man's sounding board since he was yay high!' he gestured at Ellie. 'Any trouble, always comes to his uncle first, don't you? But this one's... this is different, isn't it. I understand the stress it put you under Will,' he continued. 'We're talking about a murder. Did you hear what happened, Ellie?'

'Someone... there was an accident down the alley, in Farringdon,' she said.

'Yes,' he said. 'Barbaric. This guy was just making his way home from work and someone appeared out of nowhere and killed him on the spot. Can you imagine?'

The room fell silent. Ellie was staring at Solly. Solly was staring at me. I was staring at the floor.

'People can't get their head around it. A promising, decent young man like that, killed over nothing. It's such a waste.

People want to know why this is still happening, you know. London's supposed to be a modern city. It's not Johannesburg. We're supposed to feel safe from these people,' he said solemnly.

I glared at him.

'It could have been our Will!' he said to Ellie. 'He's roughly the same age as the bloke. Think of that.'

'Nobody can ever feel completely safe,' said Ellie. 'I don't think you can ever feel completely safe, walking around London at night.'

'What do you mean?' Solly asked.

'I mean, *everyone* I know has some story about something that's happened to them once,' she said.

'But not everyone gets killed, right?' said Solly. 'Not everyone dies because they just wanted to walk home from work.'

'No of course not,' said Ellie, 'it's really sad.'

Solly was already finishing his beer. He drained it in three swigs. Ellie got up and went to the kitchen to fetch him another one. This time, even with Ellie out of earshot, there was no whispering. He just looked at me, stony faced, in silence. I glared back at him with such intensity it felt like my eyes might burst. My vision was shaking a little. Not with fear, with anger.

Ellie returned and placed a bottle of beer in front of each of us. Solly picked his up and took a sip. 'You know something?' he said, reclining and stretching his legs out in front of him. 'I don't believe in capital punishment, but I do believe the world would be a better place without people who go around doing things like that.'

Ellie nodded.

'I'm not saying they should be hanged or anything,' he said, looking to Ellie for agreement.

'I know,' said Ellie, sipping her beer. 'I get what you mean. How are you feeling about it, Will?' she asked me, out of nowhere. 'The case.'

'Yeah, fine,' I said. 'Fine. I didn't see anything so I can't really contribute anything to it.' I shrugged and took a sip from my beer.

'Yeah. You were there though. That's the problem, isn't it?' said Solly. 'Nobody can work out how you managed not to see anything, when you were *there at the time*!'

'That's just it,' I said. 'I wasn't there when it happened. I missed it.'

'Yeah,' said Ellie. 'And the police don't believe you, right?'

My face was red hot, I could feel it. I could feel their eyes burning into me. I felt like I was being cross examined by them both, but Ellie wasn't aware she was doing it.

'Meanwhile, the bloke they've pulled in, says he didn't do it,' said Solly. 'His defence team's been trying to source any CCTV from around there, and all that.' Solly continued, looking at me.

'There will definitely be something. It's Central London,' said Ellie.

Forty-Four

Solly asked her to join him on the sofa, and she did. He was looking right into her eyes as she spoke, holding her gaze for far too long. He asked her about her childhood, where she went to school. She answered him so sweetly and honestly each time.

My blood was boiling at how naïve she was being. It was like she was hanging off his every word. She kept laughing at his jokes. She wasn't flinching when he touched her. It was weird to watch.

It didn't feel like I could intervene. She seemed perfectly comfortable. Happy, even. She'd taken an instant liking to him, I could tell. Was she… *flirting with him?* I looked him up and down: his saggy eyes, his oily, lank hair and stale breath… I just could not compute what I was seeing. *She's actually having a good time with this guy.*

He kept doing this thing with his hand. He had a ring on the little finger of his left hand. Every now and then he'd double-tap that finger on the side of his beer bottle, so it made a little '*clink-clink*'. A ridiculous little tick. I shuddered for a moment at how much bacteria must be on that ring.

I wanted her to notice what a creep he was, and cold shoulder him a bit. That might put him off, I thought, make him want

160

to leave. He was there to intimidate me, of course. To let me know he could still ruin everything if he wanted to.

He wanted me to know he could influence Ellie and make things more difficult for me. He wanted me to know he could cost me that, too. What was so frustrating was, she was making it easy for him. It was hard for me to catch her eye because she was angled slightly away from me. I'd have to walk all the way to the other side of the room to get her attention.

Ellie then asked him about his job. He told her he was between jobs but made a lot of money playing poker. He told her about how he'd *won* or *ranked* in this prestigious tournament and that. Probably bollocks. He told her he was regularly featured in articles about the best British players. Again, most likely nonsense. He brought his profile up on some website and showed it to her on his phone. She was really impressed. He told her this absolutely insane story about how he'd saved a dog that was being abused by its owner. All this shit about how he'd nursed it for months and taught it to trust humans again. And then he went on about how he's also known for having a natural expertise with horses. He certainly knew how to generate a lot of horse shit.

Then he told her he'd been dating, but he was finding it hard to meet people. She told him some of her embarrassing dating stories. The beers kept coming; they were getting along like a house on fire. The whole thing was making me nauseous.

Eventually I think she got the hint. She turned around and asked me if we 'needed to go and start dinner.' I said yes we did, and jumped to my feet. I watched Solly ogle Ellie as she got up from the sofa. He caught me looking and winked at me. I momentarily fantasised about pushing my thumbs into his eyeballs.

As we showed him out, he was clearly overjoyed with his successful evening of getting under my skin. He could tell I was livid, and he was absolutely delighted with himself. He stood across the front door frame, with his palms on either side of the frame. It was bizarre, like some sort of alpha male ritual, but performed by an absolute runt.

'Excuse me, Ellie, I hope you don't find this rude, but we've had such a nice time, I wondered if you wanted to take my telephone number. We should get together for a beer next week?' As he said the words 'we should get together', he double tapped his pinky ring again. I tried not to laugh at how fucking obtuse he was. He was absurd.

Then something unbelievable happened. Ellie said, 'Yeah sure, I'd like that. My phone battery's died, hold on.' She went and got a biro from the kitchen.

When she came back, she cradled his filthy hand in hers and wrote her telephone number on it. I think my jaw was hanging open. Solly kept glancing at me while she was doing it. He was losing his fucking mind with excitement. He was physically twitching. To be fair, my mind was blown, too. *What in the fuck was she doing?*

Solly thanked her and hugged her (again, holding it way too long). He turned to me and smiled. 'Thanks so much for your hospitality, Will. Send my love to your mum.' He held out his hand for me to shake. I stared at it for a moment. I could feel Ellie's eyes on me.

I limply shook it, and he was off into the night. With my girlfriend's telephone number.

Forty-Five

As I closed the door, Ellie went straight back into the living room and sat down on the sofa. I walked back into the room slowly, genuinely not knowing what to say. I looked at her in utter disbelief. I felt like I had just had this whole education about her.

She looked at me coldly for a second, then away. She seemed so emotionless, like she didn't care about what had just happened. I was speechless. *What on earth had I just sat through?*

I cleared my throat. 'Can I just...' I tried to speak but I couldn't. Ellie finally looked at me. Her expression wasn't what I'd been expecting. She looked furious. With *me*.

'Will,' she said quietly, 'I'm not going to get angry or upset with you. If you want me to stay here one second longer, you'll need to tell me what is going on.'

'I'm sorry, what?' I tried to digest what she was saying.

'Okay. Goodbye Will,' she said. 'Good luck with everything.' She stood up, picked up her bag and jacket and headed for the front door.

'Wait,' I said. 'Wait. Ellie, tell me what you mean.'

'No, I'm actually done telling you what I mean,' she said. 'Last chance: who was that?'

'That was... Solly... You just gave him your phone number,' I said.

She rolled her eyes. 'Who is he? I mean, apart from *your uncle*,' she said sarcastically.

'He's... a person who... wait a second. What just happened?' I said. 'I'm confused.'

'It was your face when I came in, Will. You looked absolutely terrified. Your skin went pale and everything. I knew something was up. I didn't know if he was your uncle or not at that point, but I knew something was wrong,' she said.

Impressive.

'He said he was your mum's brother, but you'd already told me your mum doesn't have brothers or sisters.'

'Right,' I said. Forgot I'd told her that.

'I could tell he was here for some illicit reason; I just didn't know what it was. And I could tell you were scared of something, but I didn't know what that was either,' she said.

'So you just listened to him,' I said.

'So I just listened to him,' she said.

'But why... that whole thing at the end... the phone number?' I asked.

'Wait,' she whispered suddenly. She tiptoed to the front door, pulled it open and looked up and down the corridor. When she was satisfied that he'd definitely gone, she came back in and continued. 'That person has got some sort of hold over you, hasn't he?'

I nodded.

'His entire deception about being ill when he arrived was just stupid. He was so inconsistent with where he was saying the pain was, and when I started engaging with him and he started getting excited, he'd just drop the whole thing for minutes at a time. I knew as soon as I came back in and saw your face, that he wasn't who he was saying he was, and I guessed that he's something to do with the trouble you're in. He is, isn't he?'

'Yeah,' I said quietly.

'Well, here's some good news for you about him: he's a moron. Did you see all that nonsense with his ring, tapping it on the glass like that?'

'Yeah,' I said. 'What *was* all that?'

'NLP: neuro-linguistic programming,' she said. 'He was trying to sort of... manipulate my brain a bit.'

'I forgot you did Psychology,' I said. I was genuinely surprised and impressed that Solly knew of something that sophisticated.

'He was trying to anchor my brain in good memories from my childhood and use that to manipulate me,' she said. 'Except he was extraordinarily ham-fisted about it. I knew exactly what he was trying to do, from the beginning.'

'Why did you give him your phone number?' I said.

'Because now, he's not the only one who can manipulate. Whatever your vulnerabilities, he now has a vulnerability too,' she replied. 'Me.'

Forty-Six

After Ellie had explained to me what she'd been doing, it occurred to me that I was about as much of a blunt instrument as Solly was. I'd been sitting there getting worked up at how naïve she was being, when in fact she was pulling Solly apart, finding out who he is and making inroads to catch him off-guard in future. She'd been the best ally I could've hoped for, and I hadn't even warned her what was happening. I felt annoyed with myself for underestimating her. Unlike Solly, I'd known her for a while.

Now she knew about Solly, and she'd immediately, seamlessly stolen a march on him. I realised at that moment, it wasn't just necessary to tell Ellie everything that had happened, it was essential.

One thing I knew for sure was that if I lied to her any more, it'd be the last I saw of her. And at that moment, she felt like my only support in the world.

'Ellie… I've done something bad,' I whispered, looking at the floor.

'I need to tell you what it is, but…' My eyes and throat began to swell with tears. 'I can't tell anyone.' I focused on one spot on the ground. This tiny, discoloured dent in the floorboard.

I could sense that I'd upset her. I dared to look up at her for a moment and saw that she too, had tears in her eyes. 'Do you understand?' I said. She nodded; completely dumbstruck. Whether the thought had already been lurking in the back of her mind, or things had just fallen into place in that moment, she instantly seemed to have calculated what had happened.

'It was you?' she whispered.

'It wasn't... on purpose. I promise. None of this was on purpose,' I said, before the lump in my throat stopped me again. 'One day everything was normal, and I just...'

She slowly sank down the wall and sat on the living room floor. I walked around and sat down next to her.

'Do you ever wish you could just go back for one second and change something?' I said. 'Surely it can't be just one chance, surely you should be allowed a second chance?'

She sighed.

'You can go, if you want,' I said.

She stared back in silence.

'It just feels so...' I started, 'everything just came at me so fast. I panicked; I was trying to... defend mys— I didn't have time to...'

Ellie reached over and placed her hand on top of mine.

'So, this person Solly,' she said, deep in thought. 'He saw it?'

'He got it on camera,' I said.

She shot me a look. 'Where's the video?' she asked.

'I don't really know.'

Over the next hour, I slowly unravelled the events of that night and my subsequent meetings with Solly. I just threw open the doors and unloaded everything in my boiling, frazzled mind. Ellie sat quietly, listening, never moving a muscle or making a single sound.

Forty-Seven

I was becoming increasingly aware of my own, plummeting mental state. I'd catch myself making these little involuntary ticks. Odd little things like pursing my lips really tight or repeatedly clicking my fingers. I'd find myself pacing around my house, saying things out loud to myself, trying to affirm things, anchor myself in truth and reality. I kept reminding myself it was an accident, and that I was a good person.

I began toying with the possibility of paying Solly's bill. Taking out a loan and giving him his £43,000. I had about seven thousand, so I'd need a loan for about thirty-six. I could get that. I had good credit and I could pay it off over ten or twenty years or something.

But to do that, I'd need full assurance that the video was gone for good. I wasn't quite sure how Solly could provide that to me. The digital revolution has made information so resilient. You can delete something in one place, and it still exists in another. There's no such thing as throwing a document into the fire and destroying it, any more.

Of course, it had occurred to me that there was only one common denominator, and it was Solly. The only thing I could throw into the fire, which would completely obliterate the evidence, was Solly himself. The thought of killing him would occasionally dance in and out of my consciousness; a quick, bleak flash of fantasy that felt like pulling out in ingrowing hair.

In my mind, all this misery now orbited around him. King had come crashing into my world, but circumstances had tried to crash him straight out of it. It was only Solly who was making him stick.

It was only Solly who was goading the police into following up on me, again and again. They'd already picked their man before he started meddling.

I spent days thinking of the right message to send to Solly. I was going to offer him the money. By that time, I'd investigated the loan properly, and I could get one. I qualified for a loan for fifty thousand. Fifty thousand pounds. I'd tell the bank it was for consolidating other debts.

I could go to Solly and explain to him that it was all over. £50,000 from me would cover what he was missing, plus a bit on top. He'd have to prove to me that the video was gone. It would put him back to square one. He wouldn't need me any more. If he didn't agree to that, then he'd be revealing that his real intention went beyond just recouping his money. At that point, I'd have a problem, of course. But first, I'd try.

I sent him a message asking if I could come to his flat one evening. Told him I had something for him. He was intrigued, kept asking me what it was. I told him I'd tell him when I got there.

I arrived at his flat in the early evening. He opened the door in his underpants.

'What the hell,' I said into the air as I pushed past him into his apartment.

'Excuse me, I'm on a different time scale to you. I've been sleeping,' he said.

'You're on a different time scale, are you?' I said. I didn't even care what he meant by that.

'I've got a tournament next week. Start time's 1 a.m. You have to adjust your body clock in good time,' he said, scanning my face for a reaction.

'I don't know what you're talking about,' I said, 'but listen, I've got something for you. I want to talk to you, properly. I think I can sort all this out.'

He scoffed and followed me through to his living room.

'Put a dressing gown on,' I said, trying not to look at his saggy off-white briefs.

'Who wears a dressing gown?' he said. 'It's not nineteen seventy-three.' He plodded into the kitchen and turned on the kettle. The button he'd pressed let off a neon glow into the dingy atmosphere. He sniffed and filled a saucepan with water from the tap, before carefully placing it on the hob. 'Hungry?' he asked.

'For fuck's sake!' I snapped. 'Can you just assume I'm never hungry? I don't come here to eat, Solly.'

He giggled and plopped three eggs into the water.

'Aren't you meant to wait for the water to boil first?' I asked.

He turned and looked at me blankly. His eyes darted up to the musty old clock on the wall. 'Don't interrupt me, I need to concentrate for two minutes,' he said.

'For what?' I said.

'Until I get my eggs out,' he said, gesturing at the pan.

'You're really going to just let those eggs sit in lukewarm water for two minutes and then eat them?' I said.

'That's how I have it,' he replied, pulling two plastic chairs out of his cupboard.

'I'm here to make you an offer,' I said, once we'd sat down.

'An offer?' he said, tapping the top of an egg with a teaspoon. He peeled the shell away with his fingertips and looked inside.

It was clearly not cooked properly. You could see the yolk was fucked. It had loads of clear, uncooked bits mixed in with it.

'Solly, you know that's dangerously undercooked, right? I'm just telling you…'

'Oi!' he said. 'You're not here to review the food. What do you want?'

It was rare to be able to wind him up. The dynamic had shifted over this egg. I quite liked it.

'Can I suggest that maybe that's what's causing your intestinal problems?' I offered.

'I was putting it on, mate,' he said.

He sat there poking and picking at those eggs with his fingertips and that little teaspoon. No bread with it, nothing. Just scooping half-raw egg yolk into his mouth. He ate so fast, like his life depended on it. His dry lips would always end up covered in whatever he'd been eating.

I remembered who he reminded me of, sitting there eating his eggs. Michael Fish, the old weatherman from the telly. It was his weird-shaped head and quirky glasses. And those sad, slightly pathetic eyes. Like he was always gearing up to apologise for something.

I don't remember Michael Fish's teeth being as bad as Solly's though. His teeth sort of defined him for me, those stale, unkempt little gravestones. They summed up his oddness and disconnection from the rest of the world. Socially active people don't have teeth like that.

Forty-Eight

'I want to ask you a question,' I said. 'And this time, I want you to look me in the eyes and answer honestly.'

Solly looked at me earnestly and nodded, as he licked dry egg yolk off his fingers.

'If I told you I could end all this right now, what would you say?' I said.

He stifled a burp. 'End all what?'

I shook my head. 'No, Solly. No. Let's do this, now. Let's respect each other and finish this.'

'Okay,' he said. 'You have my respect. What are you asking me?'

'The video you have of me,' I said, 'it's here, isn't it? It's in your flat. I want you to get rid of it. But I'm not going to ask you to do it for nothing. I'll give you what you need. All of it. And maybe a little more. But you have to prove to me that the video's gone.'

He leaned back in his chair and exhaled deeply. 'Come with me,' he said. He led me out of the living room and down a short hallway to his bedroom. As he pushed the door open this weird smell like musty old chemicals hit me. By the window was a desk, with a PC on top of it. It had a huge monitor; it must have been fifty inches or something.

He typed in his password and a home screen opened. He pulled a chair back from the desk and invited me to sit. 'When you've finished there, you can look through my mobile phone,' he said.

I looked at the screen. His desktop wallpaper was one of the generic ones. The ones the computer give you automatically, just some poppy field.

He leant over me and opened the file menu. 'Take an hour, take two hours if you like. Check all the files, check the Deleted Items is empty... Your video's gone, Will. I deleted it.'

He shuffled off into the bathroom. I looked at the screen again, then back at the bathroom door. I grabbed the mouse and started clicking.

I searched his computer for any trace of the video. After returning from the bathroom, he sat down behind me on his bed. I looked everywhere, opened every video or image file I could see. There weren't actually that many. What there was, was just video after video shot from the same angle, or very similar. But they were dated, which was helpful.

He generally didn't keep old recordings for long. If he found anything he wanted on there, he'd download and edit, and then delete the old stuff. It helped him keep on top of memory space, he said. I went through his emails to check he hadn't hidden it there. I looked in his notes folders. He then handed me his phone and I looked through that.

When I'd finished, he looked at me sincerely and said, 'I'm not a grass, Will. I deleted your video. I don't deal with police.'

'It doesn't prove anything though, Solly,' I said. 'It just proves the video isn't here, on this computer, on this phone today.'

'Go on,' he said. 'What do you want me to show you then?'

'The Cloud.'

I spent another hour and a half looking through all the shit he had on there. He didn't care about me seeing it all. Some of it was absolutely bizarre. It looked like he had cameras set up in changing rooms. One of them seemed to be in someone's bedroom. Occasionally when I'd open something unexpected, he'd burst out laughing.

Late in the evening, we retired to his living room. 'I haven't got you on video any more Will. Relax,' he said. 'I can tell how much that got to you, me having that. I'm sorry.'

I ignored him. So much of what came out of his mouth was just pure fiction. I wasn't there to satisfy his ego or play his game this time, I was there to do business.

'I have this idea,' I said, 'that I think could work for both of us.'

Forty-Nine

I told him I'd 'buy his debt'. Meaning I'd pay him £43,000, and this person who owed him the money would become my problem. (Which I didn't intend on ever solving). I explained to him that he'd be getting his money back, in full. Then, I said, as a thank you for what he'd done for me, I was going to give him another £5,000 as a gift. In return, the video would be permanently deleted, and we would never come into contact with one another again.

He listened to me, absent-mindedly running his fingers through his sparse, grey chest hairs. When I finished speaking, he leant towards me and simply said, 'I like it.'

'Will you agree to it?' I said.

'I get my money back, and you give me a special "thank you",' he said thoughtfully. 'It makes sense.'

'Yes it does,' I said, 'it does make sense, doesn't it.'

'Where are you getting the money from?' he asked innocently.

'Savings,' I said, without missing a beat. *I knew he'd ask that.*

'That's good savings. How did you save all that up?' he said.

'Working,' I said dismissively. 'I can get you the money in about a week.'

He pretended to think deeply for a moment, like he was calculating everything. 'Let me think about it,' he said.

'What's there to think about? You get your money back, and you get a thank you from me.'

'I know…' he said, 'it's just… I need to think about all this properly.'

'Meaning?' I snapped.

'Meaning,' he said, rising and running his fingers around the waistband of his underpants, 'this whole thing has been costly for me. Not just the money I've lost, but… *emotionally*.'

For fuck's sake.

'To tell you the truth, it's all made me a bit depressed,' he whinged. 'It's rendered me more or less, housebound. You've caused me a lot of stress, you know.'

'That's why I'm thanking you, Solly,' I said through gritted teeth. 'That's why I'm giving you this extra gift, the extra five thousand pounds. You can buy a new camera.'

'Five grand isn't going to buy the box the camera comes in!' he scoffed.

'Five grand is five grand!' I said. 'Buy a car with it, buy a new wardrobe! It's five grand, for nothing!'

'Is that what you've worked my price out to be, then?' he said thoughtfully. 'Five grand?'

'No, of course not,' I laughed. 'I'm offering you forty-eight thousand altogether!'

He looked furious all of a sudden. 'Well, hang on a fucking minute, you said that was *my* money. You said you were buying that debt off me! That's not a gift from *you*!'

I couldn't believe my ears. I couldn't tell if he was deliberately being obtuse, or he really thought that. I just went along with him.

'Fine! Okay then, that's your money, yes! From the poker

thing. And I'm giving you another five. Just to say thank you and goodbye – and no hard feelings and all that.'

He looked at me coldly. 'Five grand? You want to throw five grand at me after all this trauma you've caused?'

I tried to placate him. 'Solly, remember I have to get the forty-three thousand together to buy your debt off you, too. So I don't have much else, or I'd give you it.'

'Five grand's a nice, round number though,' he said. 'How'd you land on that?' He was blinking faster. It was like getting angry had set off this weird tick. He was blinking at about three times the rate and he'd stopped making eye contact with me. He was talking to me but staring at the ground behind me.

He started pacing up and down his living room. He looked absolutely ridiculous in his underpants. His shrivelled, sagging skin was like an uncooked roast chicken.

'You've upset me now,' he said eventually. 'I tell you what, you've upset me now.'

'Why?' I said quietly. He was starting to make me feel nervous. I hadn't seen him like this before. He was breathing really loudly through his nose at this point.

'So have you discussed this with the girl then?' he asked eventually.

'Discussed what, with who Solly? Nobody even knows I'm here.'

'Oh shut up!' he barked. Something I'd said had really irked him.

'What's the matter?' I said.

'Are you *thick*?' he shouted back.

'Solly, I'm really sorry if I've caused you offence somehow,' I started.

He stopped in his tracks. 'Yeah, you've caused me offence. I'd say you've absolutely caused me offence, yes. You've added a bit of insult to injury here, haven't you?'

'I don't know what you mean,' I clamoured. 'Is this because I offered you five thousand?'

'Let me guess; you told her you could buy me for five grand, did you?' he asked.

'*Who?* Ellie?' I asked.

'Yes, fucking Ellie,' he said, 'what did you say to her?' He still wasn't looking directly at me.

'I… promise you Solly, she doesn't know I'm here, she doesn't know I'm offering you this.'

'Right,' he said. 'Well, why don't we start by treating me like a fucking human being, then?'

'How do you mean?' I said.

'Well, instead of shoving five grand at me as an apology, how about actually *acting* apologetically, how about *actually* trying to treat me nicely?'

'But Solly please,' I said. 'Come on, I'm buying your debt!'

'*That… Is… Already my money!*' he shouted.

I held my hands up to placate him. His body language was like an angry toddler.

'Call me over, next week, we'll have dinner. You can cook, and we can all talk. At the end of the meal you can make a toast. You can tell everyone how grateful you are to me for how I've helped you in your life – *and be sincere about it* – and do it all in front of her, so she sees you thanking me.'

His behaviour was confusing me. He seemed vulnerable all of a sudden, irritable and defensive. It was like that figure of £5,000 had genuinely hurt his feelings. But now he was asking for something much less. He just wanted me to put this weird show on, in front of Ellie.

'Yeah, okay,' I said. 'I'll do it.'

'Right,' he said, 'next week it is. How about Tuesday evening?'

'Fine.'

'And I want you to think again about the money,' he said.

My heart sank. 'What do you mean, *think again about the money*?' I snapped.

He reached behind his radiator and pulled out grey vest. The thing was covered in thick dust. He pulled it over his head.

'What I mean is, I'm a high earner, I'm in the *higher quartile*, or *top per cent* or however you say it.' He stood with his hands on his hips and regarded me. 'You don't fob me off with five fucking grand. Is that a joke?' He headed off to the toilet again.

I was fuming. He was being completely resistant to the idea that my paying the massive fucking forty-three grand debt should in any way count towards 'his gift'. He was being totally illogical. It was like he'd just decided that was now my debt, and it was separate from the negotiation.

'Fine,' I said, when he returned to the living room, 'I'll give you six and a half.'

He turned to look at me. He looked physically pained by my suggestion. 'Think of it like this,' he said. 'Imagine you owed a debt of gratitude and apology to some rich banker. You wouldn't just toss him six and a half grand and expect him to be satisfied, would you? You'd need to give him something *valuable*. You wouldn't insult him with six and a half grand, he'd laugh at you. So why are you offering me six and a half grand. Why aren't you offering me something *valuable*?'

I didn't know what to say. I shrugged. His stupidity was impenetrable.

'What do you want?' I asked wearily. '*What do you want?*'

He plodded into his kitchen and started uncorking a bottle of red wine. 'Let's just calm things down for a minute,' he said, 'you're stressing me out.'

He came back and sat down with a glass of wine in his hand. He pushed his nose into it and took a big, deep sniff. I looked back at the bottle on the counter: it was some cheap plonk. He was treating it like it was a rare vintage. Idiot.

179

'Okay, how about this,' he said eventually, holding up the glass and eyeing the liquid, 'forty-three.'

'Forty-three what?'

'Forty-three grand.'

'The debt?' I said. He'd lost me.

'Yeah, that's what I'm owed, that's the debt you're having off me, thank you. But I think you should match it, as a thank you to me.'

'What do you mean? You want me to pay you forty-three thousand pounds, twice?'

'No, you only have to pay it to me once. The other forty-three is just the debt, you'll be getting that back.'

What an arsehole. He'd doubled it. He knew I had no intention of recovering that debt, so he knew in effect he was asking me for eighty-six thousand. Suffice to say, I had no way of getting that kind of money.

Fifty

Money was never the boss of me. Dad raised me to think more clearly than that. Money is useful, but it's not the key to enjoying life. I understood from really early on that accumulating money isn't the objective. Too many people become slaves to it.

Working hard gives a sort of satisfaction in itself. I can understand people becoming addicted to that. But I don't really do well with people who just want to be rich. I've always thought, after you've reached the point of comfort, excess money is just about power. I could never be bothered chasing power.

I'd always kept money on quite an even keel. I made a reasonable amount, and mostly I spent it. I'd put a modest amount away every now and then, when it was convenient, and I was happy enough with my slow, gradual savings pot. I wasn't feeling pressured to start ramping up my capital in the world.

So when Solly made this demand, I knew immediately it was impossible. Even if anyone would lend me that amount, which they wouldn't, it would take me a lifetime to pay it back. What he was proposing would still be affecting me when I'm fifty.

'This is a big deal, Solly,' I said. 'You're not being reasonable any more, you know that, right?'

'*I'm* not being reasonable? Have you *heard* yourself?' he said incredulously.

'Yeah, you're not. You're asking me for money you know I don't have.'

'You can get forty-three grand together, you're a grown man,' he said.

'Eighty-six,' I said.

'It's not eighty-six,' he said, 'because I've told you where you can get forty-three of it. You just need to find forty-three to come from *you*.'

'You're crossing a line here,' I said, 'you won't be able to come back from this.'

'Meaning what?' he said. 'Are you threatening me?'

'I'm just telling you,' I shot back, calmly as I could, 'I have no chance of getting that money.'

'So, what are you going to do?' he asked with a gentle smile.

I walked over and stood in front of him. He didn't look at all scared.

'I haven't decided yet,' I said quietly. We stood there for a moment in silence. He looked up at me with those stubborn, green eyes. There was nothing in those eyes that suggested he was going to back down.

He knew I'd have to pay him.

Fifty-One

After that night of Solly's visit to my apartment, Ellie and I didn't speak for more than a week. It was hard to know who was hiding from whom. She knew far more than I'd ever intended her to. He'd created this shitstorm where I had to tell her something.

I didn't want to hide from her, I missed her. Without knowing it, she'd been my ballast of sanity since that night with the banker. She'd kept me in touch and made me feel like everything wasn't lost in the world. I wondered, though, if I had a moral responsibility to let her go. I'd lived it myself: when something like this appears in your life, your first instinct is to just ignore it, hope it'll disappear from your orbit. I couldn't get rid of it from my orbit, but she could. So I didn't contact her.

When she appeared at the door of my apartment one morning, I thought I was going to weep tears of joy. I just held her really tight, standing in the doorway. We were there for ages, in silence. She didn't smile at me or anything, just came in and put her bag down and said, 'What does he want?'

We sat on the sofa in my living room, and I told her what he'd asked me for. Forty-three thousand reclaimed from his debt, and another forty-three thousand from my pocket.

'And the debt... is it real? Is the person real and do they really owe him that money?' she asked.

I shrugged.

'What I mean is, does Solly know that really, this is an impossible ask?' she said.

'I don't know,' I said.

'I think maybe you should find that out, just so we know where we are, and what his real intentions are.'

'Has he contacted you?' I said nervously.

'No,' she said, 'I haven't heard anything from him.' For some reason that actually surprised me.

'Ask him for the person's details,' she said, 'tell him you're going to speak to the person today and see how he reacts.'

I sent him a text message saying, **'I'll get the debt back today. What is the person's name and address?'**

He texted me back, literally seconds later. **'ANTOINE BECKER, 12 PERCY CIRCUS, LONDON. 43K.'**

I showed it to Ellie. He was real; or at least, Solly had sent me a real person's name. I messaged him back, asking him what date he'd taken the debt on, and what date he was supposed to have paid it by. He didn't reply. I tried phoning him and he didn't answer. Predictable.

'I wonder if it is a real person,' Ellie said, studying her phone.

'I doubt it. It's a fucking game,' I said.

'I've got the house on Google Maps,' she said. 'It's a *nice* house.'

'Yeah, I know Percy Circus,' I said. 'It's near King's Cross, it's posh.'

'So, he's never told you *anything* about this Antoine person?' she asked.

'Only that he's a family man, he's older than Solly and that he's not dangerous,' I said

'So why doesn't Solly go and collect it himself?' she said sceptically.

'Well yeah. But then why does he do anything he does,' I said.

'But I mean… literally. Why doesn't he go and get the money himself, if it's this much, it's this overdue and the person isn't dangerous? It doesn't make sense.' Ellie was zooming in as far as she could on Google Maps.

'Are you seriously thinking about me going and asking him for that money?' I said.

'*We*,' she said. 'I'm thinking about if *we* should go and ask him.'

'Ellie, what the hell…' I said quietly.

'I'm not talking about threatening him,' she said. 'We just go over there and have a look.'

'Why?' I said.

'Well…' she started, 'I don't really know, but… what happens if you don't pay him all this money?'

'I'm not going to be able to, it's a fact,' I said sharply.

'So, what happens?' she said.

'Well he was hinting that the guy they've got for the… the initial crime, his legal team is looking for CCTV. I guess he'll… just give what he has to them.'

'And then what?' she said.

'Well, then I suppose they'll be able to clear him, because they'll have the evidence,' I replied wearily.

'Can you tell it's you? On the video?' she said.

I nodded. I felt sick.

Fifty-Two

We sat there for hours, trying to think of different angles and ways to approach the situation. It was important that she knew certain things. I needed her to know everything the police had and didn't have, for a start.

I noticed she'd never make eye-contact with me when I talked about it. It was like she really wanted to help, but it was paining her to hear it. I thanked every star for Ellie. I had a person I could trust, who understood the extent of the mess, who was a more careful and methodical thinker than I was. And most of all, she didn't seem to be judging me. She seemed to understand.

It all kept coming back round to Solly, of course. I could take the loan, recoup Solly's debt, pay him all the money, but there would still be no guarantee that he'd stay quiet forever. He'd become the focal point of this problem.

'He found out what your financial limit was and deliberately set the target to twice that,' Ellie said. 'He doesn't *want* you to win.' Ellie offered to go and talk to him, one-on-one. There was no way in hell I would let her go round there on her own. She suggested she invite him out for drinks, in a public place, where she'd try to talk to him. I still wasn't keen. I agreed to let her do it, on condition that I'd be somewhere nearby.

She messaged him and asked him if he fancied meeting for a drink, somewhere in Farringdon. He didn't reply for a good six hours. During that time Ellie and I must have nervously checked her phone screen at least two hundred times. When he did reply, it was to my phone. He'd sniffed us out.

'DO YOU TWO THINK IM A DONKEY?' his message had said.

I messaged him back, pretending I didn't know what he was talking about, but he was onto us. It wouldn't have surprised me if he'd somehow known she was in my flat, at that very moment.

That evening I sat at my kitchen table. Ellie was sitting on the worktop.

'I'm stuck, aren't I?' I said. She looked across at me sadly. I knew she wanted to say something reassuring, but she couldn't. Eventually she said, 'My dad's got a really good job, we could –'

'Stop.' I said. 'Just stop.' My eyes filled with frustrated tears. She just wanted to help me. She just wanted to pull the trap open and rescue me. But it wasn't her fight.

I took a long, deep breath and blew it back out. I could feel tears beginning to roll down my face; it was too late to stop them. Ellie jumped down from the worktop and rushed over to me. She pushed my chest to indicate she wanted me to move back from the table. Then she sat on my lap.

'Ellie…' I said softly, 'it's over.'

She shook her head. I nodded and sniffed.

'I can't escape it. I tried, and I can't. I wanted to… I wanted it to be different, for us. I *wish* it could have been different.'

'It's only over when we say it's over,' she said, cradling my hot head. I winced as this whole wave of sadness crashed over me. I was now fully crying into the poor girl's chest. The more kindness and resilience she showed, the more pain I felt. Because I knew it was over. He'd won.

'Ellie I'm going to have to do it, you know. I'm going to

have to hand myself in. He's not going away, ever. And you know what? I don't care any more. They can take me. The only thing I care about, is now I have to miss out on *you*. You're what I wanted. And now because of this fucking shit I have to give you up. Someone else gets to have that life, *with you*. Do you know how that makes me feel?'

She didn't reply. I sensed I'd gone too far. We hadn't been dating long enough for me to be talking like that, of course not. When I summoned the courage to turn my pathetic, tear-stained face up at her, she was staring intently at the fridge. She looked deep in thought.

'What?' I whispered.

'That's what we'll do,' she said. 'Tell him you're done, and you're handing yourself in.'

'What good does that do?' I asked. 'Then it's game over, he's won. He'll be delighted won't he.'

'Not really,' she said. 'If that happens, *what* has he won? He won't get a penny off you, because he won't have anything to hold over you. He won't get his forty-three grand *debt* back, because he won't have anyone to go and claim it for him. He won't have anywhere to go, anyone to wind up. And his video will be worthless.'

She had a point.

'What do you think will happen though, if we call his bluff?' I said.

'Well, most likely, he'll lower his terms,' she shrugged. 'He'll think, "Well, I need to get *some* value out of this video." He'll make you a better offer,' she said confidently. 'But we'll have to make it convincing.'

Fifty-Three

I went to Solly's the next morning, unannounced. There was a dark grey cloud hanging over London that morning. The sky was threatening to burst with rain at any moment as I walked through Farringdon to his flat. We'd had a few days of unseasonal warmth, so I guessed this must be the payback. It looked like a storm was brewing.

He answered the door wearing a full black suit. Apart from the fact that the jacket was two sizes too small, and the trousers were three inches too short, it was the smartest I'd ever seen him. He still hadn't trimmed his eyebrows. After letting me in, he went and sat by the window in the living room, where he had been smoking. He said he had a funeral to go to, that afternoon.

'Whose funeral?' I asked.

He ignored me.

'Whose funeral is it?' I asked again.

Slowly, he turned to look at me, and smiled. 'Nobody you know,' he said.

'I've come to tell you something,' I said.

Raindrops began to strike the window. Slowly at first, then steadily growing louder and more frequent. He kept looking out. I'd never seen him this distracted.

'I'm handing myself in,' I said. 'To Probert and Kane at the police station. Today.'

He cracked his knuckles.

'That's all,' I said. 'I thought you should know. It's over.'

He didn't respond.

'So goodbye Solly, and good luck.' I turned to leave.

'Why did the girl give me her telephone number?' he asked in a low, quiet voice.

'Who. . . Ellie?' I said. 'You'll have to ask her.'

'Shall I tell you what I think?' he said. 'I think it was a confidence trick.' He inhaled deeply from his cigarette, leant his head back and blew a plume of smoke into the air.

'What are you talking about now?' I said.

'A confidence trick,' he said. 'That's where you use a person's confidence, to trick them.'

'Well, I wouldn't know about that,' I said.

'Neither would I,' he said thoughtfully. 'My brain just doesn't work like that.'

I resisted the urge to comment. Then he turned and looked me dead in the eyes. 'Hers does, though.'

'Ellie was trying to help me negotiate with you. She's my friend,' I started.

'Your friend! You've been fucking her and fucking her!' he barked.

'Whoa,' I said, 'what the fuck?'

'Well, you have, haven't you? And then you thought, "I know, we'll let Solly think he gets a turn at fucking her, that'll keep him quiet".'

I laughed uncomfortably.

'Using her body as a weapon,' he said quietly, as he turned back to the window.

'Look, I think you might have read a bit too much into this...' I started.

'She flirted with me and tossed my mind around like a rag doll,' he said.

'Nobody flirted with you, Solly,' I said coldly.

'Negotiate, you said. She was *negotiating* with me, was she?'

'No, I didn't mean *negotiate*...' I started.

'Do you know what the word for that is, Will?' he asked. 'What's the word for a person who uses sex to negotiate with?'

I kept staring at him, as calmly and neutrally as I could.

'It's a whore, isn't it,' he said. 'That's it.'

Inside me, there was an explosion. I could feel every bone and sinew in my body wanting to launch itself at him. But I didn't react.

'Enjoy your life,' I said. I walked to his front door and closed my fingers over the handle. *Just go, Wilbur. Just go home. Just go home to Ellie.*

'The whore twerked at me for hours, I didn't know where to look!' he shouted out to me. 'First thing she did was pulled her bra straps down for me, showing me everything.'

I pulled the front door open. I wasn't going to let him provoke me.

'If you're going to go back to her, I suggest you take this with you,' he called out.

What is it? I couldn't see. I was halfway out of his front door. He hadn't moved from that spot by the window. But I couldn't resist the urge to see what he was talking about. He'd said enough about Ellie. He'd pushed things far enough.

'I suppose she's led you to believe she hasn't been in contact with Old Uncle Solly, has she?' he called out. 'Women will do *anything* for the safety of their man.'

What the fuck was he talking about?

'Correction,' he shouted. 'Not *all* women. But this one... she'll protect her man at all costs!'

I quietly closed the front door again. Whatever I thought

about what was coming out of his mouth, I needed to know what he was holding.

When I returned to his living room, he had something on his lap. It looked like it could be a picture frame that'd been wrapped in Happy Birthday wrapping paper. When I strode over to him to take it, he flinched. That was satisfying. The fucking worm.

He looked up at me from his chair, as he thrust his hips out and reached into his pocket for his bag of tobacco. 'Good luck Will,' he said, 'handing yourself in.'

'Thanks,' I said, turning to leave.

'Let me know when you're locked up, I'll send her a text when she's back on the market!' he called after me.

Breathe.

Fifty-Four

In the train back to St Albans, I laid that thing out on one of the drinks tables. There were a few other people in the carriage. I wasn't sure whether to open it. I was worried it might be booby-trapped in some way. Maybe he'd tricked it to fling acid at her or something when she opened it. I wouldn't put anything past him.

A few people got off at Seven Sisters and I had half the carriage to myself. Nobody had an eyeline to it. The suspense was killing me. I needed to know what it was. I didn't believe any of that garbage he was spouting for a single second. But I still needed to know what this thing was.

I leant away from it and peeled the corner of the wrapping paper away with my fingertips. Nothing. I tenderly ran my fingers around the perimeter of it. It was a picture frame, no doubt about that. I nervously poked at the middle part, where the picture goes. I couldn't feel anything unusual, or any sort of mechanism.

I stared at it. *Some sort of chemical weapon? Some sort of anthrax?* Ridiculous. He wouldn't know the first thing about getting anything like that. I stood up from my seat gingerly and peered down the carriage. There was just one bloke down there, a fat guy with a baseball cap on. I couldn't see anyone else.

I decided to open it. I braced myself and gently tore away the wrapping paper around the edge of the frame. I lifted the paper and peered inside. Couldn't see any powder or anything. It was just a picture frame. I pulled it out fully.

It was a picture of me, holding a pint of beer. I tore the rest of the wrapping paper away and took in the whole image. I was in a pub. The Three Kings. I could tell by the decorations on the wall. They had all sorts of quirky stuff on the walls in there.

I guessed it must be a picture from that night. The night with the banker. I was wearing the same clothes. I could see the polar bears on the jumper. I didn't understand. I turned it over, nothing on the back.

Fifty-Five

I propped the picture frame up in front of the TV in my bedroom and lay on my bed, staring at it. It was a perfectly innocent picture of me. It looked like it had come from the CCTV in The Three Kings. They had a little TV up on the wall in there behind the bar, showing a colour feed of the CCTV. He must have gone in there and asked them for this.

The frame looked normal enough: a cheap, dark brown wooden frame. I took the picture out, there was nothing on the back of that either. I called Ellie and told her the full story of my encounter with Solly. I omitted the parts when he called her all those names. I just said he seemed angry with her, too. And that he said she'd 'tried to con him'.

I told her about the weird thing he'd said about the picture frame: *'If you're going to go back to her, I suggest you take this with you.'* She asked me to send her a photo of it, so I did. She'd gone really awkward. She asked what else he'd said to me. I told her I couldn't remember much else, except that he seemed annoyed with her for 'conning him'.

I said I'd keep thinking about it. She offered to come over and I said no. I wanted to drag her through as little of this as possible. I knew I'd be completely miserable, and I just needed to think. Solly didn't seem to have taken the bait.

On my way back from London I'd stopped in at Boots in King's Cross. Got one of those big bottles of flu medicine from the pharmacy, with the extra-dopey shit in there. I knew I'd run out of weed, and I needed something to help me sleep. I cracked the lid open and sniffed it. It smelled fantastic.

Sweet, chemical deliciousness. I filled the little measuring cup and necked one. *That is going to do fuck all.* I took a big swig from the bottle. Must have drained about half of it.

I took another quick swig and put the rest in the fridge. *It's nicer cold.* My phone rang. Julia from work calling me. I'd told them I had flu, a week ago. *How long's flu now?* It used to be two weeks for flu, didn't it?

I turned my phone off and took a bottle of prosecco to the shower.

Fifty-Six

At around midnight I awoke on my sofa, in a towel. I felt like I'd been hit by a truck. I'd also left the living-room window open, and it was ice cold. I got up and slammed it closed before going into the kitchen for a glass of water and a swig of Night Nurse.

I stood in front of the fridge drinking it and gazed at a photograph of me and a couple of mates in a bar from a few years before. I looked so relaxed. My biggest worry at that time was getting enough cash together for a few beers in the evening.

As I scanned the kitchen, I wondered what would happen to all my stuff if I went inside. Do I get to break the lease with my landlord? Or does someone else have to pay for my rent, until the lease is up? I guessed that would be Dad. I placed my glass carefully in the middle of the sink and headed up to bed. I lay on the top of the covers, staring at the ceiling for an hour or so, before the Promethazine dragged me back under.

It must have been about two in the morning when I heard a crash from the living room. It wasn't a clink, a crack or even a clatter. It was a crash. It sounded like a saucepan or something of that sort of weight hitting the ground. I sat up in bed. It had definitely come from the living room of my apartment.

I sat listening for a minute or so, craning my head to somehow try and take more sound in. Stillness. I looked around me for a weapon, something to protect myself with. The best I could find was a football pump on the floor under my bed. It was a foot-long, hollow, plastic thing with a tiny, thin metal adaptor poking out of the end. I pictured hitting someone with it and put it back. *That's not going to do shit.*

Without making a sound, I crept out of bed and tiptoed across my room to the door. Slowly, I leant my body forward to peer out into the darkness of the hallway. I couldn't detect any sound or movement at all. I edged out into the hallway and craned my neck to peer into the living room. Nothing. I crouched a little and crept closer to the living room door, to see further around the corner. 'Who's there?' I said quietly. 'Who is it?' I knew exactly who it was. I edged into the living room, reached my hand around the corner and turned the light on. The place looked untouched. It was still immaculate from when I'd blitz-cleaned it a few days before. I walked around the room, checking every curtain and cupboard. It was all clear.

The sound of my front door closing cut through the apartment. That sound was so distinctive: it was a heavy door, and it made a distinctive *ker-klunk*. I peered out at my front door. It was closed now. I ran out, pulled it open and looked down the corridor. 'Solly?' I called out. My voice echoed down the hallway. I looked out of the window at the small garden area outside. Just cold stillness. You could see the silver of frost on the grass. Then I heard something again. A noise from down the corridor. Scuffling feet.

This time, I was in no doubt as to whether it was a hallucination born of tiredness and over-emotion, or the real thing. I heard someone's footsteps. I grabbed my keys and ran down the corridor.

When I got to the stairwell, it was completely silent. The

lifts were still out of service. I peered down the stairwell. Something moved down there. A hand maybe, on the stair rail for a second. Just for the briefest moment, then it was gone.

I listened out for any sound. Nothing. I paced over to the communal window and pulled the slide bolt to one side. The window unlocked with a stiff crack and I shoved it open, blasting myself with a big, cold gasp of night-time air. I shoved my head out and peered below.

Something caught my eye in the shadows near the fence. I squinted through the tiredness, trying to focus. I was sure I'd seen something move. I stared at that same section of shadow for a good minute or so. I knew he was there.

I leaned forwards and shouted out into the night, 'I know you're there Solly, you fucking freak. You think this kind of shit frightens me? Go fuck yourself.'

I slammed the window closed and headed back to my apartment and bed.

I knew it was Solly. This kind of oddball, faceless manipulation was his speciality, I knew that by now.

Fifty-Seven

The following morning, I felt like absolute garbage. It turns out there are consequences to over-dosing on flu meds. I felt laggy as hell, it was like having slow Wi-Fi, but in your brain. I needed coffee, I put a Moka pot on the hob and turned the TV on in the kitchen.

The news was on. I wasn't in the mood for thinking about anything heavy, so I turned it straight back off again. I sat back in my chair and closed my eyes. I thought about Richard King. I thought about his parents. They must have remembered him as a little boy. I'd avoided doing that for so long, but it felt like that medicine I'd taken the previous night had really weakened my brain.

I thought, as time passed, it would gradually get easier to deal with thoughts about that night. But it was getting harder. I was finding myself accidentally straying into that mental territory more and more. It kept coming back for me. Sometimes it felt like I'd never know true peace again. I fell back to sleep in my kitchen chair.

About an hour later, I was awoken by a loud sound outside. A booming croak. Like a megaphone on a really loud setting, being suddenly turned on or off. I knew that sound; I'd heard it before. I rose from my chair slowly. *He's done it.*

I didn't even need to look out of the window. I knew that sound came from a police car. It was a tiny little bit of siren leaking out, they'd do it sometimes to get people's attention when they're moving through traffic. I ran over to the window and peeped over the ledge. My stomach dropped to the floor. There they were.

Probert got out of the car first. As he did so, he looked right up at my kitchen window. I didn't even bother to duck down. I just stood there, gazing down at him. I was half in a trance anyway from all that sedative stuff.

He stood by his car and gazed back up at me, with his hands on his hips. Neither of us smiled or acknowledged each other. Then Kane got out. He said something to her, and she looked up at me too. They both headed towards the front door of my apartment.

I pressed the buzzer to let them up. I poured myself a coffee and drank as much of it as I could. I sensed I was going to need it. The bleariness from that flu stuff was real; I felt like I was underwater.

When I opened the door, Probert asked if they could come in. *They weren't there to arrest me.* I guided them into my living room. Both were ashen faced. They didn't look in the mood for socialising. 'Your boss said you were sick,' said Probert.

'Yeah I… I was,' I said, forcing a cough. 'I'd still keep your distance.'

He looked me up and down as if he didn't believe a word of what I was saying.

I don't have to convince you I'm really ill, mate. I sat at the kitchen table. Probert sat opposite me. Kane stood, next to the kitchen door. *Why was she blocking the exit like that?*

Probert sniffed and pulled a notebook from his pocket. He read out loud from the book, 'Mikkel. That mean anything to you?'

I shrugged.

'Mikkel? No? Okay, how about this one,' he read from his notebook again. 'Timberland Brown Courma Classic, 6-inch Men's Boots. Size nine.'

I looked between him and Kane. 'Well that's… my boots.' I said.

'That's what, sorry?' said Probert.

'My boots, that's my Timberland boots I gave you.'

'That's right,' said Probert. 'They *were* the boots you gave us.' He took his iPhone out of his pocket and turned the screen to face me. A chill shot right through my body. It was the photo; Solly's photo, from the frame.

'What we can't work out, Will,' said Probert, 'is why you keep lying to us.'

Fifty-Eight

I sat there in shock, staring at that photo. I felt sick. He'd done it. The game was up. I glanced up at Kane, by the door. They'd finally nailed their man.

'Someone sent this to Jacob Evatt's defence lawyer,' Probert said solemnly. He theatrically turned the phone to face him, then back to me. 'It's a photograph of you,' he said.

'Yeah, I know,' I breathed.

'Early in this investigation,' he said, 'you told us you hadn't seen or heard anything in that alley. We really pushed you, you really reached,' he said. 'D'you remember?'

I nodded.

'And then we went for that walk, didn't we?' he said. 'You walked down there with us. And the only stop you could remember making, was at the top of the alley, to put your headphones in your bag.'

I nodded.

'Then we asked you to drop in the clothing you'd been wearing that evening. You dropped in three items: one brown Uniqlo rain jacket, one pair of black Levi's jeans and a pair of dark brown Timberland boots.'

I nodded. He pointed the screen of his phone at me again.

'This is a still shot from CCTV at The Three Kings pub, earlier that evening,' he said. 'It's been verified. The video still exists.'

'Okay,' I said.

'Now, would you look at those boots?' he said.

I didn't need to look at them. My body went weak. It was happening. They were here to take me away. It felt like everything had gone into slow motion. The pair of them just stared into my soul.

My lungs suddenly felt drained of oxygen. I tried desperately to draw in more air without making it too obvious.

'You can see quite plainly that the boots you were wearing that night were a different colour from the ones you told us you were wearing,' he continued. 'You can even tell from that picture that the eyelets for the laces are different. They're not the same boots,' he said.

He was right. The fact of it was, I didn't know there was this kind of colour footage from that night, that close up.

'They're the wrong boots,' I said quietly. 'I'm sorry.' I scanned his face for a reaction. He was furious.

'The jumper you were wearing was lost by a laundrette; then you give us the wrong boots,' said Kane.

'It's almost like you don't want us to have what you were wearing that night,' continued Probert. He leant closer to me and stared into my eyes. 'Why?' he whispered.

I didn't react. I was frozen still in my chair.

He leant back in his chair and folded his arms. 'Why doesn't Wilbur Cox want us to have his clothes from that night?' he said into the air. Then he locked eyes with me again. His eyes looked so different now. Cruel and disbelieving.

'We'd like to have a look through your wardrobe with you, Will,' he said eventually.

I agreed and walked them through to my bedroom. Kane

put gloves on and picked through my clothes while Probert and I stood and watched. She took two pairs of black jeans she found in the laundry basket and bagged them to take back to the station. She couldn't find the boots though, of course. A quarter of an hour in, there was a knock at my front door. They both looked at me.

'Can I go and answer it?' I asked pathetically. Probert nodded.

It was Ellie. She'd already seen the police car outside. When I pulled that door open, she didn't look the tiniest bit afraid. She was straight into battle mode. She marched past me to where they were rustling in my bedroom. I got there just in time to see her make eye contact with Kane, who was kneeling on the floor.

'Excuse me, what's this?' Ellie said.

'Police search,' said Kane abruptly. 'You are?'

'Do you have a warrant for this?' replied Ellie. She looked down at the evidence bag next to Kane, which contained two pairs of my jeans. 'Wait, wait – you *do* have a warrant for this, right?' Ellie said sharply.

Kane rose to her feet. Ellie put her forefinger behind her ear sarcastically and looked between them. She had them on that one.

She told me later that she was worried one of them was just going to pull something out, and she'd have to look at it and say 'okay, carry on then'. She had no idea what a warrant looked like, and neither did I.

They halted the search. I said they could still take my jeans if they wanted, and I didn't care. I knew the pairs she'd picked up weren't the ones, anyway. They didn't want them any more. I think they could tell from my reaction that they were worthless.

Ellie led them back to the kitchen to continue interviewing me. Probert was quietly seething. He looked beet red.

'They were called Mikkel,' he said to me, as I sat down.

'What was?'

'The boots you were wearing,' he said, 'they were black boots from All Saints, size nine, and I believe the product name was "Mikkel".'

The name did sound familiar. Maybe that was what they were called. Maybe they *were* from All Saints. But I wasn't telling him that. They were long gone.

'I thought the ones I gave you were the ones I was wearing,' I said. 'I'm sorry. You can have all my other boots if you want them.'

Probert smirked. 'Oddly enough, you don't seem to have a pair of those Mikkel boots any more,' he said.

'I throw shoes out all the time,' I said. 'I walk on the side of my heels, so—'

'So, the boots must have gone the same way as that jumper,' he said. 'Just *pfft*.'

'The boots looked pretty new in that picture,' said Kane.

'Well, they weren't.' I hit my fist down on the worktop, causing a loud thud. Everybody looked at me.

Probert broke the silence. 'You know, they have a pretty unique sole, those All Saints boots?'

'No,' I said.

'They're a narrow shape, and they have this little diamond pattern in the rubber,' he said. 'It's totally different from a Timberland sole.'

I looked at Ellie. She looked terrified. I was mortified that she'd walked in on all this.

'Can I tell you something interesting, Will?' he said. 'Someone wearing a pair of All Saints boots walked right up to Richard King's body, after he'd been knocked to the ground. Stood over him, we think.'

I swallowed hard.

'Not many people have stood over a dead body,' he said, gazing into my eyes. He leant close to me, until he was inches from my face, and whispered. 'You've been hiding something for a long time, haven't you?'

I stared back at him, then glanced at Ellie.

Probert was still staring into my face. 'What are you keeping from us, Wilbur?'

Fifty-Nine

What could I do, at that point? The game was up. After they left, I sat at the kitchen table with my head in my arms. Ellie stared out of the window.

'You were willing to let them take those pairs of jeans,' she said.

'They aren't the ones,' I mumbled into my arms.

'And the boots?' she asked nervously.

'Gone too,' I said. She let out a deep sigh.

'It's over, isn't it,' I said forlornly

She didn't answer for a long time. Maybe a few minutes. Then she just said, 'No.'

Ellie thought the fact Probert was getting angrier wasn't a sign that the police were getting closer. She thought it was a sign of the opposite. She thought Probert seemed like someone who'd *lost* something, not found it.

'For him to talk like that, and not arrest you... they're grasping,' she said. 'If they had enough to arrest you, he wouldn't have told you about that, just now. They can't piece things together. They know you were there, but they can't understand what happened. That's why they've still got that other guy in for it. They keep getting new bits of information and they can't piece them together into a coherent picture.'

'So in other words... they're on the brink,' I said.

'No, not necessarily,' she said. 'They don't have the evidence. They clearly just don't have what they need. That's why they're still fishing like this, so long after it happened.'

'It feels like they're getting closer,' I said.

'They'll only be able to get closer if they find new evidence,' she said, 'and they're hoping they can pressure you into giving it up to them. Don't.'

She was right. As long as they didn't find any more evidence, they still didn't have anything on me. Except that I'd lied about the boots, and probably the jumper too. They knew I was lying, but nothing more than that.

'There's only one end left open,' she said thoughtfully.

'Yeah,' I sighed.

'And as long as it's left open, information is going to keep leaking out,' she said. I nodded gravely.

'I need to shut him up,' I said. 'I just need to shut him up.'

'You need to shut him up,' she echoed quietly.

'Threatening him won't work,' I said, staring at the table.

'No,' she said quietly. 'I don't think it would.'

We sat in silence for a while, both racking our brains.

'You could just *tell* him?' she said.

'How do you mean?'

'I don't know really... the problem is that he keeps moving the goalposts. So you could just give a fixed amount of money, whatever you decide, as his *thank you* or whatever, then... just tell him that's *it*.' She shrugged.

'That doesn't stop him just going to the police anyway,' I said.

'No, it doesn't,' she said, 'but it's your way of saying you're out of the game and it's up to his conscience what he does next.'

It didn't seem like much of a plan at all. Leaving anything to Solly's conscience did not seem smart. But it seemed like the only alternative left to killing him.

Sixty

My sick note expired and I had to return to work. It felt really strange going back, even though it'd only been a week-and-a-half off. I'd completely disconnected from that world. They buzzed about, talking about things that were so insignificant, and they did it with such energy and enthusiasm. *I used to be like that.*

People could tell I wasn't on the ball. Folks at that place were mostly intuitive, they were good at giving me space. I was given a project to work on: some new business pitch. I sat in one of the side offices pretending to read research papers I'd printed. What I was really doing was planning my visit to Solly. My last throw of the dice.

I was going to give him one last try. Try to persuade him, to plead with him if necessary, to just back off and stop being a prick. Ellie had approved it as a plan. I wasn't going to go with any cash, but I was ready to offer him ten thousand pounds. All my life savings, plus this month's pay. He could have it straight away in cash, if he wanted it. But that would be all.

I'd appeal to his better nature. I'd tell him he'd cleaned me out, and that we didn't need to get any more silly than that. I'd explain to him that I just couldn't raise the figures he was talking about, but that I'd given him everything I had. I was to tell him that ten grand was a *thank you*. A thank you for helping me through a difficult period in my life. Nothing more, and nothing less.

If he still wanted to share it with people, that would be up to him. It wasn't a stable position to place myself in, but Ellie was right: it was the last gamble I had that was worth taking. Appear out of all the madness and chaos with an olive branch, and just *see* what happens.

He agreed to meet me after work, at his apartment.

Sixty-One

Solly Green was an eccentric man, no doubt about it. But there was no charm in his eccentricity. It wasn't quirkiness, oddness or kookiness. It was just this raw detachment from integrity that made him really difficult to connect with.

I could tell he was a loner. He'd said it himself. That was the one saving grace with Solly, nobody really wanted to listen to him. He rattled around in his own little bubble, with his cameras filming the world outside.

The block he lived in just had this atmosphere to it. It was like all the happiness had been sucked out of that building years ago and never been replaced. Even when you approached it, it looked sad. All this chipped white paint facing the street, that'd been dulled for decades by car exhausts and all London's other pollutants. The reception area inside had this awful 1970s brown tint over the glass of the floor-to-ceiling window. It made everything seem so gloomy in there.

People adapt, I suppose. What can seem dull and depressing to an outsider can feel familiar and comfortable to a long-term resident. And everyone I saw there seemed to be long-term residents, plus some Chinese students. I feel bad when I see foreign students living in expensive shitholes. Someone saw them coming.

When I arrived on Solly's floor, the hallway lights were out. With only a few ceiling windows in the hallway, it was pretty dark. I could barely see where I was going. That *must* be a fire hazard.

Solly opened the door as I approached and held his hand out to me. 'Will, I'm sorry,' he said. 'Can I just apologise for how I was, last time?'

I couldn't get past him because he was blocking the door. 'What, you mean calling my girlfriend a whore and everything?' I said.

'Please, please don't be sarcastic or mean,' he said, 'let's get off on the *right* foot together. Let's come together and sort this mess out, today.'

'That's fine,' I said, 'I'm not going to shake your hand. I don't mind being civil and everything else.' He looked at me hopefully for a few more seconds, before dropping his hand and stepping back to let me past.

The evening was drawing in and his living room was dark. I tried to turn the light on as I went in, but nothing happened. 'Power cut,' he said, lighting a candle. Outside was dark too, even the streetlamps were out. A proper power cut: it looked like half of Farringdon was out.

'I'm sorry,' he said, 'it's cold in here isn't it. It'll warm up when these candles are lit.' He scurried off into his kitchen.

'I'm not bothered about the temperature,' I said. I was trying not to get frustrated. I was trying not to let him get under my skin.

He was so irritating. The way he ducked and dived about, the way he kept fingering his ears and nose. His whole over the top *what-can-I-do-for-you-today* attitude. *Squirming little wretch*.

I hadn't forgotten all that stuff he'd said about Ellie. All that other stuff too, implying she'd secretly gone and done some disgusting deal with him. In his fucking stupid, perverted fantasies maybe. I knew Ellie wouldn't do anything like that, of course, that was ridiculous. He'd been trying to dig me out; trying to goad me into attacking him, so he had more to hold over me.

I watched him rummaging about, I realised I'd never really *hated* anyone before. I didn't hate Richard King; I didn't know him. But I really hated this little man rummaging about in the half-dark in front of me. Nobody had ever disgusted me so much with their behaviour and outlook. I genuinely didn't care if he lived or died.

I thought to myself, *if he fell down and had a heart attack right now, I'd just walk away*. I wouldn't call an ambulance; I wouldn't even tell anyone. I'd just leave him there, to suffer. I wouldn't feel guilty. He wasn't a person of value to the world.

But I was there on business. I couldn't let my loathing for that spiteful little man affect what I needed to do. I was there to ask for my freedom. He returned with his hands full of small, white candles and carefully lit them. When he'd finished, he sat down in his armchair and lit a cigarette.

'Solly,' I said, 'I'm not here to say nasty things to you, or to threaten you, or to pretend I'm going to go and call in any debt for you... I'm here to talk to you and try to sort this out. I realise I've been responsible for bringing a lot of trauma into both our lives; that was my own mistake. I wish I could take it back, but I can't. I wish I could.'

He nodded sagely.

'Given that I can't turn back the clock now, all I can do is ask you to forgive me for that. I've decided to give you all the money I own. I have seven thousand pounds of savings in a Nationwide account, and then another three thousand in my current account. I have an overdraft of five hundred pounds on my current account, you can have that too. That's ten thousand, five-hundred pounds.'

He leaned back and smoked, thoughtfully. 'And my debt?' he said.

'Your debt is nothing to do with me, Solly,' I sighed. He frowned and looked me up and down.

'Okay fine. I'll clear your debt, too.' *I'll take out the fucking loan after all then.* Amazing how easily he was able to grab another forty-three grand off me. 'And that's me cleaned out. That's everything I have.' I continued. 'But it's yours. After that, what you do is up to you. If you want to tell things to the police, I can't stop you. But I'm asking you not to. I'm asking you to accept my apology… and my thanks for the… the way you've helped me.'

A smile crept across his lips. 'You got desperate, didn't you?' His rampant arrogance was one of the most disgusting things about him.

Sixty-Two

'I'll disappear,' he said eventually. 'If it makes you feel more comfortable, I'm willing to disappear.'

'Disappear where?' I said.

'Abroad! I don't know. Costa Rica or somewhere,' he said.

'Is that how you'll spend the money?' I said, feigning interest.

He laughed into his hand. 'Yeah,' he said. 'That's how I'll spend my money.'

'I'll give to you it monthly, five thousand a month for eleven months, then all the remainder on the twelfth month,' I said sadly.

He nodded and scratched his chin with a dirty fingernail. I wondered how the hell I was going to afford those repayments.

He smirked again, pretending to rub his nose with his sleeve to disguise it.

'What's so funny?' I said.

'Nothing,' he said.

'No come on, tell me what you keep laughing at,' I said. I was trying not to become irritated, but he was making it so difficult. He knew exactly what he was doing.

'Okay, okay,' he said, 'it's just, I really don't need your money. I've tried to tell you that.'

I gritted my teeth. I wouldn't crack. 'I know you don't need it,' I said. 'It's just a… gift. And the debt.'

'What fucking debt!' he giggled. 'There isn't a fucking debt, you wally!' He was bent over double, laughing to himself.

I took a deep breath. 'Okay fine, good one. You got me. There isn't a debt. But I'm still going to give you this ten thousand, because it's a gift, from me to you. And I wish you luck with… everything.'

His smile suddenly dropped. 'Are you living with the girl now?'

I rolled my eyes. 'No, we've only been dating a few months.'

'How comes she didn't come round with you today?' he said.

'I don't think she'd like it here,' I replied coldly.

'You'd be surprised,' he said.

'What does that mean?' I shot back. I could feel my adrenaline engines whirring up in my gut. I needed to slow them down.

'Do you like her birthmark?' he said. 'Cute, isn't it?'

I didn't respond. He gestured for me to sit in one of his stupid little chairs.

'She doesn't have a birthmark,' I said, pretending to yawn.

'She does mate! It's up by her tits, up here!' he pulled his jumper up to show his scrawny chest and jabbed a finger at his upper ribcage. 'Ask her to show you it!'

I took a couple of long, deep breaths.

'Will,' he said, *'Will?'* He'd developed this new, incredibly irritating way of saying my name. He'd really over-pronounce the consonants to make it sound extra naggy and infuriating. 'She's got nice tits, hasn't she?' he said. 'A proper, natural woman.'

I stood up from my chair and walked over to him. I knelt gently down on one knee in front of him and took a deep breath. 'Solly, I'm going to go now. I'll ask you please to stop insulting my girlfriend. I'll bring you your money. I'll bring it to you in cash. When do you want it?'

He looked incredulous. 'Tell me what I said that was insulting!' he said. 'The only person being insulting here is the person trying to pay someone off!'

I stood up to leave. My heart was racing. I hadn't felt this angry in a long time. I needed to get out of there. My teeth were grinding involuntarily. I could feel my heartbeat through the back of my eyes. I turned and made for the front door.

'Here!' he called after me. 'Here's what I want, and we can call it all off.'

I stopped by the front door, without turning back to face him.

'A photograph. Of the girl,' he said. 'Nude. Front-on. I want to see it all. And smiling. Make sure she's fucking smiling, not that miserable face of hers.'

I slowly turned back to face him.

'I make fifty grand in one evening, half the time,' he said. 'I'm not interested in money, I've tried to tell you that, all along.'

I nodded for a second and looked at the ground. 'That's what you want, is it?' I said. 'That's how you want me to pay you?

'*Finally*,' he said, 'we have a deal!'

I looked up at his face. He was grinning again. 'Would you like to know what happened when she came round here?' he asked, calmly and politely.

Every cell in my body was rattling. Everything in me wanted to run at him and rip that rotten tongue out of his head. I stared into his eyes. He stared back at me. There was no fear in there. There was no doubt, no part of him that was wearing down. He was never going to tire of it. I decided right there, I'd have to finish it myself. I was going to hand myself in to the police.

Sixty-Three

I went straight from Solly's flat to Ellie's. I messaged her to come and meet me at the pub near her flat. By the time she got there I'd already drunk two pints. I told her about my exchange with Solly, and that he wasn't going to budge.

I told her about the whole mad exchange. This time I told her about his weird stories about her having visited him at his flat, and that stuff about her having a birthmark on top of her ribcage.

'Well... yeah I have,' she said.

'What?'

'Yeah, look,' she pulled her top up to reveal a little birthmark that looked like a sailboat, at the top of her ribs, underneath her bra.

'Huh...' I said. 'How have I not noticed that before?'

'Well it's not that prominent, is it?' she said.

'But then... how on earth does he know about it?' I said.

She shrugged. 'Social media?' she said. 'Bikini pictures online somewhere?'

We both came to the realisation at the same moment. The pervert had been going through her social media photos.

We sat there mostly in silence for an hour or two. The

jingling fruit machines would occasionally jolt through my consciousness and remind me this was real. Eventually, we both finished our drinks and got up to go. I told Ellie I was going to hand myself in. For the first time ever, she didn't object. She just looked at me, glassy eyed, and continued putting her jacket on.

'My dad knows a lawyer,' she said, as we headed back in the direction of her flat. 'It's his cousin's wife; she's supposed to be really good. She was like some young hotshot or something. She's older now though.'

I sighed and we continued walking in silence. Ten minutes later when we stopped at a zebra crossing, I handed Ellie my phone. Without saying anything she punched in the details of the lawyer. This was really happening.

Sixty-Four

I made an appointment to meet the lawyer. When I made that appointment, it still hadn't fully sunk in that I'd actually have to do it. I'd actually have to sit there and tell a professional person, everything that'd happened. When I woke up that morning, a freezing morning in late January, I felt terrified.

I'd only had a few hours' sleep. I kept tossing and turning, imagining this panel of lawyers behind a big table, frowning at me and asking me to elaborate on things. *Do I need to wear a suit for this?* I owned a suit, but it had been a bit too big for me before and now, with the weight loss, it would look awful. I got up at half seven, showered, ate breakfast and dressed in the smartest clothes I could find. Grey trousers, a white shirt and a blue jumper.

I felt reassured by how professional the place seemed when I arrived. It didn't look like some bullshit provincial firm. The place was beautifully kitted out with glass tables and soft leather chairs. The receptionist offered me a drink; I asked for water.

Then this lady came out to greet me. Her name was Victoria Palmer. She was in her late forties or early fifties. Her thick, dyed brown hair, grey at the roots, was tied in a messy bun and her glasses sat perched on top of her head. She was wearing a dark grey skirt suit and low, black heels. She walked quickly and assertively, her heels thudding across the wooden floor as she approached me.

'Wilbur?' she said, holding out a hand to greet me. 'Vicky Palmer.'

'Yes,' I replied quietly, shaking her hand. 'Hi.'

She was extremely posh. She showed me into her office and sat me down, closing the laptop on her desk and pushing a bunch of papers into her top drawer.

'Now I think the best way to approach this…' She continued, without looking up at me, 'is if we use today as your opportunity to talk me through what's going on, and not leave anything out. I'm going to record you; is that okay?' She produced a silver Dictaphone from the drawer and held it up in the air as she continued organising her desk. 'Does that sound okay?' she repeated, looking up at me.

The Dictaphone scared me. The Dictaphone represented everything finally going on record. It would all be coming out of my head and into somebody else's for the first time. That was scary. Once I let the genie out of the bottle, there'd be no putting it back in, I knew that.

I wasn't sure if I could trust Victoria Palmer. I wasn't familiar with lawyers. Everything I'd read about this lady sounded okay, but I was still unsure about what to expect. I'd envisaged a lawyer who really cared about me and in this brisk first encounter she wasn't really giving that impression.

I leant forward, staring at the table. 'Look, I… I don't know how to say this to you, but… I'm really scared to say this, I'm scared to speak. I've been holding something in for months and I need to tell somebody… I need help… but I'm really worried about talking to anyone… it implicates me, quite badly.'

She glared back at me for a moment, before her expression softened. She leant back a little in her chair and sighed, plugging the biro she'd just picked up into her bun. 'Ok Wilbur—' she started.

'Will. Will, please,' I interrupted.

'Will,' she corrected herself. 'You've found yourself in some bother that requires legal expertise, so I'd suggest to you, if you need to tell somebody, your lawyer is exactly the person you should speak to. In fact, I'm the only person I'd suggest you speak to.' She looked at me gravely as she said that last part. I could tell she was reading my reactions as she said things, scoping me out.

As we spoke, she grew on me. I liked her sense of no nonsense, and she was reassuringly posh. She was extremely switched on and perceptive. I trusted her; something told me she was a person who could help. I needed to check something before I started, though. 'And if I tell you something that—'

'Anything you tell me is bound by professional privilege, whether or not you go on to be charged with anything – and whether or not I eventually represent you. It's a fundamental principle of the justice system.' She leant forwards and held her hand up as if to throw the spotlight back to me. Instinctively, I turned around and looked behind me. Then I leant towards her, looked into her eyes and spoke in a low voice, 'Well, first of all… I don't know how to say this. I killed somebody.'

Palmer didn't bat an eyelid. She calmly removed the biro from her hair with one hand and reached for an A5 journal on the desk in front of her. 'Hold on,' she said. 'Can we start with your full name please, and where you live.' She pushed her glasses down onto her nose with a single flourish of her wrist, and we were off.

Sixty-Five

I told her everything. Everything that was in my head, I poured into hers. That night with Richard King, the police coming after me, the clothes I put into the charity shop, the clothes I'd given the police. It all came tumbling out. Then I told her about Solly's video and the fact he had released a screenshot from it to Evatt's defence team.

'Who is Evatt's defence team?' she asked abruptly.

'I don't know,' I said.

For the most part she just sat quietly listening, occasionally asking me to repeat things or to explain them more fully. She had this tendency to look behind me while I was talking, which at first was unnerving. I think that was just how she listened. She took notes on the pad occasionally, but for the most part she listened and absorbed.

She was ferociously intelligent, I could tell. She was absorbing such huge amounts of information from me on the spot and was instantaneously building this picture in her head and simultaneously challenging it. She wasn't the warmest person, nor the gentlest communicator, but her cool assertiveness gave me confidence.

Throughout this whole thing, I'd just wanted someone who

knew what they were doing to look at this logically, but without thinking they might turn on me. I felt that Victoria Palmer might just be my person. She'd introduced herself as 'Vicky', but I liked the sound of 'Victoria Palmer'; it sounded legal and serious.

When I finished, she turned to a new page of her notebook and wrote out a basic timeline of the events, starting from that night in October. She must have asked two hundred questions about that night – and about Solly too. She wanted to know every detail about our conversations and what he'd said to me – the specific language he'd used and the technical setup in his apartment of sin. She didn't seem that bothered by my descriptions of Solly either. I guessed she must deal with freaks and weirdos all the time. When I finished, she gently closed her book and stared at the table.

'The thing I don't understand is… why not go to the police? I mean, why not go to the police straight away?'

'Because I didn't want to go to prison for the next ten years, because someone fancied having a go at me one night, for no reason—'

She held up her hand, submissively. 'Okay, okay yes, I get that,' she said. 'I can understand that… But am I right in thinking you intend to go to the police now?'

I nodded.

'Yes,' she agreed. 'It does sound like that would be a good idea, for your own safety if nothing else. This *negotiation* with the blackmailer could go on indefinitely; and it'll only get worse.'

I took a deep breath. It was so good to have a real-life adult helping me.

'You've done exactly the right thing by coming and discussing it with me beforehand,' she continued. 'That means I can help you manage this process of your confession now. Small details are probably going to make the world of difference. If you were trying to escape detection now, the best strategy would certainly be silence. But you don't have that luxury, do you? You've correctly identified that you have to attack this situation, at this point. You'll need to present your version of events clearly and as precisely as possible; we can't allow for any inaccuracies.'

I nodded, before reaching into my pocket and placing Solly's USB stick on the table. 'That's the only copy I have,' I said.

She picked it up and examined it briefly, before dropping it into her desk drawer.

'Aren't you going to have a look?' I said.

She ignored me. 'Our biggest threat at this moment, is time,' she continued pensively, locking her desk drawer with a little key. 'It sounds like the police are quickly becoming more... vigilant towards you. I think we might see those inquiries gathering pace now.'

That sentence was like a punch in the stomach.

Palmer took a sip from her coffee. She noticed I was uncomfortable. She was going through the process of ripping the plaster off.

'You committed an illegal act, and you don't want to be locked up for it, because you see it as an accident, a blip, something that perhaps you feel shouldn't be punishable. But it is, of course. There's nothing we can do about that. But if we act quickly, we can manage things in your favour.'

'So, what happens next?' I asked.

'Come back tomorrow,' she said. 'I'll work on this overnight and put a document together for your confession tomorrow. I'll come with you to the station in the morning.'

This whole conversation was like having my fingernails pulled out.

'Can I talk to my girlfriend about it?' I asked.

'I'd suggest you don't contact anyone at all, for now. Give me some time to work on a strategy for the police confession tomorrow. Get some rest tonight.'

Ha ha! Rest!

Sixty-Six

I got home and thought about what to have for dinner. The thought of any food turned my stomach. My stomach had shrunk into this incompetent little prune. It didn't do well with solids at that point.

I smoked a joint and drank a couple of bottles of beer, and then I started cleaning my flat.

It wasn't a regular clean, where I go round with a bin bag, then just sort of straighten everything up and hoover the carpets. It was a ferocious, uncompromising clean. I scrubbed the grout between the bathroom tiles until it was ice white. I deep-cleaned the carpets with the special powder. I scratched the crap off the edges of the window frames. I bleached the bathroom until it made you squint to open the door and look in. When I'd finished, I cleared the last items my laundry basket and hung everything out to dry. Then I lay on my bed, staring at the ceiling, occasionally breaking to go to the toilet. The TV remained on, playing inane stuff at super-high volume. *I wasn't doing well with silence.*

Later in the evening, I was still lying on my bed, staring at the ceiling. An old episode of *Grand Designs* was playing on the TV. My whole head felt hot, like my brain was overworking.

More than anything, I just wanted a day or two with Ellie, where none of this had happened. I was terrified about what the morning would bring.

Someone outside was setting off fireworks. It was noisy out there, as if someone was setting them off right next door. I don't mind fireworks but was not in the mood for them at that moment. I went to the window to see what was going on. They were making such a racket out there. I guessed they must be some of those massive, expensive ones. I couldn't see anything going on. Just the bare branches of the trees framing the road. Glistening wet from rain that had only recently stopped. I could see lights on in people's windows up and down the street.

Nobody has anywhere to go early in the new year; it's cold and miserable and party season's finished. No reason to go out, really. I stood there looking up and down the vacant street. I felt a pang of jealousy for all these normal people, with their normal lives.

And then I saw him. A man, standing on the other side of the street, staring directly up at me. I made a point of looking around some more, scanning the whole environment, before looking back at him again.

He was still looking at me. I recognised him from somewhere. This awkward gait and pointy features. And leaning forwards on the balls of his feet like that, slightly stooped. I squinted a little, trying to focus on his face some more.

I cursed myself for not getting my eyes tested. They weren't 20/20 any more, this situation made me sure of it. I'd have been able to make his features out more clearly in the past. I glanced up and down the road again, before turning away, taking one last look at the staring man as I went.

I took a few paces backwards into the darkness of my room. I needed to think for a moment. Why was this person so brazenly staring up into the window of my flat? Why hadn't he become awkward when I'd looked back at him? I peered forwards to see if he was still there. He was. Just standing there, staring up at me.

I nodded a greeting to him. He didn't move a muscle. I shrugged my shoulders and mimed, *'What?'* Again, he just stayed completely still, staring up. I was starting to get pissed off. I mimed *'piss off'* and jabbed my thumb sideways. He just stared back at me.

This weird feeling came over me all of a sudden. I realised where I thought I knew him from. His pointy, angry little nose and slightly squinting eyes. It was Richard King. The realisation hit me like a mallet to the side of the head.

I squinted in disbelief. That weird stoop and face like a bird; the harsh little beak-shaped face: it was *him*. I leant forwards some more to look at him more closely and my body went weak all over. It *was* Richard King. *It was him.*

Richard fucking King was standing in the street outside my flat. Every time I looked back at him, expecting to notice it wasn't him, I'd just confirm it was him again. The guy was alive. Richard King was alive and standing in the street outside.

I gripped the window ledge and stared out at him, trying my best to look intimidating. He just stared back. He didn't move an inch. I wanted to shout something, but I couldn't. I couldn't make myself speak. My mind was racing with possibilities at this point, but I couldn't verbalise any of them. I stood at the window watching him. My hands were soaked with sweat, I rubbed them down my T-shirt.

Then he moved. He reached down slowly into his coat pocket and touched something in there. I ducked for cover. I cowered, listening to the sound of the crackling fireworks for a few moments before slowly raising my head to peer over the window-sill again. His hands were back in his trouser-pockets now he was completely still again, staring up at me. I'd had enough.

I threw on a tracksuit and charged down the stairs. I ran out and around the side of the building to the road. There he was. He was *real*. Standing there, in flesh and blood.

My chest tightened as I got closer to him; it felt like my lungs had shrivelled to a tenth of the size. He didn't seem to notice me marching towards him, he was still staring up at my window. My sweaty hands were balled into anxious fists.

As I reached the edge of the road, I realised it was not in fact, Richard King. This guy was older, at least ten years older than King had been, and now I got up close, I could see he also had darker hair and larger, more robust nose. As relieved as I was about that, there was still the delicate matter of who he was, and what he was doing staring up into my bedroom window. I stopped, facing him across the road.

I gathered my breath. 'Can I help you, mate?' I said.

He looked towards me for the first time. 'Excuse me?' he said.

'I just wondered what you wanted,' I said. 'Why you're staring at me, in my house.'

'I'm sorry, I have no idea what you're talking about,' he said.

I rolled my eyes and started crossing the street towards him. 'This is Solly, is it?' I asked. 'Are you Solly's little mate? Aren't you a bit old for all this?'

The thought of this little dickhead believing he had the tools to push me around was irritating me now. Especially when I realised he must be a mate of Solly's. *What a weird bunch of individuals.*

'Piss off yeah, just move on,' I said, stopping a few steps away from him.

'I'm sorry mate, I really don't know who you're talking about, I wasn't looking into your house.' He took a hand out of his pocket and pointed upwards, where fireworks were popping and splashing across the sky. I looked back at him with a frown.

'It's the Social, I think,' he said. 'They didn't do their New

Year fireworks thingy because she was ill, she had the flu. So, I think they're doing it tonight.'

I looked up at the fireworks again, and then at my bedroom window across the street. The streetlight outside my window threw such a glare on it, he hadn't been able to see me looking out at him. I looked at the ground for a few moments, and then back at him.

'Sorry,' I said. 'I thought you were somebody else.'

'No worries,' he said eventually, looking back at me with concern. 'Take it easy.'

Sixty-Seven

The next morning when I woke, I didn't enjoy my normal first few seconds of bliss, that momentary illusion before I remember the realities of my current situation. But I didn't feel the crushing sense of helplessness, either. In some fucked up way, I felt like I was taking back control. In some fucked up way it felt exciting.

I sprang up from my bed and powered around the flat, preparing myself. I was looking forward to just waking up every day without these big secrets hanging over me. I was ready to give my brain a full enema and blast all the dark corners out.

I was going to meet Victoria Palmer at 10 a.m. and the plan was that we'd visit Islington police station at lunchtime. I wondered about calling Dad but decided not to. I'd call him when I could answer the questions he'd have. I'd call him when I could offer him some sort of certainty, at least. I was determined to minimise the damage on Dad's life.

I couldn't bear to see Ellie in the morning, I didn't want to look at her. I was fully aware of what I was losing, it was too painful to draw it out. I sent her an email telling her how sorry I was for how everything had turned out. I told her I wished more than anything I could've had a future with her. Losing my freedom was beginning to feel less painful than the part about losing Ellie.

I caught the 8.45 a.m. train into King's Cross, arriving in London at about quarter past nine, giving me enough time to get a coffee and make my way to Victoria's office at Nash Xavier Legal. The journey felt so quiet and peaceful. It felt like the world was taking a step back from me, getting out of my face a little bit. I'd had this knot in my lungs for months and hadn't even known it was there. It felt like it'd loosened today.

Victoria was waiting for me in reception and greeted me with a smile, leading me straight through to her office. 'I see you already have a drink; would you like anything else?' she asked as we breezed through reception.

'Double vodka please,' I said. She smiled.

It was so quiet; it didn't look like the reception staff had started for the day yet. I quite like being in commercial places when they haven't yet woken up for the day, don't know why.

'No thanks,' I replied. My stomach felt like a tumble dryer with thirty tennis balls in it, I was so nervous about what she was about to say to me. Whatever strategy she'd come up with was going to make a huge difference to the next decade of my life, at least.

The instant she sat down in her chair; she was all business. No quick social chat, no soft introductions, just straight to the action. She pulled a pile of paper on her table in front of her and straightened the corners, as though they were notes she was about to make a speech from.

'Are you first-aid trained?' she asked, suddenly.

I frowned and shook my head.

'Never been a lifeguard or anything?'

I shook my head again.

'Can you do CPR?' she asked.

'I could have a go,' I replied. 'You just pump the chest, right?

And it's to the beat of "Stayin' Alive" by the Bee Gees. I saw that advert.'

Palmer eyed me thoughtfully, 'For a moment, I want to separate the issue of obstructing justice,' she started. 'You have obstructed justice, and you will be held to account for it, but that part of this matter sits in the shadow of your first indiscretion and the things that happened subsequently. Do you follow?'

I nodded.

'What I mean is,' she continued, 'the way that you've behaved since the event has been guided by stress responses to the event itself, but also other mitigating things... the only crime that you *opted into freely*, you could argue, was the decision to strike this man Richard King.'

'Yes,' I said, nodding for her to continue. I was conscious of how much I was frowning at her. It was like waiting at the dentist's.

'So, that decision is what we need to pay most of our attention to. That decision is really the fulcrum of all of this, from your perspective.'

I made a mental note to look up the word *fulcrum* later. It sounded like a word I would like to use more.

'The complication, though, is that we know this footage of you exists, but it's private footage. The police currently don't have it, but we have to behave like they eventually will. Because I think they will, once this person Solly thinks he has got maximum value from it. Private footage may not be admissible as evidence ultimately – but it can implicate you circumstantially enough to see the CPS make a real case of this.'

She turned her computer screen around to face me and pointed at a still image of me standing in front of King in that alley. 'Self-defence is a problem,' she continued. 'To judge something as self- defence, body language and directions of motion are really important. Now, I think you can make a strong case from the footage here, that King certainly initiated contact, and certainly persevered with goading you after you'd tried to pass. But this part is a problem,' she motioned at the screen again. 'The point where you had passed one another, he wasn't moving, and you stepped towards him before you hit him.'

I sighed. *What an idiot.*

'If you hadn't stepped towards him, it could've made the world of difference. I know how simplistic it seems, but semiotics and direction of motion are really what tend to make the difference when it comes to courts making these decisions – certainly when it comes to prosecutors constructing arguments.'

'So, I can't claim I was defending myself?' I asked. 'Even though he'd come after me and shoved me and called me a pussy and all that?'

'It's very hard to measure, but I would say no,' she replied sharply. 'The action you took wouldn't be deemed proportionate enough to the level of threat, you see.'

'*Really?*' I shot back, quite angrily. 'Remember, I didn't know he was going to just die like that. I thought I was just punching him.'

'Yes, I agree,' she said. 'I agree that your intention was only to punch him and that's a point we need to stick around very vociferously… but it is still very unlikely to qualify the act as a reasonable act of *defence*. There's a big chance a jury would say you weren't under significant threat by that point, and that you just felt extremely irritated. And in legal terms, irritation is a world away from fear, as a motivator.'

I tried to stop my blood from boiling.

'So *that's* not frightening?' I snapped, finally. 'What happened to me *isn't* frightening or threatening? People are just supposed to live with that, are they? Being shoved and called names as they walk in the street?'

'Will, please understand, I'm not questioning your moral culpability. I'm telling you how a court will process this information.' She replied to my outburst with absolute placidity, like a parent to a toddler. 'I'm not saying you don't have any options and I'm not saying you don't have grounds to defend yourself… Okay?'

I nodded. I wanted to speak but for some reason I could feel a lump growing in my throat. It was beginning to feel like I *didn't* have any options. But I had faith in Victoria Palmer, at least.

I looked around her office. It was packed with stuff, but tidily kept. Lawyers are analogue people, they love having physical copies of things. There were shelves behind me full of legal texts and the walls were decorated with sketches and artworks in baroque style wooden frames. The radiators looked ancient, but really cool: those huge, old bronze looking things with the oversized taps on the side and the branding embossed into the plates. I guessed the rug under my chair was probably worth more than I was.

After a moment, I felt like I could speak again. 'So… what are my options? I mean, what should my… *angle* be?' I asked, quietly. It felt really wrong, saying those words.

She looked up at me. There was a sadness in her eyes for the first time, like it was all going so well and then I'd really disappointed her. She breathed in deeply and exhaled slowly, as though she were trying to slow the tempo of the conversation.

'I think we need to talk about what you mean, by *angle*,' she said eventually. 'I *cannot* tell you the charges you're facing won't be serious. I cannot point to an exit door that you can just leave through,' she said gently. 'The first thing you need to do is reacquaint yourself with the gravity of the situation. Stop thinking in terms of angles and solutions and start thinking in terms of practicalities. Like I said, we have to assume the police will ultimately have access to every piece of information, so it's safest to assume that eventually they'll know exactly what happened... *physically*. And the visual evidence looks bad.'

She nodded towards her computer screen. 'What they don't have, and what you *can* affect, is the context of the thing. Context couldn't be more important, and context will be the difference between a harsher sentence and a more reasonable one. So, we're going to make sure they have the context, in your own words. It'll be your most important commodity in this entire case, because to a jury it'll be the difference between an unlucky man and a ruthless, violent man. We're going to concentrate on context. Accuracy and context.'

I stared blankly at her. I didn't know what to say. *Accuracy and context? That's all I have?*

She held her hands up as though she could anticipate my doubt.

'Context is far more important and defining than you might be thinking—' she started.

'Look... I didn't mean to kill anybody,' I interjected.

'No,' she shot back. 'No, you didn't. You were in a state of fear and you struck somebody.'

'And then... I left him there for dead and hid for three months,' I replied, defeated. 'What's the context and specifics we'll apply to that?'

'*Specifics*,' she replied sharply. 'Being *specific, and accurate*. What you just said was far from specific and accurate.'

'I think that's pretty specific and accurate,' I replied, quietly. I didn't want to argue with her, but I didn't want to lie to myself either.

'First of all, you aren't qualified to say you "left him there for dead",' she said bluntly, 'because you wouldn't know how to check a person's vital signs with any degree of accuracy. You said yourself you don't know anything about first aid. That's called a *verifiable fact* and it's important because it supports the *context* that you exited a conflict situation at the first, safe opportunity – rather than you "left him there for dead". Context. Accuracy. Specifics.'

She pulled a lever arch file from the floor and placed it on the desk between us. I could see she'd written 'Cox, W. January' in permanent marker. There were only a few pieces of paper in there, the top few were loose. She took them off and slid them to me.

At the top of the document, it said, *Wilbur Cox: Confession*.

Sixty-Eight

She was right; there was no *angle*, except that I had not intended to cause serious harm. It made a big deal of suggesting I didn't know he'd been fatally wounded just before I'd left – which I sort of didn't.

She'd made an even bigger deal of the horror and fear I'd felt afterwards and how it had prevented me from coming forward to the police.

Solly wasn't mentioned. She explained that that was a matter to be dealt with separately. This document was just the facts about that night, narrated to minimise my culpability.

'Can I say something to you, Will?' she asked when I finished reading and looked up. 'You mentioned yesterday your fears around getting a lengthy prison sentence. It doesn't need to be that way. It's entirely possible we can negotiate a shorter term, perhaps a few years, which you'll be able to chip away at, with compliance and good behaviour. It's also highly unlikely we'd be talking about the high security sort of setup... nothing is off the table at this moment but it's very important we remain assured and alert, do you understand? It's not over yet, so hold your head up. It's an important moment to stand up for yourself.'

'A few years' didn't exactly seem like something to aim at, for me. I didn't want any years. 'Is there any scenario where I don't go to prison?' I asked tentatively. 'I mean… is there any eventuality where I'm sort of, *let off*?'

'I think it's time you were more realistic about your prospects,' she replied coldly. 'I understand your mitigating circumstances, and the things you've faced have been horrifying for you as much as anybody – but we aren't going in there to proclaim you as innocent, remember. We're going in there to explain the *context* around *why* you did it, to *frame* it in *terms* of your innocent motives.'

I looked at the bottom of the confession. She'd left a space for me to sign and date it. I looked up at her again.

'A few years?' I asked quietly.

'We can't guarantee anything,' she replied. 'Personally, I think *a few* is much more realistic than ten.'

Eventually I held out my hand and Victoria Palmer passed me her biro. I signed it and passed it back to her.

'You're doing the right thing, Will,' she said, as if she had heard my heart racing from beneath my shirt.

I took a deep breath and wrung my hands.

I still couldn't get my head around the idea that in a matter of hours I'd be confessing to the police, probably even Kane and Probert. And that I was going to be locked up, and have to leave my life behind, just like that. I felt like I should've planned it better, maybe spent more time working on the things I wanted to do before I went away.

But I'd lost that opportunity because of Solly and his pressure. He'd forced me into shopping myself. One way or another I was going to take that bastard down with me, that was for sure.

Sixty-Nine

We took a taxi to Islington police station. When we arrived in the reception area this horrible feeling came over me. All those posters on the wall with images of shadowy muggers and dark figures in hoodies doing their evil deeds. I wasn't one of them.

I stood behind Victoria as she spoke to the person on the front desk: a blonde in her early twenties. Victoria explained who we were and that we were there for a meeting with D.I. Probert and Sergeant Kane. She said she'd try to locate them and asked us to take a seat.

We were waiting for less than two minutes when an enormously fat man in his late fifties came bustling out and jabbed a sausage finger at me, half-shouting in a Scottish accent.

'Are you here for Probert?'

I looked at Victoria and nodded back to him. He beckoned us to follow him and plodded off down a corridor towards the interview rooms.

He had a different uniform from the others: a black jacket that was sort of double breasted with some fancy epaulettes on it. I don't know if it was his girth, but he had a lot of presence. As we walked, I listened to him breathing heavily through his mouth.

I guessed he must have been at least twenty-five stone. His

arms swung beside him like big jambon pendulums, propelling his enormous frame forwards. He looked all business, this guy; he didn't look capable of laughing, he seemed so intensely dour. His skin looked pallid and desperately unhealthy, covered in red spots and shaving nicks. Around the bottom of his neck, just above the collar of his shirt, was this glistening ring of sweat. In the morning. In the winter.

He waved us into an interview room and asked us to take a seat.

'They'll be along shortly,' he said, eyeing me suspiciously.

Victoria had already called and explained to Probert that I had a written confession I wanted to deliver to him and Kane. I wondered how much this fat guy knew. I bet they were all talking about it in the station.

When he left, Victoria told me he was the big cheese, the station Superintendent, and that his name was Porter. She said he was hard work and that we'd better hope he wasn't involved in my case. *That's all I need.* Panic started rushing through me. It was all becoming a bit too real.

Victoria smiled encouragingly at me. 'Relax,' she said, 'and remember, you shouldn't need to speak today. They'll want you to elaborate on your confession, but we aren't going to do that. Don't let them tempt you into a conversation that cannot benefit you today. "No comment, on the advice of my lawyer".'

I put my hands into my hair and had a good old scratch at my head. It's something I do when I'm stressed.

It only took a matter of minutes for Kane and Probert to appear. We were offered drinks, they sat down, and we began the formalities. Victoria explained to them that I had a written confession, which she would be reading to them. She added that for now, I did not wish to answer any further questions regarding the confession.

Neither of them seemed very pleased at all that I was handing myself in. I just didn't get that.

I wasn't expecting *gratitude*, but I suppose I expected relief or at least some sense of satisfaction. They both looked really confused and anxious. That's the only way I could describe it.

I didn't have much time to think about this new little mystery of the coppers' odd reaction. They just kicked things straight into life, like they were in a hurry, rushing through the time and date and passing around the room for everyone to introduce themselves for the audio. And then suddenly, they just stopped.

All the rushing around just stopped and this silence fell over the room. Probert held out his palm to Victoria and nodded at her. She looked awkward for a moment before leaning forwards and clearing her throat.

'My client Mr Cox has instructed me to read a prepared statement on his behalf,' Victoria began. 'Mr Cox wishes his statement to be processed today but does not wish to answer any further questions at this point.' She eyeballed Probert like a 1950s headmaster regarding a naughty little boy.

Go, Victoria Palmer!

Probert glowered at the table. He in turn, looked like a moody teenager. He sat with his arms folded, listening to Victoria, as if she was about to tell him something he'd heard a million times before and couldn't be bothered to sit through again.

Victoria pulled her glasses down onto her face and began to read my confession.

Seventy

'... I felt happy and calm; I was looking forward to getting home to relax and watch television before work the following morning. I estimate that I had consumed four to five pints of beer, but I had eaten only hours before and was not feeling drunk. I took my usual route home, following the alleyway which connects Turnmill Street and Clerkenwell Road, adjacent to the building works.

Approximately thirty metres into the alley I was approached by a person I now know to be Richard King. I sensed from King's movement and behaviour as he approached, that he was mildly intoxicated. As he came within conversational distance of me, Mr King was behaving in an overbearing and aggressive manner, shouting insults towards me and striking me with his shoulder as he passed. I believe this was an attempt to knock me to the ground...'

Victoria Palmer read the document slowly and deliberately. She didn't stop once, even to glance at her unimpressed audience. I didn't look at them either. Just sat staring at the table, occasionally glancing up to look at the page Victoria was reading from.

It felt so uncomfortable. Porter and Probert looked like they were in pain, listening to it. I couldn't work it out. *We're doing your job for you here, guys.*

'*... When this failed, Mr King directed a personal insult at me. He referred to me as a "Pussy". I believe he was trying to compare me to a female body part, to somehow suggest I was a weak man, to try to aggravate me and to provoke physical conflict.*

I felt safer not to turn my back on Mr King, so I turned to face him and asked him to leave. We had a heated verbal exchange, during which I felt overwhelmed with fear and concern for my personal safety. I took the decision to try to incapacitate Mr King momentarily, so that I could escape from this situation and get to a safer, more public space.

Without considering the consequences for a moment and over-whelmed with fear and anger, I struck Mr King with my right fist. This action was very out of character for me; my only intention was to briefly distract Mr King so that I could make a safe escape. I had not intended to cause him lasting harm of any kind...'

Victoria stopped reading for the first time to take a sip of water. I noticed Probert shake his head at her, like he'd heard enough. She took a tissue from her pocket and wiped her nose. Victoria worked to her own beat, I appreciated that about her. She'd be good at my job.

I was glad to have her on my side. This didn't feel like it was going smoothly, though. You could cut the atmosphere with a knife.

'*... I did not find out until the following day that Mr King had in fact fatally hit his head in that same alleyway. I do not know for certain if the particular fall that caused this fatal injury was caused by the contact from me, but I realised the following day from news reports that he had died, and I accept responsibility for the consequences of my own physical altercation with Mr King that night.*

I deeply regret not handing myself in to the police subsequently. Following the incident, I felt paralysed by the horror of what had happened, and I suffered severe post-traumatic stress which rendered communication extremely difficult.

I was fearful of contacting the police because I was fearful about being punished unduly heavily. Despite feeling remorseful I am still relatively young and do not yet have children. I did not want the consequences of this accident to affect me heavily in later life, so I did not contact the police. Instead, I withdrew into a place where I could reconcile the trauma in my own mind. Today, I wish to confess to this crime and intend to comply fully with the justice system…'

After Victoria finished speaking, there was a good thirty seconds of deafening silence. I braced myself to dig in. I knew the questions would be coming and Victoria had been absolutely clear with me to deflect them. *'Don't get dragged into a dialogue,'* she'd said.

I knew that the next few minutes might be some of the most important in my life. I took a few deep breaths and looked up at Kane. She was staring directly at me. Probert was, too.

Probert finally broke the silence with a question. 'Is that a false confession, Will?'

Seventy-One

A bizarre sequence followed. Victoria and I momentarily lost the thread of what was going on, as Kane joined Probert in pursuing this unexpected narrative. We kept looking at each other, both our minds whirring, before squinting back at these two officers who had apparently lost the plot.

Probert fumbled his words as he tried to reason with me: 'Will it's... I want you to think about this. I want you to shut out all the noise and just think about... the real world.'

Kane interjected. 'Will, I'd just ask you to take a step back and think about this situation, and where you've got to. You're here now and we can help you out, but... I don't think what you're saying to us here is exactly true, is it?'

I sat, open mouthed, looking between them. Victoria, who'd clearly been furiously trying to recalculate the situation, took a deep breath and asked, 'What do you mean, Police Sergeant Kane?'

'Can I see that?' Kane held her hand out towards the confession letter in Victoria's hand. Victoria calmly took two copies from her file and handed one to Probert, before passing another to Kane.

The pair sat, scrutinising the pages, occasionally glancing at one another. I could sense exasperation. Something very odd was going on. Immediately, I thought of Solly. *Wherever there's confusion and misinformation, he won't be far away*, I thought.

It's hard to overstate how disorientating this felt. I'd come to confess to something. I'd been building myself up for this moment psychologically, since the night it happened. But for some reason, the police weren't accepting what I was saying. Not only that – they were accusing me of lying.

These people had been chasing me down for months. Only days before, Kane had left me a voicemail message asking if I could bring those additional pairs of Levi's jeans to the station. They'd searched my house without a warrant. They'd sat in my kitchen and more or less confirmed to me that my time had run out.

I'd spent so much time agonising over this moment, my *moment of enlightenment* that would clear up this whole mystery for everybody once and for all, and they were trying to block it. Somehow, somewhere along the line, they'd got something badly mixed up. It felt like they didn't want to accept what I was saying. Or that they *couldn't*.

Victoria had seen enough. She decided to withdraw me from conflict until she could work out what was happening. She asked if we could take a moment's counsel. Probert was in the process of agreeing when Kane interrupted.

'Will, we think you're confessing to a crime somebody else committed and we need to know why. We think you *know* Jacob Evatt killed Richard King, and we think somebody has coerced you into making this confession today. What do you think about that?'

My mouth fell open again, I couldn't help myself. I had to consciously remind myself to close it.

'Yeah, take a moment to confer with your brief,' said Probert, rising and nudging Kane with his elbow to invite her to follow him. 'But please think really carefully about what comes next, Will. It's quite important at this point that you don't mislead us or waste any time. Richard King died from a hematoma to the brain, which was caused by being hit with a twelve-kilogram scaffolding pole. We have an eyewitness, and we have a confession. So, for you to appear today and claim that in fact, *you* killed King, is... a little frustrating, not to mention entirely unbelievable. Can you understand that?'

I looked at Victoria. I couldn't quite take it all in. Probert seemed sarcastic, almost mocking in his tone. He was *mocking* the suggestion that I'd been involved.

'I don't...' I started.

'Will, whoever has asked you to come here today has committed a serious crime. But don't forget, if what you're saying is not true, you're committing a crime too. Do you understand?'

'We'll erm... we'll pause things there, I think,' said Victoria.

Kane sighed and shook her head at me. Probert slammed his folder shut and shoved it under his arm. They both looked exhausted. I'd really rattled them with this; I just had no idea how or why.

Seventy-Two

Probert suspended the interview and the two of them left the room. I glanced at my reflection in the mirrored wall adjacent to me. It occurred to me that they'd probably gone to smoke cigarettes and look at me through there.

As soon as the door clocked closed, Victoria turned to me and snapped with an ice-cold glare. 'Don't say anything at all. Do you understand? My professional advice to you is not to respond to a single question with anything more than a "no comment". I think there's a lot more to this that we'd realised.'

'*What?*' I shot back.

For the first time, Victoria looked flustered. She asked me to wait for a moment while she went to speak with Probert and Kane. We both agreed that we should hear what the police had to say, before surrendering any more information.

They were all gone for a good twenty minutes, before Victoria returned, looking pale. She shot me a quick smile and fanned her face as she sat down. 'Goodness me!' she said, 'right…'

I sat there in utter astonishment as Victoria explained to me that the bust up between Evatt and King had been far more significant than we'd realised. She rushed me through the events:

they'd scuffled briefly in that bar, with Evatt shoving King against a wall by his throat, before security staff, bar staff and some local white knights had wrestled them outside.

A few of Evatt's hangers-on had inflamed matters and initially prevented King from leaving. Evatt had caught up with him and had him in a headlock in the street. He'd pummelled the back of King's head with punches from close range until eventually the security staff from the bar intervened again and pulled the pair apart. They sent King on his way and held Evatt up for as long as they could, with the help of some willing lads from the bar across the street. Someone had asked King where he was headed. And during the period he'd been kept busy by the helpful lads from the neighbouring bar, either Evatt, or Evatt's girlfriend had somehow become party to the information that Richard King would be heading in the direction of Old Street station.

Evatt had appeared to leave the scene with his girlfriend but once they were out of sight of others, he took off after Richard King, alone. Evatt knew the route well and had felt confident he could find him and cut him off. He was incensed by a comment King had made about his girlfriend.

King had called Evatt's girlfriend an 'ugly pig', by all accounts. I didn't see a photo of what she looked like. King was an oily character, by no means tough, but a wind-up merchant, who didn't seem to care much about his own safety. He knew how to push people's buttons.

The police had more or less been able to track most of King and Evatt's journeys with CCTV. They'd seen King stop at a newspaper stand near Farringdon station and talk to the proprietor. They'd seemed to have exchanged some sort of cross words; King had flipped his hand at the guy as he turned away.

The vendor had long since closed for the night; he was there waiting for a delivery before he could go home. King approached him and asked him if he sold cigarettes. The vendor explained that he didn't, and that his stand wasn't open for business, in any case. King didn't seem to care that the guy didn't sell cigarettes, or that he was closed. He decided he wanted to buy his cigarettes anyway.

He'd drunkenly pulled his wallet out of his pocket and coins had splashed out everywhere.

A two-pound coin had rolled under one of the heavy display units and King had bent right down.

He was almost crawling underneath the stand to look for it. While he was doing this, Jacob Evatt casually walked past the magazine stand in the background. On the CCTV footage, you clearly saw the moment where he clocked King.

As King tried to get back to his feet, he'd hit the stand heavily with his head and nearly knocked it over. The owner of the stand had taken objection to this, which had caused the argument between the two. The vendor said he hadn't taken it too seriously as it seemed like 'the usual kind of drunken nonsense'. King left and headed down Turnmill Street, which is where things got hazy, because of the CCTV blackspot there and down the alley. Probert said something about six or seven cameras in Turnmill Street being non-operational, and that there were no cameras on the back of the building that lined the alley, because it was listed; nobody was allowed to mess with it. Apparently, it was actually the second crime that had taken place down there that had basically proved 'unsolvable', and it had been causing problems for local government. The council had plans to try and improve visibility down there. They were just moving very slowly.

King had set off down Turnmill Street and had bumped into Evatt a minute or so later. Or rather, Evatt bumped into him. Evatt had seen the argument with the newspaper vendor and had been lying in wait for King. He'd taken a piece of scaffolding pole from near the entrance to the building site and brought it down across the back of King's head. The newspaper vendor heard it, heard King cry out, and saw Evatt running away down Turnmill Street.

The eyewitness had been crucial in nailing Evatt, who had eventually confessed. He admitted that King hadn't been moving when he fled the scene. He'd pulled King into a doorway, disappeared down the road and got into a taxi at the bottom of Turnmill Street. Evatt had been utterly perplexed as to why King's body had shown up so much further down the alley.

But King had got up again, minutes later. Evatt hadn't known this. The newspaper vendor had gone to help him. The police said the vendor had kept changing his statement, which hadn't helped.

They thought he'd probably overstated how well King had seemed, to make himself feel better for not calling an ambulance. They guessed he'd just wanted to get home after a long day.

He'd said King was 'physically okay, but seemed drunk, and was escalating in and out of anger'. He'd seemed confused about the whole thing, he didn't seem to remember who Evatt was, or why he'd hit him. But he refused an ambulance. He'd seemed a little bit disorientated but could walk and talk okay. He said he was going to go home and sleep it off. Evatt's DNA was all over him by that point, of course. And the police believed he'd already been dealt his fatal blow.

I pointed at the two-way mirror. 'Are they watching us, from in there?' I whispered.

'No,' replied Victoria.

'How do you know?' I said, glancing at it again.

She ignored me and pushed on. The case against Jacob Evatt was, she said, *quite far down the line*. She said she detected that the police were glad to have nailed Evatt. They didn't appreciate me messing with their case. They told Victoria they'd found me a 'hostile witness' throughout, and that part of the reason they'd found it hard to gather evidence against Evatt was because their only witnesses were me and the newspaper vendor, and we were 'each as unreliable as the other'. I guess each of us had our reasons.

King's body was covered in trace elements of Evatt's clothes, and not mine. King's skin under Evatt's fingernails, and Evatt's under King's; six different imprints from Evatt's sovereign ring on King's skull; King's hair, saliva and as well as traces of his blood on Evatt's jacket and T-shirt – even an imprint of King's teeth on Evatt's wrist. And nothing of mine.

I'd touched him twice: with the shoulder of my jacket, and with an unseasonably gloved hand. And those gloves – and all the clothes I was wearing – were now god knows where. So, as confusing as this was initially, coupled with Evatt's nature, it was relatively easy to understand how the police had filled in this blank so erratically. They had nailed Evatt, a known crim-inal. They didn't want some bumbling Advertising dweeb to steal their glory with a leftfield intervention.

Seventy-Three

That had been one of the things that had confused me from the very beginning. The fact that I'd managed to hit the guy in such a way that he'd fallen and died. I suppose I had been surprised at how easily he fell down. And then there was that walk of his.

Victoria explained to me that when I'd mentioned the state of King's clothes as he'd approached me, it'd made her wonder if he had already been in some sort of physical altercation before I'd met him. But his walk was what really stood out for her. I'd described him staggering slightly, leaning slightly off centre. But I'd said he was okay focusing on me, okay talking. Then, when she'd seen Solly's video, she'd really started to wonder if Richard King had already been dealt a serious head injury, before he came across me.

'There's this… scaffolding pole. Or scaffold-joint or whatever it was,' she said. 'Striking someone across the back of their head with something that heavy, when they're off-guard… that's far more likely to have caused a fatal internal injury than a punch to the jaw, from…' she trailed off and nodded at me.

Of course, I agreed with her.

'Another thing to consider: a sudden, sharp increase in

257

aggression is very possible after a traumatic brain injury... it's entirely plausible that the *reason* he behaved so aggressively towards you was in fact as a *result* of this ghastly blow he'd taken about ten minutes before,' she said.

I was reeling. 'But then... that makes no sense; how come he was able to communicate with me? He seemed... normal. A *bit* drunk but, you know... *normal*,' I said.

'Richard King died of a hematoma,' she said. 'A trauma causes injury to the wall of a blood vessel, so blood is haemorrhaging out into the surrounding tissues. But the brain isn't designed to absorb that much extra fluid, so it gradually creates pressure as it gathers and clots. It doesn't happen immediately. It can take an hour, a day, a week...'

'So does that mean...' I rubbed my head aggressively. Fucking strip lights overhead were giving me a headache. 'But I still... *hit him*.' As I whispered it, I glanced at the two-way mirror.

'Yes, well, I doubt you would have helped matters,' she said, 'but he looked like he was showing possible symptoms of bleeding on the brain when he accosted you.'

'Okay...' I said cautiously, 'so what happens now?'

'The police... are not accepting your confession, at this point,' she said.

'Sorry... *what*?' I said. 'What does that even *mean*?'

'This isn't something I come across very often,' she began, 'in fact it's the first time in twenty-five years of practice I've ever seen anything quite like this.'

Victoria removed her glasses, folded them and placed them on the table. 'The police,' she said, 'like anybody, have a job to do, and they take satisfaction from doing it well.'

'Of course,' I said.

'In this instance,' she continued, 'a known criminal has committed a brutal assault very publicly, and despite initial difficulties gathering evidence, they've finally managed to nail him. Do you understand what I am saying, Will? They've finally managed to nail Jacob Evatt. His trial is due to start in a few weeks; the CPS thinks it's a slam dunk...'

'You're saying they don't *want* my confession?' I said, wincing and closing my eyes to absorb it all.

'I don't know,' she said. 'I don't think they know *what* to do with it.'

'Well...' I started. *Yeah, what do I expect them to do with it?*

'In their world, you aren't valuable,' continued Vicky. 'A bedroom weed smoker from an advertising agency doesn't hold any value for them. This man who has confessed, has value. Real value and...' she raised her eyebrows in a gently mocking expression, 'accomplishment.'

'I don't smoke weed,' I said automatically.

She nodded. 'And to answer your question, Will, that's how I know they're not watching us,' she said, nodding at the two-way mirror. 'This is a game of incentives. We're dealing with human beings. They want to *win*. Plus, that's not actually a two-way mirror, it's just a mirror.'

I watched her talking, with a blank expression. It wasn't really sinking in. The atmosphere wasn't quite adding up.

Surely this is brilliant news? Am I out of here?

Victoria seemed so calm. She was maintaining her British reserve. 'But now they're concerned about *why* you've come here today, and who is putting pressure on you to confess to it.' She calmly picked up her glasses, placed them on her head and closed her file. She stared at the table, deep in thought. Like me, she was trying to pull all the loose threads together and summarise the position.

'They just don't seem to be *entertaining* the idea that you could've done it,' she said eventually. 'I think they're blinded by the physical and circumstantial evidence around Evatt... and the motive of course.'

'So, what happens now?' I asked. I wondered for a moment whether we could just walk out, now. *We definitely could.*

Victoria tapped the table, as though she were trying to wake me up. 'Remember Will, there's evidence out there supporting your version of events. The oddity of this is that your version of events implicates you and the police are refuting it, in favour of a version that doesn't...' She put her head in her hand for a moment as she strained to think.

'We have to work on the assumption that that evidence will eventually find its way to the police, and that it implicates you,' she said. 'Eventually it'll be revealed to them, one way or another. If we allow the police to proceed with this fantasy, you might be out of the spotlight in the short term, but you'll be spending your life waiting for Solly Green to expose you. And then what happens?'

'Yeah,' I said quietly. I didn't want to hear it, but I knew she was right.

Seventy-Four

Fifteen minutes later Probert and Kane bustled back in. She was properly staring me down. They were both stomping and huffing and making too much noise over everything. It was like watching a pair of moody teenagers arrive for class.

Probert pulled his chair up close to the table and loosened his tie as Kane re-started the recording. He rolled the sleeves of his shirt up and took a tiny piece of cloth out of the top pocket of his jacket. We all sat and watched him rub the lenses of his glasses for a minute; it was quite hypnotic. They looked like expensive glasses.

There was a real steeliness about him now, like he was fed up with the niceties.

'Do you know what a patsy is?' he asked me eventually, clearing his throat and placing his glasses carefully back onto his face. He really spat out the 'p'.

'Really?' exclaimed Victoria. She wasn't impressed by Probert, I could tell. He rubbed her up the wrong way. I sensed this case was not her first encounter with him.

'It's American slang. There was this character, on Broadway,' he said, 'called Patsy-something-or-other, and the joke was that this person always got blamed when anything went wrong.'

'Okay…'

'So people say that's where it comes from, but it was before that really, because it came from words that already existed in different languages floating around working class America, like *Pazzo* meaning "fool" in Italian or a *Patrick*, which was sort of an Irish underground slang for a *sucker*, one-born-every-minute type of thing. You know?'

I looked at Victoria and then back at him. 'No comment,' I said.

'The point is,' he continued, 'everyone knows what a patsy really means; it's a bottom-feeder, someone who can be manipulated and pushed about, right?'

'Look,' I said. 'I know what you're saying. But… I'm not being that. Nobody has asked me to come here, I've come here myself.'

'Wilbur,' said Probert blankly, 'I'll remind you this isn't a game. There are consequences to everything, that I don't think you've fully considered.'

I kept glancing at Victoria. She looked nervous as hell; it was like she wasn't sure what I was about to give up.

'Can I ask you something?' Kane interjected. 'Let's say you did this. Let's say Evatt didn't catch up with King at all, and it was *you* he met down Turnmill Street. Why hand yourself in? You knew we had someone else for it, the whole world did.'

As usual, she seemed to have been the one who smelled that drop of blood in the water first. Although Probert didn't look surprised when she'd asked it. I wondered what they'd discussed in that fifteen-minute period between Victoria leaving them, and their coming back into the interview room. *Why was she tugging at this thread, now?*

I took a deep breath. And then another. Something inside me gave in. I felt my face contort and my eyes begin to well with tears. I put my hand over my mouth and whispered into it.

'Victoria, I'm sorry,' I began.

I looked up at Kane. For the first time ever, I was able to hold her hawkish gaze. For the first time since I'd met her, I didn't feel like I was scurrying for cover.

'Because it does you in,' I whispered to her. 'Honestly, it just...'

I pressed my trembling hands into a ball and squeezed them together tightly. I took a deep breath and sunk down to rest my forearms on the cold table. 'Someone else getting the rap for it doesn't stop it from eating away at you,' I whispered into the plastic tabletop.

I couldn't look up and see the expression on Victoria's face. This was not part of the strategy. I wasn't supposed to talk about any of it, but I couldn't stop myself.

'I thought I was a suspect,' I said quietly. It felt like it was all coming out now, I couldn't stop it. 'I thought you were coming after me. I needed to like... *conclude* it.'

I sat up and rubbed my eyes, wiping my nose with my sleeve. 'It was a genuine accident. It was a mistake. If I could do anything to take it back, I would.'

Kane listened intently before turning to face Probert. They eyed each other for a moment, before Probert touched Kane's arm, as if to gesture she hold questioning.

'Will,' he said, more calmly now. 'Take some time. Think about it. Think about what you're saying and *think about what we are saying to you.*'

The way he was looking at me didn't match the calm of his words. He looked like he could burn a hole in me with his eyes.

I was scared to make eye-contact with Victoria at this point. I could see in my peripherals, she was staring at Probert, trying to decipher him.

'Why don't you go home and sleep on it?' he suggested.

'I... don't have any comment,' I said, nudging Victoria.

She swung around to look at me, as though she'd been snapped out of a trance. 'Erm…' she started.

'Go home and sleep on it, Will,' said Probert. He had this look in his eye, like he wanted to turn the tape off and throttle me.

Seventy-Five

In hindsight, the suggestion to postpone for a day was in fact D.I. Matt Probert deciding he didn't want any more of this conversation to be on tape. After ending the interview, he led us back out into the corridor.

'We'll talk more in the morning.' He pointed to a Toilets sign at the end of the corridor. 'Please, take your time, freshen up. Police Sergeant Kane will show you out when you're ready.'

Victoria power-walked off to the Ladies with her files and iPad tucked under her arm. 'I'll meet you downstairs,' she called over her shoulder. The amount of tea she got through, it was surprising she didn't need to go more often. I wondered for a moment if lawyers had to take their files into the actual cubicle with them. I guessed they did. You can't exactly just leave them on the side, by the hand dryer. They must put them on the floor of the cubicle while they go.

I ducked into the Gents for a splash of water on my face. When I got in there I stood and stared at myself in the mirror. It was dimly lit in there; the slimline window running along the top of the wall cast these horrible shadows across my face. I looked so haggard and startled. It had become my default look at that point.

I washed my face at the sink, with the hand wash. It smelled surprisingly nice; fresh and lemony. As I stared at my damp face in the mirror, I took stock of things. Things were starting to fall into place in my mind. I wasn't sure if I was the luckiest, or the unluckiest guy in the world, but I was slowly realising that my part in the events of that night were more of a footnote than a headline. What I'd done, and what Solly had *seen*, had happened in the shadow of this whole bigger context.

I went into a cubicle. I don't use urinals; it is a recipe for getting urine splashed over your trousers. I heard somebody come into the bathroom, so I turned and locked the cubicle door behind me. I heard the person's shoes scratch up to the urinal and stop there. But there was no further noise. No noise of a fly unzipping or anyone doing the business. Someone was just standing there.

I finished and flushed the loo. The flush was loud and abrupt like an aeroplane toilet; scared the life out of me. As I unbolted the door, the person turned around from the urinal to face me. It was Probert.

I quickly nodded a greeting and walked past him to the sink. As I washed my hands, I tried not to make eye contact with him, but I could feel he was still watching me. As I turned around to dry my hands, he spoke,

'Is that yours?' He pointed back into the cubicle I'd come out of.

'What?' I said, taking a few steps back towards him to peer in. As I reached him, he grabbed me and shoved me back into the cubicle. I bounced off the open cubicle door and spun around to face him.

'What the hell?'

Probert held his finger to his lips. 'Shut up,' he whispered, '*shut up.*'

He stepped into the doorway of the cubicle, blocking my

exit. 'Listen to me,' he said, grabbing my bicep really tightly with his hand. 'Listen to me!'

I held my hand up and winced. He loosened his hand.

'Okay, okay!' I repeated in a whisper. *'Fuck!'*

He forced me further into the cubicle and closed the door behind him. 'Sit,' he hissed.

I put the toilet seat down and sat on it. He stepped forward so he was standing right over me.

'I don't know if someone's in your ear, or if you're just really, really stupid,' he said, in a harsh whisper.

'What do you mean?' I protested, also in a strained whisper.

'Pack it in. Leave it. Fuck off. Whatever this is, whatever this whole game is, *leave it*. Do you understand what I'm saying to you? How are you this fucking stupid? *Leave it.*'

He crouched to eye-level with me. 'I really, really don't want to see or hear anything else from you,' he patted his chest. 'Detective Inspector, yeah? I can make life extremely difficult for you, and I don't want to. Yeah?'

I tried to respond but I was lost for words. I didn't have any intention of having this guy making life difficult for me, too. I'd rattled him, somehow. He was normally so calm and in control. It was like he had lost it, all of a sudden. He seemed so skittish, full of this nervous anger.

'I came here... to tell you... *confess* to you that—'

He launched himself at me, grabbing my throat with one hand and putting his hand over my mouth with the other. 'You are a *liar*, Will. And I don't think I want to listen to any more lies from you. *Stop* fucking lying to the police. Stop fucking lying to us.'

'I'm nmot fbuckinm lyimng,' I shouted into his hand.

He tightened his grip on my mouth, it was really pressing my teeth into the skin of my mouth. He was stronger than he looked. When I first saw him, I had him down for a pen pusher.

I had my hands around his wrists, trying the wrench them off. It was no use. I loosened my grip. He had me leaning right back on the toilet seat now, his face right up to mine.

After a while, he let go of me and leant backwards against the cubicle door. He sighed and rubbed his face.

'You're undoing years of work, Will. I think you need to understand, people have died for this moment. Someone died for this, right now.'

I had no idea what he meant by that. 'I know. I know somebody died,' I said quietly.

He shot me a look of disdain.

'Not the fucking insurance salesman,' he said. 'An officer. One of ours.'

Seventy-Six

Probert explained to me that, for just over two years, he had led a task force trying to close a net on Jacob Evatt. Evatt, a high priority criminal with a history of serious violence, had dropped completely off the police radar. His illegal activities instantly fell from frequent to zero. The authorities suspected something else was going on.

Evatt had very swiftly moved upstairs, from a street-level operator to an international drugs trafficker. He'd inherited a haulage firm from his dad and spent years creating a network with brokers around Europe. He was bringing huge quantities of coke into the UK via the Channel Tunnel.

Probert was an up-and-coming detective who had excelled up until that point. He was appointed to lead the task force to bring Evatt's racket down. And he'd hit stumbling block after stumbling block.

'Can we talk out there?' I asked him, jerking my thumb hopefully in the direction of the door.

'Then came the bust,' he said. It had started when a truck entered the UK from the Netherlands and was intercepted at Customs. It was found to contain seven suspect packages. 'Cocaine,' said Probert. 'Fourteen kilos.'

The driver reckoned he wasn't aware of what had been packed and he agreed to let Special Ops place audio and visual surveillance in the back of the truck. They got him to tell them his destination, which was this farm in rural Essex. Then he'd agreed to continue his journey there, as if nothing had happened.

Meanwhile Probert's team, with the NCA, were all over it. The truck was then allowed to proceed to its destination. When the stash had been unpacked by two staff members, Probert's team, with Special Ops in tow, had swooped and arrested them. But Evatt wasn't there.

When Special Ops stormed in, an encrypted phone was seized from one of the men working there. By a major stroke of luck, the screen was still unlocked, and the arresting officers could scroll back through the conversation on there. The phone had been passed to a young constable named Archer, from Probert's team. She'd been told to scroll back through the chat log to get as much information as she could.

She'd seen conversations with a person with the screen name *K2*, whom the police believed to be Jacob Evatt. She'd seen evidence that that person was heading up the operation and got a lot of detail. But the screen on the encro phone had timed out and locked. Both the staff members they'd arrested pretended not to know the passcode to reopen the encrypted device, and it's never been reopened since.

So, the only usable evidence trail to Evatt was in Constable Archer's head. But the police didn't think to step up security or protect her. She'd just continued work, as normal. And then one morning, she went missing. She hadn't shown up at the station for work.

The assumption was that one of Evatt's lot, or someone instructed by Evatt, had taken her from her apartment in the early hours. She'd never been seen again. Not even a body to bury. She'd just vanished, and they'd long since presumed her dead.

The police had tried and failed to penetrate Evatt's operation for years. They were getting more and more desperate to nail him.

'And then one night,' said Probert, 'Richard King happened.' He lifted his hands to the sky as if to say, *hallelujah*.

He took a deep breath and looked me in the eye. 'And then... Wilbur Cox happened.'

Suddenly, he held his finger to his lips. He turned to face the direction of the main door, even though he couldn't see it. Someone knocked on the door out there. Now this wasn't the cubicle, this was the outer door, the one that led to the main corridor. Probert rose and turned to open the cubicle door.

'Will?' called a familiar voice. 'Is everything okay?

I stared wide-eyed at Probert. It was Victoria. He looked back at me. He moved his hand away from the lock of the cubicle.

I froze. I opened my mouth to speak but wasn't sure what to say. Probert reached past me and spun the toilet roll holder a few times. Then he stood up straight and glared at me. It was like he was saying, 'Your move'.

For a moment I thought about shouting to her that Probert had followed me in there. But I couldn't bring myself to do it. It didn't make *sense* to do it. It didn't make sense not to do what he was asking me.

'Will?' she called again 'Are you in there?'

'Yes,' I called back, 'all good. I'll be out in a sec.'

I looked up and nodded at Probert, before barging past him, out of the cubicle.

Seventy-Seven

When I went home, it was rush hour in London. It felt incredible, being in the middle of all that noise and energy again. I breathed it all in. I took my time on the journey home, smiling and nodding at passers-by. I couldn't quite contain myself.

Getting home felt strange. I didn't feel like I wanted to be tucked away there any more. I'd spent months hiding in that place; now I wanted to get out into the world again. It felt like being in a weird vacuum, being back in that same kitchen, but with the weight lifted off me. It just didn't quite feel normal, yet.

But I still felt a stone lighter. My breathing was different; I felt like I was taking deeper breaths. It occurred to me that my jaw had been a tiny bit clenched, for months. My only ambition was to get back to *normality*, as soon as I could. If I never saw another police car – it would be too soon.

I wanted to tell Ellie first. I wanted to take her away somewhere and spend time, just me and her. She'd ridden this wave with me and kept me alive, and sane. I owed her some happiness now, and I finally planned on giving it to her.

The spectre of Solly was impotent. I wanted him to know that his video was now useless, and that he could go and fuck himself with it. I texted him.

'Can we meet?'

An hour later, he replied.

'PHOTOGRAPH READY?'

'I'll be round at eight' I replied.

I called Ellie; I was dying to tell her what had happened at the police station. I also wanted to thank her for how she'd stuck by me and not freaked out. I called her a couple of times. She didn't answer. I left a message saying I'd come and see her later. I then took the decision to go to Solly's first. I had this idea that I could settle things with him and be home in time for dinner with Ellie.

How wrong I was.

One thing I should have learned by that point was that when it came to Solly Green, nothing would ever be straightforward.

Seventy-Eight

I got to his flat at quarter past eight. The train was delayed. He sniffed at me as I entered his flat. 'You've been burning those frankincense sticks.'

I had literally no idea what he was talking about. Naturally, he still had this cocky air about him. He still thought he was in control of me. *Bursting his bubble is going to be satisfying as hell.* I stood at his living room window, facing out. He had a great view from up there.

'I've come to tell you something, my man,' I said smugly.

'Oh?' he replied casually.

'Yeah. You see, it's erm… it's over,' I said. 'It's all over, brother. I went to the police.' I turned around to see his reaction; he looked unmoved.

'Aren't you happy for me?' I said. 'I'm still here! I've told them, and I'm still here.' I had been hoping the opening statement would have more impact on him than that. He was playing it cool, the bastard. I wasn't going to let him spoil my moment. I walked over and took a seat in his armchair.

'Richard King died from a blow to the head… from Jacob Evatt,' I said. 'You didn't know that did you? He was already on his way out, when I hit him. He had this… bleeding on the

274

brain. Your video just shows me punching someone, but that's it. It wasn't *me* who killed him.'

He stared at me sadly for a moment, before wandering into his kitchen and pouring himself a glass of wine.

'Would you like a glass of Sauvignon Blanc, Will?" he asked.

'No.'

He lifted the glass to his lips and took a deep gulp. The glass was covered in oily finger marks. 'I told you Will, I deleted that video,' he said. He slammed the glass back on the countertop and burped into his hand.

'Yeah, sure you did,' I said. 'Well, now it doesn't matter if you deleted it or not, it's not useful to Evatt's defence team.' It suddenly occurred to me that Solly's armchair was probably the most germ-ridden thing I'd ever made contact with. I casually got up and stood by the window.

'In case you forgot,' he said, 'you asked me to delete it. You asked me to do that for you, so I did.'

I faked a laugh and shook my head. *Pathetic*. He'd enjoyed his moment of power, but now it was mine.

'You said what you were giving me was just a *gift*,' he said. 'A thank you.'

'Well, I seem to recall you sending an image to Jacob Evatt's lawyer, a few days ago,' I said.

'That wasn't from that video,' he said.

'What difference does it make?' I shot back. 'You tried to screw me over; you failed. Now you can just crawl back into your perverted little hovel up here, carry on living your weird little existence and stay the fuck out of mine.'

'This is exactly what I expected,' he said to himself, quietly. 'Ungrateful little turd.'

I turned around to look at him properly for the first time. He was wearing some sort of harem pants.

'What?' I said. He looked even more decrepit than usual now, it was like he'd physically shrunk a few inches.

'Do you really think I give a shit about giving you a gift?' I said. 'You're literally the worst person I've ever met. You tried to bully me into giving you all that shit, and you knew exactly what you were doing. You tried to ruin my life and you failed. So guess what? You can't any more. Fuck you.'

'Have you considered the impact you've had on other people's lives?' he asked. 'Do you think maybe you've ruined a few lives, by murdering an innocent man?'

'I just told you, I didn't kill him. They've examined his body or whatever. It wasn't me. What you saw on your video amounted to someone punching a... like a *dead body*.' My toes curled as I said that. That didn't sound so good spoken out loud.

'Disgusting, Will. I knew you'd try to screw me over,' he said. 'I knew this was coming.'

'Nobody is trying to do anything, Solly. I'm just telling you: your plan didn't work.'

He still looked calm, smug even. I'd expected him to fall to pieces when I revealed all this to him, but he was holding it together.

'You made a lot of false promises to me,' he continued. 'You told me you'd sort out that debt, you told me you'd pay me ten thousand, you told me you'd get me some nice pictures of that girl.'

I rolled my eyes.

'Nobody gives a fuck, do they?' he said. 'Do they? Why should you pay up to Solly? Why be grateful to Solly? Why bother? He's nothing.'

The pity party had commenced. I sat down in one of his plastic chairs. He sloped over to his smoking chair by the window.

He sat there in silence, puffing on his cigarette. 'Last year, I had a septic condition,' he said. 'Dirty blood, you know?'

I didn't know, but I let him continue.

'I got so fed up, I drank like a fish to try and take the edge off. Then eventually I went unconscious. Right there, where you're sitting.'

I looked down at the floor, half expecting to see an oily body stain or something.

He glared at me unmoving, 'Three days, I was there for. I kept waking up and dipping out again, waking up and dipping out again. When I finally got the strength together to get myself up, I was nearly finished. I went up to the sink there and drank all this water, then I called an ambulance. The woman doctor at the hospital told me she didn't know how I'd survived.'

'Sounds grim,' I said dismissively. It did actually sound pretty sad. But whatever. I took my phone out of my pocket to see if Ellie had got back to me. Nothing.

'Even the hospital didn't care. They just seemed cross with me, for taking up their time.'

'That's a very sad story,' I said sarcastically.

'Nobody really cares, do they? They care about their *own* thing. It's like what I told you about the Chinese. Nobody really cares about anyone else, when it comes down to it.'

'Sure,' I said, 'we're all just out to get each other, right?'

'Not *all*,' he corrected me. 'People look after their own. If it's their husband, or wife, or son or daughter, or even their "friend", they help each other.'

'Sounds like a pretty good system to me,' I said.

'Yeah I bet it does,' he said angrily, 'because you're inside it. You've got people looking out for you. What do I get?'

'You get the same as everyone else; you get the opportunity to be a good person and to live a good life,' I said, brushing imaginary dust off my knee.

'I get fuck all,' he snapped. 'Nobody gives you anything. They *make* you *take* it. If you don't *take it*, you don't get anything. It's a knife-fight in a phone box.'

'Okay, so there you go, you do have something,' I said. 'You have an extremely fucked up view of the world.' I got up to leave.

'That's all I *had*,' he said. 'That's all I had when I played by the rules.'

'Meaning?' I said.

'Meaning, things are different now. I have something.'

'I don't know what you mean,' I said, zipping up my jacket.

'For one thing, I have a girlfriend now,' he said with a faint smile.

'Okay, well, good luck with that,' I said. 'I'm going to go, Solly. Goodbye. This is the last time you'll see me, and it's the last time I'll see you.'

'Before you go, there's something we need to discuss,' he said quietly. 'I'm afraid you might be a bit cross with me.'

278

Seventy-Nine

I braced myself for another wave of inconsequential shit.

'Let me guess, you've met up with Ellie privately again, and given her a right good seeing to?' I said, with a mocking smirk. 'I've been meaning to ask her to stop doing that.'

He glared at me intently. I was enjoying the shoe being on the other foot.

'Everything that comes out of your mouth is garbage,' I said. 'You're a pathological liar.'

'That's a bit rich!' he laughed.

'Nothing I did was deliberate,' I said, slowly and calmly as I could. I could feel my adrenaline beginning to rise again. He just knew how to get under my skin.

'So the banker just walked into your fist and died?' he asked, stubbing his cigarette out. 'What a nice fairy story. Listen, I'm glad you came, I do need to talk to you. I need to own up about something.'

'Okay, but just don't bring my girlfriend into it,' I snapped. 'I've heard enough about her from you.'

'Right... but that's just it,' he said. 'I'm afraid I do have to tell you something about her.'

As much as I didn't take anything at face value from him any more, he looked so serious. I took a deep breath. I'd allow him one last mindless storytelling session.

'Right,' I said, 'go on then. What now?'

'I've been… let's just say I've had my *concerns* over her. Since that night, when she tricked me, I mean. I don't think of her as a person of integrity. You need that, Will. When you get to my age, you realise you need people with *integrity* around you.'

'Right, okay, I'll keep that in mind,' I said, 'people like you, you mean?'

He wasn't distracted by my snarky comments. He looked focused and serious. For the first time in ages, he was holding eye contact with me. His eyes weren't as darty and evasive as usual. He was talking slower and more purposefully.

'You're a good man, Will,' he said. 'You've been dealt a difficult hand in life, and she took advantage of you. Of your vulnerability. She's used that, to get close to you. Can't you see that?'

'Yes, I see it! Oh my god, you're right!' I said animatedly. I was ready to just sit and bat his rubbish away with sarcasm. It was over. He was back to being a nobody.

'You're an orphan aren't you?' he said. 'Not a real… orphan, in the old-fashioned way, but your parents didn't care about you, did they? You sort of raised yourself.'

I shot him a look. *How did he find out things like that?*

'Both my parents are alive so no, I'm definitely the opposite of an orphan. I was raised by a single parent, it's not unusual,' I said sharply. 'You are aware it's not still nineteen-thirty-two, right?'

'Yes, yes I *know* that,' he said, putting his hand over his chest. 'What I mean is, as a person who was raised in a stable home, by two parents who *both* loved him, I feel a bit of natural pity for you… I know it must be hard… to understand relationships. Especially women. You never had a woman in your life growing up, you're naïve to their ways,' he said.

'Are you going to teach me?' I smirked.

'No, I'm not going to try and teach you anything,' he said, 'because you're too arrogant to learn. But what I *could* do for you, is help *her* to understand how to be more of a decent partner.'

'What does that mean?' I said.

'It means, I think now she understands how to be a proper girlfriend,' he said. 'I showed her.'

281

Eighty

Something wasn't right. By this point I'd come to know Solly's characteristics and mannerisms quite well. He wasn't behaving like he usually did. Normally he was like a dog, desperately waiting for a ball to be thrown; there was this jumpiness to him, like he found it hard to keep his enthusiasm in.

But this time, he wasn't like that. He looked calmer, more assured. I didn't like it. I needed to stop him talking about Ellie. While I knew it would all be lies, he just knew how to get into my mind and mess with the way I felt anyway.

'I went to visit her in Battersea last night,' he said, 'because I was upset and sad.'

This vicious chill shot through me. It would never stop surprising me, that talent he had for spying on people and gathering information. But, so *what* if he knew where she lived?

'You see, I've been keeping an eye on you. For your own safety. I knew you went to a solicitor, and I anticipated you'd be handing yourself in. Now Will, I thought that was a bad decision on your part, and I expected you'd be going away. Which means your life would have changed; *her* life would've changed. And I did *not* think she was ready for it.'

'You don't need to worry about my relationship,' I said. This weird feeling was beginning to set in. Spreading out from my stomach, all over my body. I'd had enough of him.

'I decided to do my part for you. She once suggested that I meet her for drinks, and to have a chat, so that's what I went to do. I took a nice bottle of wine.'

'Okay and what did her three housemates think of you?' I said mockingly.

'A concert,' he said, 'they were at a music concert.'

'Oh, how convenient,' I said.

'You don't believe me,' he said. 'Go on Facebook. The girl who got all the tickets was called Laura Cavanagh, she's one of the house mates. She got the tickets two weeks ago and she posted on Facebook that they were all going.'

Ellie did have a housemate called Laura Cavanagh. And she had said something about a week before about them going to a Harry Styles gig. But as he'd said, all of that information was readily available on Facebook. I could only assume he was once again, taking pinches of truth and conjuring up wild stories from them.

'Listen, Solly,' I said irritably, 'how many times have you made shit like this up? How much more of my time do you really want to waste?'

He just gazed at me coldly.

I took my phone out of my pocket and called Ellie's number.
Still no answer.

Eighty-One

I stormed out of his living room and ripped open the front door. My chest was wound into a tight ball, my vision had gone sharper. Something was up.

I turned to him on the way out and said, 'You do realise, if you've actually gone round there to her house when she was alone, I'll come back here and kill you? And I really fucking mean it.'

His eyes opened wide. 'You would? Well, I suppose then I should be honoured. I'm in the presence of an *actual* serial killer. *Wilbur Cox, the Farringdon Ripper!*'

'*Fuck* you,' I snarled, slamming his front door.

I tore off down the corridor. I guessed I could get to Battersea in a taxi in about twenty minutes, if traffic was light. I pressed the Call button on the lifts and waited. I pulled my phone out of my pocket and tried calling her again.

It rang and rang. I thought she wasn't going to answer again. But just as I was about to hang up, the ringing stopped. *She's answered it, thank god.*

Silence on the line.

'Ellie?' I said nervously, 'are you there? Can you hear me?' I heard her take a deep breath. *Was she crying?*

'Ellie, talk to me,' I said. 'What's happened?' I could hear her sniffing and staccato breathing softly in the background.

'*Ellie!*' I shouted.

She hung up.

The lift arrived, the doors opening in front of me with a *ding*. My stomach had dropped to the floor. *What had he done?* I turned and walked back up the corridor. I didn't know what I was doing, my body had gone into auto pilot. I had to try and shake it out of him.

When I turned the corner to face his apartment, there he was. In the doorway with his hands on his hips.

'Come back Will, you silly boy. We haven't finished talking,' he said.

I felt my legs start driving faster towards him. I was fully running.

He closed the door just as I reached it. I banged on it hard with my fist and booted the bottom of it, hard as I could.

'Open it!' I yelled. 'What have you done?'

'Will, you're overreacting,' he called from behind the door. 'She's safe and well. But if you want to come in, I'll need you to calm down.'

I needed to know what was happening.

'Let me in,' I said. 'I'm not going to fucking touch you, let me in.'

I forced the rage and violence down into the pit of my stomach. I had to make him talk. I had to get it out of him.

Eighty-Two

He sat by the window and rolled himself another cigarette. I stood by living room door. I physically could not sit down. I could feel my teeth grinding together.

'She's safe,' he said. 'I wanted to help her understand what it means to be a girlfriend.'

'I don't know what that means,' I shot back.

'Respect. Obedience. Discipline,' he replied.

I stared at him. 'Are you going to start telling me what you're talking about?' I was trying to sound authoritative, but my voice had gone weak.

'I got there late evening,' he said. 'It's a nice place, old, converted town house. I suppose you've been there, haven't you?'

I didn't flinch; just stared at him.

'Anyway, she was in the living room wearing not very much at all, watching television. I could see her from the street. I knocked on the front door. She took so long to come and answer it, I lost my nerve. Ended up ducking down the side of the house when she came out. I was nervous.'

I tried to remember if Ellie's house had a side passage. I was pretty sure it didn't. It was attached to other houses, on both sides.

'Why is she crying?' I said, as calmly as I could. My legs felt like lead, all of a sudden. He motioned for me to sit. I dragged a plastic chair over to him and sat down. I couldn't show him that he was getting under my skin, that would make him worse. I needed to pretend I was calm again.

'What, now?' he said. 'She's crying *now*? Did you speak to her?'

'Yes I did. She was crying.'

'And it was definitely *crying*?' he said. 'She wasn't, I dunno, *laughing* at something?'

My hands tightened around the lip of my plastic chair. I was trying not to clench my jaw. He'd notice that.

'She was so full of malice, from the beginning,' he continued. I didn't respond.

'She's a piece of work, you've got there,' he said, wagging his finger at me playfully. 'When I went round the back, the back door was open, so I let myself in. I opened my bottle of wine, an expensive fucking bottle, twenty-five quid bottle, and I poured us two glasses. They've got these huge wine glasses, like deep bowls. Fantastic, I'm going to buy some of those.'

I watched the excitement grow in him. He was a shit merchant: at his happiest when he was parading a big ball of dung around.

'Any questions so far?' he asked, with a raised eyebrow.

'No questions,' I replied quietly. 'Carry on.'

'I took those through to her in the living room. I thought we could just relax and watch some television together, before I spoke to her seriously, I mean. But she was extraordinarily surly when I surprised her: *a bitch*! And remember, it was her idea to have a drink together!'

He got up and scurried into the kitchen to pour himself another glass of wine. 'She screamed at me and told me to get out. I'm just standing there like a wally with these two wine glasses.'

I watched him carefully as he spoke. I knew not to take anything at face value. Without doubt, he'd be taking a bit of truth and bending it to seem more dramatic: his trademark. It was another one of his bizarre wind-ups.

'Can I ask a question,' I said. 'Was the television new? Had it just been delivered? Because they don't have a TV in their living room, you div.'

'Laptop then! Whatever!' he said.

'Oh, so the TV has now shrunk to a laptop,' I snapped.

'A laptop on the coffee table I think, yeah that's what it was, not a TV,' he said, holding his finger in the air as if he was correcting a line for the court record.

'You really are a fucking buffoon,' I said. 'There's no alleyway down the side of her house, for a start.'

'There is!' he shouted, 'there fucking well *is*!'

'Go on,' I said. 'Finish your story.'

'I was trying to, *thank you*,' he said irritably. 'I actually don't have all night to talk about this!'

'Then she pushed past me and covered my merino wool jumper in wine, look!' He pointed at a jumper that was laid out over one of his disgusting little radiators. It was beige, but it had a big, splattered stain down it, a South America sort of shape.

'This is so boring,' I said. I wanted him to tell me why Ellie was crying and not speaking to me. What he'd *actually* done.

'Then she got upset, started calling me every name under the sun and pushed me against the wall. She *knows* I'm a frail man with a bad back and upset guts, she's still pushing me around like a rag doll.'

'Ellie? This is five-foot-three, eight-stone-wet-through, Ellie?' I said. 'She started flinging you about, did she?'

'Yes, she fucking well did!' he said.

One thing he'd said had been bothering me. I couldn't stop

thinking about it. The thing about the wine glasses. Ellie *did* have massive wine glasses in her kitchen. They were novelty ones, each of them held a full bottle. They did look like big, deep bowls.

That was nothing he couldn't have known from just snooping around her house, though. He could've known that by looking in her kitchen window. But he *couldn't* have looked in her kitchen window, because there's no access to the back, from the street. I was pretty sure about that. Like, 99 per cent certain.

Eighty-Three

I knew he was talking shit, but that one part about the glasses was confusing me. I let him continue. I needed him to get to the point. The nugget of truth that he was spinning all these lies around.

'I explained to her that that's exactly why I'd come by. To talk to her about being a lady and behaving in a way that's appropriate as a girlfriend. I pointed at my jumper and told her that was *exactly* the kind of thing I was here to talk to her about. And do you know what she did? She laughed at me.'

I snorted. He looked me up and down angrily.

'So I told her if she didn't start dealing with me in a more pleasant manner, I should become cross. And we'd skip all the niceties and go on to the important matters.'

I felt my fists clench. It was so obvious what he was going to try to say. He was more maggot than person. I mustn't react. I definitely must not hit him. *Stay fucking calm, Will. Stay in control.*

'And then she threatened me. She picked up this thing, like a… what do you call it, a… like a slider… for opening envelopes…'

'A letter opener?' I said. 'A Victorian letter opener, is that what she just grabbed? You moron.'

'Stop calling me names!' he hissed at me. He had this bizarre way of going from passive and calm to really angry, in a split second.

He was a weak liar. His story was so lame and ill-conceived. He'd struck gold with those wine glasses; I don't know how he got that, but the rest of it was pure nonsense. The TV in the living room, the passageway down the side of the house, the fucking letter opener in the hallway, like he's in some mental live action game of Cluedo.

I pulled my phone out and tried Ellie's number again. This time she didn't answer at all. She was screening my calls. *Why?* My mouth had gone dry. I put my phone back into my pocket and snarled at him.

'What the fuck did you do, you rat? Get on with it.'

'If you call me any more names, I won't say another word,' he said. 'I mean it.'

I sighed and gritted my teeth. I couldn't look at him any more. I looked down at the floor.

'Go on then.'

'She starts waving that thing around, like a sword. And I'm trying to calm her down. She's still calling me *F*s and *C*s and every name under the sun, telling me to get out of her house.' He shook his head and looked at me sadly. 'She was vile, Will, she was the farthest thing from ladylike.'

'So, then what happened?' I asked in a low voice. I accidentally caught his eye again. He had this dumb expression of pain and sorrow.

'Well, she's ended up poking it up against my neck, trying to force me out; and I'm just trying to calm her down, telling her she's being over-emotional,' he said.

He paused and sighed deeply. 'Women can become over-emotional, it's… well I couldn't take any more of it,' he said. 'She was being so nasty and disgusting, the things she was saying to me. So I gently restrained her on the stairs and held her mouth shut for a little bit, to give her time to calm down and think. But she *would not* calm down. So I told her it was a good opportunity for our first lesson.'

'You're so embarrassing,' I said quietly, avoiding his gaze.

'And then she squealed like this really awful, scream, from right down in the guts,' he interjected. He was staring into my eyes. He leant towards me and whispered, 'Primal fear.'

I closed my eyes and sighed. 'This is the most cringeworthy shit you've ever made up, and that's saying something,' I said, getting up to leave. 'I'm done.' It was a dumb fucking bluff, from the archdeacon of dumb fucking bluffs. *Fuck him.*

Then he said, 'She wears these little hot pants to bed, doesn't she? Little cotton things. Sky blue, they were.'

How did he know that? He'd just been spying on her at night, I guessed. Through the windows. He's clearly just been spying on her, right? I could feel my blood turning into lava. I knew he could see it in me now, I'd be bright red. There was no point trying to hide what I was feeling. He always found a way to tease it out.

'Will, I told her very gently that I had to show her how to be a proper woman,' he said, 'for *you*, for the tough years ahead! And then I...' He trailed off and moved his hand to his chin, leaning towards me to try and place his other filthy hand on my knee. I recoiled. He sighed and stood up, sticking his head out of the window onto the balcony.

'Need to cool down,' he said. 'Will you fetch me my wine?'

My entire body was shaking. I knew he could see that my hands were shaking. I ripped my phone out and called Ellie again.

'Is she at home?' I said. My voice was obviously shaking and weak, I couldn't override it.

'I don't know where she is, Will!' he blurted with a grin. 'I'm not the woman's keeper! You need to relax. If you smother her, she'll go looking for other men. Calmer men.'

It felt like my body was ready to leap at him, all by itself. Without my mind's permission, if necessary. I hadn't felt anger like it before.

That night with Richard King, he'd made me angry, but it was nothing like this. Solly knew what he was doing. I knew what he was doing, but I couldn't stop it. He was trying to tempt me to hit him. I guessed he was trying to make me attack him, so he had more collateral, more power.

That thought gave me pause for a moment. I took a long, deep breath. What *was* his long game? To force me to hand more money over to him, more personal stuff? To try to take more control of me. It was like he'd planned it all out, this staged takedown.

But the more I thought about it, the attack on Ellie didn't make sense. It'd be a hugely destructive thing to do, for someone so calculating. He'd be locked up, immediately. For all his madness, Solly seemed smarter than that. He was a shadow-creeper, not someone who'd risk prison. He was lying.

I needed time to think. 'Solly, where's your bathroom again?'

Eighty-Four

He guided me down the hall to a bathroom that looked straight out of the 1960s. It was carpeted, for a start, which is disgusting. This dense, fluffy, peach coloured carpet with occasional discoloured areas. In the corner there was a stained bathtub with a tiny, dried out bar of soap propped at one end. All the taps were dense with limescale and every corner was thick with mould.

I put my sleeve over my hand and slid the lock closed.

'If you do a big shit you might have to flush twice,' he called through the door.

I ignored him.

'Did you hear me?' he called again.

'Right,' I called back irritably. The fucking toilet had an actual bit of that rank carpet fitted over the top of it. I couldn't bring myself to sit on that.

I perched on the side of the bath. I had to make contact with Ellie somehow. I opened Facebook on my phone. It was something I didn't do often. I guessed I'd probably have a wave of notifications on there. The first thing I saw was a message from Ellie. Four messages from Ellie. Heart racing, I opened the chat.

A straight shot of pure relief flushed right through me. She'd lost her phone. But she seemed okay; she seemed fine. She had just been worried about me, and what was happening with the police.

Pure relief.

She'd been burgled. Someone had broken into her house while she was in the shower the night before and stolen a few random items, including her phone. I looked up from my phone and smirked grimly at the door. *He's done me again.* That had been him, when I'd called. In my panic, he'd managed to convince me it was her, crying.

She'd been trying to get hold of me on Facebook, Instagram, even LinkedIn. She didn't have my phone number, since it was stored in her mobile. She'd sent a temporary number for me to contact her on. I quickly composed a text message to her, letting her know I was at Solly's apartment, and that it was Solly who had burgled her. I'd had enough; I decided to confront him straight away.

When I opened the toilet door, I saw he'd retreated to his smoking spot by the window. The door to the living room was ajar and I could just about see him through the gap. He was lighting a cigarette, with his feet propped up on the windowsill. To my left was his bedroom. I wondered if he had Ellie's phone in there. I fantasised about marching back in and presenting it to him.

I pushed the bedroom door open and scanned the room. Just his dusty computer, wardrobe and ancient-looking double bed and bedside drawer. The bed, wardrobe and bedside drawers were connected, a creepy little unit he or some other madman had purpose built for the apartment. I quickly shuffled through the drawers. The top one had just lots of papers and assorted junk. The bottom one had a multipack of Walkers crisps in it. *He'll have been sucking on those in bed.*

I quickly peered into the wardrobe. Some bizarre get-ups in there, stuff I really wouldn't have expected. One jumper with all this fake bling sewn into it. Like what a teenage hip-hop fan would wear. Plenty of autumnal browns and beiges. But no sign of any phone. *He'll be getting to the end of that cigarette now.*

I gave up on the search. What did it really matter, anyway? On my way out, I ducked down and made a cursory glance under the bed. I cringed at how much dust and hair and other shit was accumulated under there; it was dense. I rose to my feet too quickly and had a head-rush. I reached out to steady myself on the door frame.

Wait a second. Back there, among all the shit under his bed, I'd seen something I'd recognised.

Eighty-Five

I remember this business guru in a talk once, saying the two most important things to invest well in are a good bed and a good car. I think basically his point was, having good sleep and reliable transport are important comforts in life. One of Ellie's important comforts was having cool underwear, and I think it was similar logic, for her. She'd spend a fortune on underwear, she said it made her feel good.

Anyway, she had these sort of neon sets. There was a neon pink and a neon yellow. I remember them because she had them delivered from ASOS one morning when I was there, and she'd shown them to me. They were made of this soft fabric that was pretty cool, it just looked impossibly bright. Proper illuminous type of colour.

When I'd ducked down and looked under his bed, I'd caught a glimpse of this luminous pink mound of fabric. It looked *just like* that colour.

I edged back into the hallway and peered through the gap in the door. He was still slumped in that position, fresh smoke rising from him. He was singing to himself. I couldn't work out what it was, but he was singing something. Something about a sombrero.

I darted back into his bedroom and dived under the bed. There wasn't much space under there; I had to really squeeze to fit under. I shoved myself back to the corner and grabbed the neon thing. I pulled my phone out of my pocket for some light. And there it was. It was Ellie's bra.

One of the cups was hanging out of the side of this old suitcase. I craned my head to try and look out into the hallway. I would give myself another ten seconds, then I was out. I unzipped the suitcase halfway around and prized it open, shoving my phone up to the gap. He'd taken the full set of pink under-wear. This is what he must have decided to steal, when he'd burgled her.

I grimaced and shoved the underwear to one side to see what else was in there. A wine glass. It was one of the big glasses from Ellie's kitchen. It still smelled of wine and it had stains from her lip gloss on the rim. I craned my neck to peer back into the corridor. *He was too quiet.*

I quickly shoved my hand further into the suitcase, where I hit something hard and sharp. *A knife?* I ran my hand down the side of it; it wasn't a knife. It was a metal box of some kind. I felt underneath it. Another one. And another. *Hard drives.*

I guessed there were about eight or nine of them in total. Then there were these bags, like vacuum-seal bags. I couldn't see what was in them, it was fabric of some kind. I heard a noise from the living room. It sounded like the living-room door had moved.

I edged myself out from under the bed. I was watching the hallway through the gap, the entire time. Then I felt the tickle in my nose. That unstoppable fucking tingle. I frantically con-torted my face to try and stop the urge. All that rank dust had overwhelmed my nose, it had had enough.

At the last moment I grabbed my nose with my hand and pinched it. *Phutffff!* Jesus fucking Christ. I pulled myself fully out from under that bed. Another one was coming, for fuck's sake. I bolted for the doorway of his bedroom, savagely clawing and grabbing at my nose to *fucking* shut up.

Phtfjjshh! Jesus Christ. I pulled the bedroom door back to how it had been before, whacking dust off the front of my clothes and peered down the corridor into the living room.

I couldn't see him.

He'd gone from his spot by the window.

Eighty-Six

I stopped for a moment to think. I admit, freezing is probably my standard response. The experts say, when something bad is about to happen, it's fight, or flight, or freeze. The time I'd decided to fight, it hadn't gone so well. So there I was, reverting to safe mode, paralysed in my thoughts.

I crept down the hallway, still peering through the gap in the door. I swallowed hard and steeled myself as I gently pushed the door open with my hand. He was standing there, staring straight at me. He eyed me for a moment, expressionless.

'What are you staring at?' I mumbled eventually, bustling past him. He just kept staring. I went into the kitchen and drank some water, straight from the tap.

'Would you like a glass, Mowgli?' he asked.

'No,' I said gruffly.

I felt my phone vibrate in my pocket. Ellie had replied from her new number, asking for his address. I had to force myself not to smile when I saw it was her. I knew he was lying of course, but I was still worried about what he'd actually done to her. It was such a relief to know she was safe.

Solly poked his finger into his ear and waggled it aggressively, before pulling the finger out and inspecting it. I sensed he was

deep in thought. I replied to Ellie, telling her I'd found a suitcase under his bed. I told her it had hard drives in it, and 'some
of her stuff'. For some reason I couldn't bring myself to tell
her what *stuff*, over text.

She replied straight away. She just said:

'That's where it's going to be, Will.'

My thoughts exactly.

'Who are you texting?' he called over. He was still standing
in the same spot, facing the living-room door. Still deep in
thought.

'Mind your own business,' I said, staring at the screen, waiting
for her to respond. She was typing.

'Why'd you take so long? Did you shit?' he said eventually.

'Erm… yeah,' I said, still gazing at my screen.

'Did you flush it twice then?'

'Yeap.'

'You didn't even flush it once, you dirty bastard! It makes a
racket,' he said, as he stormed off towards the bathroom.

I heard him open the toilet seat. There was a pause, then he
closed the lid again. He returned, shaking his head.

Ellie replied. **'Take the bag. Make sure you bring it with you.'**

I thought about it for a moment. It was too big to move
without him noticing. That suitcase was about the size of a
40-inch TV, and the hard drives would make it heavy.

Then Solly appeared in the doorway and said, 'Oi, did you
go in my bedroom?'

Eighty-Seven

I shoved the phone back into my pocket. 'No,' I said, looking him dead in the eye.

'You did, you liar,' he said. 'What were you looking for?'

'I just had a look in there,' I said eventually, 'on my way back from the bathroom. I didn't know you were so precious about it, Jesus.'

He eyed me suspiciously. 'How would you like it if I went poking about in *your* bedroom?' he said eventually. *Oh, the irony.*

'I didn't poke about,' I said. 'I just saw the door was open on my way back from the bathroom, and I had a quick look in.'

'Why?' he demanded. He folded his arms like a spoilt kid.

'I was just intrigued, I s'pose,' I said. I have to stress – this questioning wasn't making me particularly nervous. I didn't find him in the least bit physically threatening. It was actually refreshing to see him reduced to seriousness. The shock of feeling suddenly exposed was finally forcing some sincerity out of him.

'Right, well next time you're curious, let me know, I'll give you the tour. Don't need to go sneaking about. And you don't use my bathroom any more, it's out of bounds for you.'

Ellie had got my mind whirring. That suitcase was his haul.

It was his treasure chest. That was why his computer had nothing of interest on it; he stored it all on those hard drives, which he kept under his bed. She was right; the video of me would be in there.

It felt like I had to move for it now. If I went away and came back, he'd have time to think more about my having been in his room. He might tag on, re-home his treasure to somewhere safer, and then this chance would be gone. I'd have to find a way to get it out of there. Preferably without him knowing.

How do you secretly move a 20 kg suitcase out from under a bed and across a hallway, without somebody in the next room noticing? I absent-mindedly checked my phone again. I made a mental note to stop looking at it so much, or I'd make Solly more suspicious. Ellie had replied saying:

'I'm on my way. Will msg you when I arrive.'

Eighty-Eight

Solly slid over and took a seat in his armchair. He regarded me carefully for a moment before asking, 'Are you okay, Will?'

I let out a deep sigh.

'Are you in a panic about what I told you? I'm sorry,' he muttered. 'It's a lot to take in. But please understand, I'm on your side, I'm trying to *help* you.'

I needed to think. I needed to stop allowing myself to be distracted by his nonsense, so I could figure out a way to get that suitcase out.

'You know one thing top poker players know, that nobody else does?' he said. He looked like he'd recovered a bit of his confidence, from before. It'd freaked him out that I'd been in his bedroom, I could tell that had knocked him.

'The best poker players know, there's no such thing as *control*,' he said smugly, raising his eyebrows and drumming his fingers on the armrests of the chair. 'I'm used to jumped up little wallies like you, coming in all guns blazing. Because I see a few moves ahead.' He staggered over to his kitchen and produced a deck of cards from the cutlery drawer. While he was there, he poured himself another glass of wine and downed it in one.

'It's called *bragging*,' he continued. 'It's when an inexperienced player comes in thinking they're holding a certain win and starts throwing all their intentions out there, for everyone else to see.'

'I have no idea what you are talking about,' I said.

'You! Coming in here today, like a fucking dog on heat! Telling me "it's over now Solly", and marching about my place like a little Sergeant Major! It's funny to me.' He giggled and poured the last of the bottle into his glass.

'Let me tell you a story about the Chinese, from back in the day,' he started.

'Why are you so obsessed with the Chinese?'

'No, no, sit down, let me tell you this, it's a fun one. So this English explorer goes to visit China and every morning at nine o'clock he'd see this guy go into the town square wearing a red hat, and then he'd wave it really aggressively, like this, for about five minutes.' He waved his right arm violently left and right. He had a huge grin on his face again.

'So then one day the explorer asks somebody, "Why does that guy go and wave his hat like that every morning?" and they tell him, "Oh, that's to keep the dragons away. Someone has been waving a red hat like that for over a hundred years and we haven't had a dragon in all that time."' He looked at me as if he was hoping I'd burst out laughing.

'Cool,' I said.

'No, no, you're not understanding it,' he said. 'It's the illusion of control. People like the thought of control. It becomes hard to differentiate real control from the illusion; people prefer to kid themselves.'

'Meaning?'

'Meaning that's *you*. You're the berk waving his hat! You think if you wave it hard enough, you've got control, don't you? But while you're waving your hat, I'm taking your house! Because what you're holding, is a bastard flush!' he grinned, shuffling the cards.

'No, I think I've got control back because the police don't want to charge me,' I said.

He finished shuffling the cards and placed the deck gently down on the table between us.

'Will, Will, Will… Who cares?' he said softly. 'Look around you. Some bent coppers don't want to charge you for what you did, because you're middle class and white? How will that go down with the red-tops?'

'*What?*'

'They've let you off, wrongly. Mistake. So, when the video comes out, you think the media will hold back?' He made the sound of an incorrect game show buzzer.

I glared at him.

'When the video comes out?'

He grinned and rubbed his chin.

'So you haven't destroyed it at all, have you?'

He rolled his eyes at my apparent naivety.

'Here's what happens next. The police get fired for being bent and you get what's coming to you. It's no different, to me.'

Eighty-Nine

Solly's new idea was to take his video to the media. 'The red tops', he kept saying. Again, I wasn't sure he knew what year he was living in. He was unbelievably resilient, I had to give him that. Every time you thought you'd stamped him out, he'd regroup and come back with a new angle.

It seemed to be about the chase, for him. The chase seemed to fascinate and motivate him. He got off on the feeling of control and the feeling of *trespassing*; he just loved having his fingers in my dinner.

It didn't seem to be about the physical rewards, for him. He didn't even seem clear on what he *wanted*. One minute he needed money, then he didn't care about money, then it became about Ellie… It was like this didn't really have an end, for him; like he was somehow doing it for sport.

There were levels to his fascination with Ellie, that was for sure. He seemed to have such violent swings in attitude towards her. And there was something monstrously sexual underpinning it all, of course. Why he had locked on to her like that, I had no idea.

I wondered what would really happen if he took his video to the *Sun*, or something like that. They'd be interested, no doubt, but would it make a difference? The case against Evatt was pretty iron-clad. They had physical evidence, a *confession*.

But the video Solly had of me was clearer than that, if you didn't have a vested interest. It clearly happened *after* King's altercation with Evatt. You didn't have to be a forensic expert to realise that. Solly could let the world know that the last blow hadn't come from Jacob Evatt, it had come from Wilbur Cox. It would surely put enormous pressure on the justice system to punish me. The more I thought about it, the more I thought it could still be the undoing of everything.

Still, I retained the veneer of calm. I knew how important that was. I smiled politely and sat down facing him. 'Okay, well if you're going to do that, I don't think I can stop you,' I said.

'You'll go down like hot Cinnabons in prison,' he snorted, taking a long sip from his wine. He set his glass down on the floor and stood up. 'Now if you'll excuse me, I shall need to go and *break the seal*.' He ambled off to the bathroom, scratching at an angry-looking shaving wound on his neck.

That was just what I needed. A minute of distraction. I could just run in there and grab the suitcase, while he was in the bathroom. I tiptoed to the door of the living room and peered across the corridor. He'd left the fucking bathroom door open.

I could hear him loudly pissing against the side of the toilet. I tried to quickly calculate how long it would take me to nip into his bedroom, wrench that thing out from under the bed and leg it down the corridor. About twenty seconds, I guessed. Not enough time. I heard the toilet flush. I'd missed it. I scurried into the living room and sat down.

I'd need to distract him until Ellie got there, then I'd make my move. I messaged Ellie, telling her to come up to his apartment, and to message me when she was there. I told her I was going to bring the suitcase out the next time he went to the toilet and leave it outside the front door for her to make away with. She'd have to make off with it in a cab, while I continued distracting him.

I sensed the wine was going to be important. That was how I'd keep him going to the bathroom. I shoved my phone back into my pocket as he re-appeared.

'So, she's managed to get in touch with you then,' he said.

Ninety

He caught me unexpectedly with that question. I sat in silence for a moment, wondering whether or not to continue the act. I decided to ditch it.

'I know you didn't do it, what you've been saying. You went to her house, but you didn't see her.'

'Is that what she told you?' he smirked. 'Fine, okay.'

'You just took her phone, didn't you?' I said, standing up to face him. 'Where is it, Solly?'

He smiled and shrugged. 'You're such an easy target, so quick to anger!'

I considered how I could keep him talking. I guessed Ellie must be around five to ten minutes away, at that point.

'I will have some of that wine,' I said quietly.

He laughed loudly. 'Oh dear! I think the penny's just dropped!' he said. Solly would regularly say things that didn't make much sense to me. He scuttled into his kitchen and pulled another bottle of white wine from the fridge, twisting off the screw top and pouring out two large glasses.

'Here, drink!' he said, handing me a glass.

As I raised the glass to my lips, he smirked. 'Cheers,' he said coldly. 'To fame and fortune! I suspect you're going to be *very* famous by this time next week!'

I took a drink from the glass and sat back down. He perched in his armchair.

'I don't think you really want anything,' I said quietly. *Keep him talking. Keep him gloating.* He smiled and took a sip from his wine. 'What I want,' he said, 'money can't buy.'

'Yeah, I know. But before that it was money, wasn't it? It's like you're constantly trying to think of new things you can harass me with. But why? What's the point of it all, Solly?'

He took a long sip of his wine and sighed. 'Can I help you, Will?' he asked eventually.

'What?'

'I mean, what are you still *doing* here? Your girlfriend is back in touch, you'd better go and spend some time with her, before you go inside.' He winked and me and picked up the deck of cards again, gently shuffling them.

I needed to keep him talking longer. I needed to get him going. I had an idea.

'Sure,' I said. 'I'll go.' I got up and headed for the front door.

He remained in his armchair, crossing his legs and shuffling into that wretched leather. Calmly, he fished his mobile phone out of his top pocket.

'Run along, boy,' he said. 'I have some calls to make.'

Ninety-One

I opened his front door and looked down the corridor. Not a sound. I theatrically turned back to face Solly in his living room, still holding the front door open.

'Hey, Solly,' I said. 'What if I said I can get you want you want?'

He didn't reply.

'Solly?' I craned my neck to see through into his living room. He was still in his chair, staring ahead into space. Carefully, with the one hand, I held the latch open and manoeuvred the deadlock button upwards, so the door wouldn't automatically lock when it closed. He didn't notice.

'Well... I'd say I need it today; I'd need it *now*, in fact,' he said, 'right now.'

'And then what?' I said, pushing the front door closed.

I walked up to the living-room door and stood with my right arm concealed behind the door frame.

'I need some time,' I said. 'She'll need to go home and erm... I'll need to explain to her what...' As I mumbled, I crafted a message to Ellie: '**Door open. Be quiet. +About to call u. ignore it.**' I shoved the phone back into my pocket.

'She can have fifteen minutes,' he said.

I feigned a laugh of exasperation. 'Fifteen! That isn't enough time, to—'

'In fifteen minutes, I call the red tops, how about that?' he said, reaching to pull his bag of tobacco out of his pocket. There was no way he had any contacts at the 'red tops', of course. It was just another thing to toy with me about. I'd worked him out by that point; I could see right through him. He was a one-trick pony.

I called Ellie. As the phone rang, he excitedly asked me to put it on loudspeaker. He came over and kneeled next to me, watching it ring. I could see big shards of dandruff on his shoulder, threatening to leap off at me.

'This is a very dangerous game you're playing Will, if this is a wind-up,' he muttered. His breath was so acidic and stale. Days of alcohol and tobacco and gross food. I prayed that Ellie had seen my message. She'd need the context for this.

'Hello?' she answered gingerly. I paused and took a deep breath.

'Ellie I'm... I need you to do something for me and it's important,' I said.

'Okay...' she said.

'I need you to... basically, Solly's g— I'm here with Solly and he's asked... he's saying he's going to call the media about... my video... the video.'

'Okay,' she said calmly. Relief. She knew what this was about. She'd got the memo.

'I need you to send a topless photograph to Solly in the next fifteen minutes,' I blurted out, all at once. Solly shook his head and nudged me,

'Nude. Fully nude,' he whispered. He put his hand on his chin and nodded at me after he'd said it; as if we were haggling over an art piece.

'Erm...' I cleared my throat. 'Sorry it, erm... it actually needs to be nude.'

'Fully nude. And smiling. The face showing, smiling,' he hissed.

'Fully nude,' I repeated grimly, 'and... smiling.' I raised the inflection in my voice when I said 'smiling', as if it was a question. This pretend exchange was making me sweat, for some reason.

'O...kay,' said Ellie. 'And... I'm not at home though, I'll need more than fifteen minutes.'

I kept glancing at Solly. I sensed he was going to clock on, any minute. But he didn't. He looked really focused and serious.

'Half an hour,' he said eventually. 'Direct to my mobile phone.' He reached over me and ended the call. 'Now that wasn't too difficult, was it? Half an hour.'

He looked up at the clock on the wall and nodded.

Ninety-Two

Solly stood by the window smoking, while I stared at my phone. I was worried about how long she was taking. I wondered if she'd been held up, somehow. I started thinking about contingency plans. Whether I could just steal the suitcase and fight him off if he tried to stop me. I decided it was a bad idea; he was too unpredictable.

After an eternal wait, the screen lit up. She'd got in and she was already outside, at the front door of his apartment. I instinctively looked up at him and he snapped into life.

'Is that her?'

'No,' I said, shoving my phone away.

'What's she said? Let me see,' he said with a grin. He was this horrendous ball of excitement. I just had to keep him here, excited and distracted, while Ellie got that thing out of there. About ten minutes, that's all I'd need to keep him for. Fifteen, to make sure she got away completely.

'You can be as secretive as you like, my friend,' he said eventually. He pointed up at the clock.

'I'm worried,' I said. 'Of course I am.'

'She'll come through for you,' he said, 'she knows what she's doing.' He reclined in his armchair and closed his eyes.

I strained my ears to try to hear her. I couldn't hear anything. She must be in the bedroom by now. I didn't crack, I didn't turn to face the door once. My job was to keep Solly here.

I nodded down at his deck of cards. 'So, you're a poker champion?'

He opened his eyes and looked down at the cards, then laughed modestly. 'I have won a few tournaments, yes. Make plenty of money from it...' He wafted his hand around his rank apartment, I assume to demonstrate wealth.

'What do you play?' I said.

'I play whatever,' he replied.

'Texas Hold 'em?' I said, shuffling the cards.

He nodded with a wry smile and watched me shuffling the deck. It was like the expression of a proud dad watching his son try to shuffle cards for the first time.

'Excuse me,' he said as I started to deal, 'what do you think you're doing?'

'Let's have a game,' I said.

'I don't play for free,' he laughed.

Keep him talking. 'So, what will you play for?' I said.

He looked me up and down with a faint smile on his lips. He was trying to think of something clever to say.

'Hold that thought,' he said, jumping up from his seat. 'I need a Jimmy Riddle.'

Oh shit. 'No, wait!' I said. 'Come on! Let's have one round! Let's see your legendary skills.'

I could see into the hallway behind him. She'd come in and left the front door slightly ajar; I could see light from the hallway spraying in through the crack. He'd notice that. Then he'd notice that the deadbolt was on.

He smirked and flourished his hand, as if to instruct me to deal. I quickly dealt us two cards each, face-down. I spread five more out on the table. He picked up his cards and snorted, shooting me a dismissive look.

'Yeah, that'll do me. I won. Thanks,' he said, and threw his cards back on the table, face-down.

'What?' I said, 'is that it?'

'Yeah,' he said, 'it's over already, I won.' He was being a child. He'd obviously got a hand he didn't like, so he was trashing the game.

I put my cards down, face-up. A three of clubs and a four of diamonds. There was nothing on for me. 'So, what makes you think you won?' I turned his cards over.

He had nothing on either. But he had an eight, so he had the higher card.

'Neither of us had shit,' I said. *Hold his attention.* 'But you had the high card. So you win that hand,' I said.

'Will, it was written all over your face,' he said. 'You can't hide your micro-expressions!' He turned to go.

'Wait, what's a micro-expression?' I called quickly. I walked around towards the kitchen, hoping he'd follow me.

'Oh, you want poker lessons, now?' he winked. 'I don't think you can afford that. I know how much is in your bank account, remember?'

I pretended to be upset, holding eye-contact with him. He took a few steps back into the living room, after me.

'This is what I'm talking about, Willy,' he said, 'the illusion of control. It's seductive.'

Gotcha. I could keep him for another twenty seconds with this, at least.

'So you know how to play around with the illusion of control, do you?' I said.

He laughed, 'You're starting to get it, yeah. I see things you don't, Will. It's all patterns; nobody thinks they're in a pattern but it's all there, in the micro-expressions and neuro linguistics. I know how to take control of a situation. Or a person.'

'So you can get other people to behave how you want them to, can you?' I pretended to be interested.

'Will,' he smiled. 'I can make anyone do anything if you give me enough time.'

'Well, you haven't been able to make me do anything,' I said.

'No,' he replied, 'that's right. And that's why you're going to prison.' He held my gaze for a few more seconds before shuffling out into the hallway. Adrenaline tore through me. *Was she still out there?*

I heard him go straight into the bathroom. This time he slammed the bathroom door behind him. I leapt up and ran to the doorway of bedroom. She wasn't there.

I looked at the bathroom door in a moment of panic before throwing myself onto the floor and peering under the bed. The suitcase had gone. As I got back to my feet, I saw track marks on the carpet, where Ellie had yanked it free. *She's done it.* I did my best to brush the track marks out.

She must have lifted that thing up to carry it out. *That'll be why she couldn't close the door.* I darted to the front door and peered down the corridor. I couldn't see her; she'd already disappeared down the corridor. A cat-like thief – the perfect accomplice. I quietly closed the front door and took a seat back in Solly's living room. I tried to slow my breathing and appear calm, but the exhilaration was immense. He emerged, wiping his hand on his trouser leg.

'How are we doing for time?' he enquired smugly.

I looked up at the clock on the wall. 'About five minutes to blast-off,' I said.

'Blast-off!' he chuckled. 'You're a cocky little so-and-so, aren't you? Are you intending on being that cocky in prison?'

'No,' I said. *Keep him talking. She'll be outside the building, now.*

'In prison,' I said, 'I will always assess every situation. I'll be careful. You taught me that.'

He grinned. 'That's good! You'll do well, I'm sure. Patience! And don't run your mouth too quickly. That's something else you've learned, I hope.'

'Yes, I have, Solly,' I said calmly. 'I have learned that.'

He sniggered and drew a deep, self-satisfied breath. 'You don't get old, without getting wise,' he said finally.

'Yeah, I know what you mean,' I said.

'Concentration, it's a game of concentration. Life, poker...' he said.

'Yeah,' I said. 'It's "busted flush", by the way.'

'What?' he sneered.

'Earlier, you called it a "bastard flush". I think it's actually called a "busted flush".'

He tried to hide it, but it knocked him off guard. That was genuinely new news, to him.

As ever, he recovered quickly. 'Different players call it different things. It's a global game. The world's not just the end of your nose. You just lost a game against me in about two seconds.' He wafted his hand at the cards on the table.

'Yeah,' I said. 'I see.'

'Do you know what I think?' said Solly. 'I don't think you'd even have known I won that hand just now, if I hadn't told you.' He leaned his head back and laughed.

I could see all his rotten teeth and black fillings. 'I don't think you're a poker player at all. I looked for you. It's not difficult to find things like that out, you know. Other people have the internet, too.'

'I'm *not* a poker player!' he gasped in faux shock, 'Oh my goodness, that is hilarious!'

'Well, let's have a game then—' I shot back.

'I'm not here to play games!' he interrupted, swiping the

cards onto the floor. He was flustered. He shot a look at the clock.

'Right, time's up!' he cried, angrily.

'Yeah,' I replied. 'Time's up.'

Ninety-Three

Solly took a seat in his armchair and began rolling a cigarette. I stood by the window, drinking my glass of wine.

'Will you be calling the red tops tonight?' I asked him. 'Are they still open?'

He scowled at me before going back to his cigarette. He was recalculating, I could tell. This hadn't gone how he'd expected it to. He hadn't expected me to call his bluff on this. He thought he was a psychological judo-master; he specialised in finding ways to get on top of you. But he'd seen his power slowly stripped apart, until he had nothing left except this vague threat to call the media. He wouldn't accept it yet, but he'd been beaten.

'Listen,' I said, 'I'm going to go. If you really want to call the media, then I guess that's up to you, but I'm going to go now, and I don't intend on thinking about you again. I wish you luck and, you know... that was... I'm sorry about what you told me, about falling unconscious and all that. Maybe you could make some friends playing cards or whatever, I dunno. Think about it, you're right, being on your own up here isn't good.' At the time I thought that garbled, half-arsed pep-talk was a cool thing to walk out on.

He wasn't happy about it though. Not at all. He couldn't let me leave like that. His pride had been wounded.

I saw this different side to Solly unfolding, as he got up and stood blocking the doorway. This panicked, frantic side. His hands were clasping and unclasping. Every now and then he'd reach up and vigorously rub his nose or mouth. He checked his mobile phone one last time and sighed. 'She was never planning on sending that to me, was she?'

'No,' I said, double-checking my pockets for my valuables.

'What was the point of that?' he said.

'I don't know,' I said, 'fun, I suppose.'

'Fun.' He echoed gravely. He stepped into the hallway started putting his donkey jacket on.

'Going somewhere?' I said.

'No,' he replied, looking at me intently.

'So what's with the coat?' I said.

He eyed me for a moment but didn't reply. Then he turned on his heel and disappeared into the bedroom. I heard him march in there and jab the light switch before stopping dead in his tracks. He was silent for a moment, then he slowly paced across his bedroom. I heard the material of his jacket crinkle as he knelt. Then he was silent again.

I decided it was time to leave. As I started for the front door, he dashed to intercept me.

'Wait. *Wait*.'

I opened the door and turned to look at him. His eyes weren't darting around any more. They were motionless, red, with blotchy eyelids. He eyed me furiously.

'What do you want, Solly?' I said. 'I'm going now. You won't hear from me again.'

I saw the muscles in his jaw move. He was having to hold himself back from going for me. I saw his eyes dart around for a weapon. There wasn't anything useful in that hallway: some shoes and an old plug-in telephone.

He grabbed the front door from me and yanked it fully open. After a moment looking down the corridor, he looked me up and down again, furiously. He'd gone deathly pale.

'Where is it? What have you *done* with it?' he said quietly. He was simmering with rage.

'What have I done with what?' I said. I plunged my hands into my jacket pocket and felt the end of a packet of sweets. I pulled it out: three Polos. I plucked one out and put it in my mouth. I motioned towards Solly with the pack and raised my eyebrows.

He nodded his head slowly and smiled. He was turning red. All that oil on his face had now turned to liquid and started cascading down his wrinkled skin. He looked hot. He looked like he was about to burst.

'Are you okay Solly?' I said. 'Can I get you a drink or anything?'

He looked up at me, then at the phone, then into his living room. He reached behind me and gently pushed the front door closed.

'See, here's the thing,' he said quietly. 'That was a good lift, but you forgot something.'

'Oh yeah?'

'Yeah. I know you didn't have time to get it out and down the corridor, and there's nowhere to stash it in the corridor, so you've concealed it somewhere here, in my flat. Now all you need is for me to think it's gone and take my eye off you. Then you'll be able to make off with it.' He cocked his head into the general direction of his apartment.

'It's somewhere in here, isn't it?' his mouth stretched into a smirk. He tapped the side of his head, knowingly.

I opened the front door again. 'Goodbye Solly,' I said.

He watched with a faint smile as I walked out of his front door and away, down the corridor. He thought it was a bluff. When I'd got about ten paces away, he started following me.

He followed me all the way to the lift. I got in and pressed the Ground Floor button. He stood at the open doors, watching me. He still had that faint smile on his face. Then it suddenly dropped.

He charged into the lift and grabbed me by my lapels.

'Where is it, you little fucking rat?' he roared, pushing his face into mine.

I wrestled him off and threw him onto the floor. He crawled back out of the lift and scurried to his feet.

'*Fuck you*! You little coward!' he shouted. 'You're a fucking ungrateful little turd!'

And he was gone. As the lift whirred down towards the ground floor, the world fell completely, perfectly silent.

Ninety-Four

Solly's activity ran far deeper than I'd given him credit for. Surprisingly enough, his drives were extremely well organised. Each of them contained folders labelled with a different person's name. One of the files was labelled *Wilbur Cox*. His penchant for filming people in compromising positions went beyond his sexual perversion. He had been using the materials to blackmail people.

He had this extortion process that was very emotionally driven. He'd get some initial trigger material and then frighten and torment the victim with it. He'd use that as leverage to demand more compromising things from them, on the premise that they could make it stop. But of course, it'd just make things worse. He'd keep gradually wrapping his tentacles tighter around people, leaching dignity from them.

But he'd toy with them throughout. It was like this game within a game. He kept all his correspondence on each file. He had details of people's families, their work addresses, bank account details. He'd copied my card details too, of course, when he'd had my wallet for that short period.

The folders contained letters to employers and spouses, as well as hundreds of voice recordings. He'd recorded most of the conversations he'd had with me, including our first meeting on the street. Each folder was a case file that could reduce the victim's life to dust, in one way or another. Most of them were sex tapes or illicit images, some of them were affairs. Mine was the only violent one. Mine was the only one where someone had died. He'd struck gold with my video. Or so he'd thought.

I never heard from him again. Although no doubt he's seen plenty of me, from up there on the rooftops. I try my best not to look up at those windows, but I always do. The tarpaulin has gone from his balcony. None of the cameras are up there any more. Ellie thinks he must have disappeared. She thinks he's gone.

We spent a few hours one afternoon deleting all Solly's folders. The first folder we looked in was that of a Chinese girl who lived in one of the buildings opposite him. She was a student; it was her first year in the country. He'd made a video of her having sex with somebody one night and was threatening to send it to her family back home. He'd made enormous sums of money out of her, the piece of shit.

We decided we wouldn't look into any of the other files, after that. Apart from feeling invasive, it was emotionally taxing to unwind what he had been doing. I shuddered when I understood why he'd wanted the picture of Ellie so badly. We opened each folder just to get the name and contact details of the victim, so that we could contact them – to let them know he'd lost his material.

When everything was deleted, we took the drives to be properly disposed of. We also got rid of his vacuum-packed bags of underwear. We got rid of it all. It felt like disposing of the horror of those previous six months; it was fucking wonderful.

I returned his suitcase to him. I left it outside the front door of his apartment early one morning. Of course, it didn't contain any of the stuff that was in it previously. It was empty, save for one thing: a present I bought especially for Solly. A red hat.

Of course, I still think of him often. He left an indelible mark on me. Never before or since, have I come across someone so detached from human decency. And yet, I did pity him. He was a person who, for whatever reason, had ended up alone with his toxic logic, and it had been allowed to fester. Ellie would continually search for evidence of him online, in the following months – she couldn't find any evidence of his existence. She continued scouring poker events, thinking that would be our best chance of finding him. I told her it was probably a fool's errand, and that he probably didn't play poker at all.

Ninety-Five

It was a hot May that year. One Saturday afternoon, Ellie and I headed down to London Embankment on the Underground. We took a little picnic with us: a bottle of prosecco, a French baton loaf, some grapes and a big lump of Irish cheese. We walked around talking for hours, before eventually sitting by the riverside to soak up the sun.

We sat by the river drinking and chatting while London buzzed around us. Ellie was sloped on me and would occasionally reach back with her hand to stroke my chest or play with my hair.

At one point I was watching this group of teenage German tourists, gathered excitedly at the water's edge for a photograph. Five or six of them clustered together, grinning ecstatically while they waited for the shutter to click. They'd got some passer-by to take the picture for them, a middle-aged man in a dark, heavyweight jacket. It was an odd day to be wearing a jacket like that. I tilted my head to watch more closely as he took the photo.

'How come you stopped talking in your sleep?' Ellie asked me. 'You haven't done it in weeks.' Without breaking my stare from this guy in the jacket, I shrugged.

'I'm serious,' she said, 'you used to ramble away so much. It actually made me pretty sad. Like you were never really resting.' She reached up and gently tapped the side of my head.

'I dunno,' I shrugged, watching the man hand back the camera and replace his dark sunglasses on his face. 'Processing, I guess...'

She nodded.

The Germans all bustled back around the camera, shouting and laughing at the photo. I kept on watching their photographer as he skited his way through the crowd into the distance, glancing left and right. It wasn't him. This guy was much younger. Moved much more freely.

As day turned to evening, the tourist crowds thinned to a gentle trickle. A street seller nearby was selling candy floss, and little gusts of wind would momentarily fill the atmosphere around us with a warm, sweet aroma. We both watched as a big, lumbering paddleboat gently ploughed past us down the river.

'What do you want to do now?' said Ellie.

'Let's just stay here for a little while,' I whispered, grasping her delicate hand.

I wasn't ready for the moment to finish. I smiled and watched the paddleboat roll gently down the Thames, churning the water into soft, white foam.

Photo credit: Carly Cussen

Royston Reeves is a psychological thriller writer from Essex, England. After spending years in advertising writing TV scripts, newspaper ads and billboards, *The Weatherman* is Royston's first novel. Reeves is a Strategist at *Playmaker Films* and he currently lives in the Kent countryside with his wife, Carly, and daughter, Hunter-Rose.

Bedford Square Publishers

Bedford Square Publishers is an independent publisher of fiction and non-fiction, founded in 2022 in the historic streets of Bedford Square London and the sea mist shrouded green of Bedford Square Brighton.

Our goal is to discover irresistible stories and voices that illuminate our world.

We are passionate about connecting our authors to readers across the globe and our independence allows us to do this in original and nimble ways.

The team at Bedford Square Publishers has years of experience and we aim to use that knowledge and creative insight, alongside evolving technology, to reach the right readers for our books. From the ones who read a lot, to the ones who don't consider themselves readers, we aim to find those who will love our books and talk about them as much as we do.

We are hunting for vital new voices from all backgrounds – with books that take the reader to new places and transform perceptions of the world we live in.

Follow us on social media for the latest Bedford Square Publishers news.

@bedsqpublishers
facebook.com/bedfordsq.publishers/
@bedfordsq.publishers

https://bedfordsquarepublishers.co.uk/